CIRCLETS & SEEKERS

ALORA'S TEAR, VOLUME IV

There's no accounting for tomorrow.

Nathan Barham

NATHAN BARHAM

BARHAM INK
MOSCOW IDAHO USA

Edited by Zoë Markham
markhamcorrect.com

Cover illustration, layout, and map by Isis Sousa
www.artstation.com/isissousa

ISBN-13: 978-0-9905965-9-2

Published by Barham Ink: barhamink.com

Ordering Information:

Quantity sales. Special discounts are available on quantity purchases by corporations, associations, and others. For details, contact the publisher at the address above.

Orders by U.S. trade bookstores and wholesalers, please contact In-gramsSpark: www.ingramspark.com.

Table of Contents

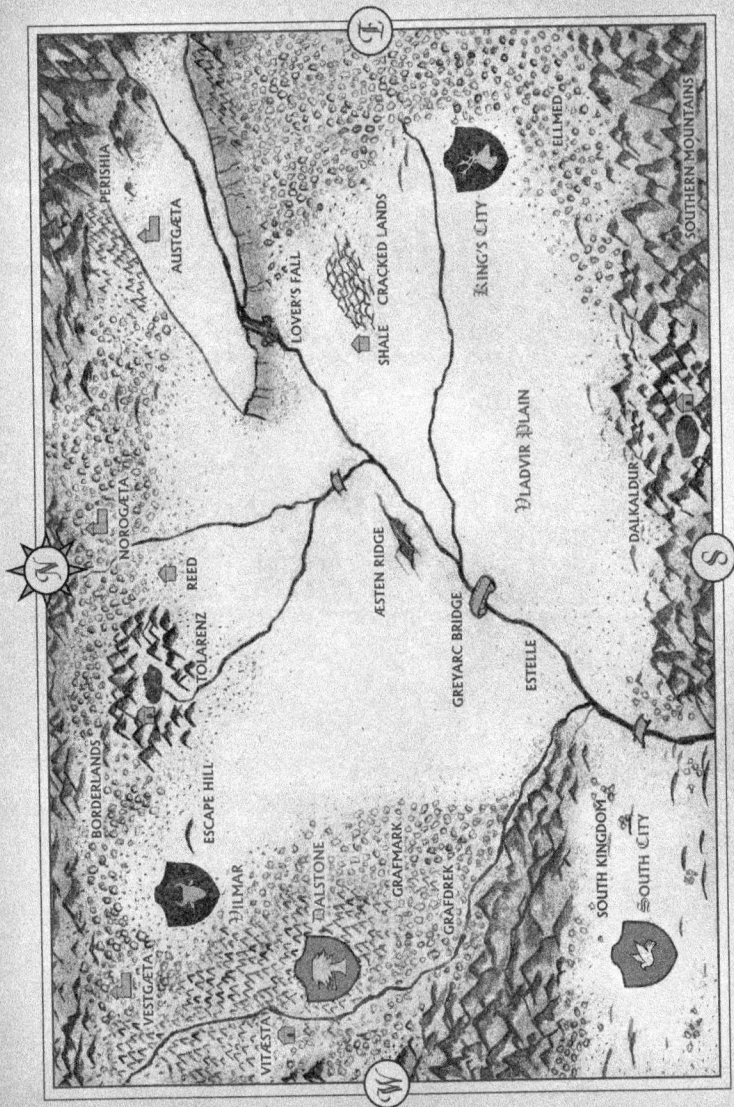

ALORA'S TEAR, VOLUMES I-III

In Summary

In the land of Vladvir, Askon of Tolarenz, half-elf and unlikely officer in King Codard's army, sets out on one final mission before taking charge of his hometown—a haven for half-elves and other outcasts—from its founder and beloved leader, Caled.

A vicious race of monsters known as the Norill have prepared an assault on the border fort Austgæta. When the King's forces are unexpectedly defeated in their surprise counterattack on the Norill stronghold, Askon sends his closest allies, John of Dalstone and Thomas of Shale, to warn King's City and Vladvir's other outposts. Sensing great danger, Askon himself races to Tolarenz to find the buildings utterly vacant and Caled murdered at the hands of a supposed ally, Iramov of Vilmar.

Iramov carries a piece of a powerful artifact which Askon believed to be only a myth: Alora's Tear. The fragment that Iramov carries allows him to kill not only Caled, but every citizen in Tolarenz save one. When Iramov escapes, Askon is left with his grief and Caled's associate Morrowmen, who informs him of the remaining four fragments of the Tear and Iramov's plan to unite them all. Morrowmen gives Askon the Time fragment, a gift meant to be passed from Caled to Askon, and tells him to warn the king.

When Askon arrives in King's City, Iramov is already there, and Askon stands accused of desertion. But Edward, Vladvir's prince and Askon's longtime friend, intervenes, escaping with Askon and Thomas who takes them to Shale in the hope they will find shelter. Using the Space fragment, Codard stages forces to intercept them, and they narrowly escape again. After reuniting with John, the group makes a stand against Iramov's forces at the Battle of Dalstone. Here Askon learns that the Time fragment can both control his perception of time and, if only he can master it, allow him to control time itself.

After the victory Askon, Edward, Thomas, and his newly met companion, Elise head for South City where they believe Morrowmen awaits with the Life fragment and the keeper of the Sight fragment, Lord Apopsé. On the path, they encounter Morrowmen and the only other survivor of the Tolarenz massacre: Askon's sister Líana who was spared only by Morrowmen's use of the Life fragment. Her injuries were such that the fragment traded years of her life for a full recovery. When Askon left Tolarenz she was a girl of ten, but when he meets her in the South Kingdom she is a woman of twenty whose skill with a sword matches and even bests his own.

Líana and Edward fall in love, and Morrowmen gives the Life fragment into Líana's care. Upon arrival in South City, Apopsé is reluctant to help defeat Iramov, despite his army's movements through the South Kingdom.

The Battle of South City ends with Iramov sending his army of undead soldiers in a horde that overcomes the gates and over-runs the city. With the help of John and the newly allied Grafmark Norill, Askon and his friends are able to defeat Iramov and take control of the fragments of Alora's Tear.

Askon returns to Tolarenz with a contingent of half-elven refugees from South City in an attempt to bring his home back to its former self. There, Edward and Líana are married, joining the fates of the human royal line and the half-elves of Vladvir.

During the ceremony, however, Askon and his friends, with the combined power of the Tear, glimpse a vision in which a young woman flees pursuit only to secret away several very famil-iar gems. Before the vision comes to its end, Askon notes an in-scription on the circlet she wears, which reads: Alora.

GIRCLETS&
SEEKERS

Prologue

"What were you doing there?" the voice demanded.

She could not reply. Would not allow herself to speak.

"There are ways," it rumbled, "to convince you to answer."

She didn't.

"It's been dark for quite some time. Maybe you'd like a little light?"

It *had* been dark. So dark. But for how long. Hours? Days? She couldn't say. Oh, but how she wanted the light. In the dark the noises played tricks on her: the *scrabble-tap* feet of vermin, heavy footsteps through the wall, an agonized scream that choked and rattled then died away. But always *his* voice came back, cold and low like the growling lions she'd read so often about.

The first room had been better: ascetic, well-lit, with featureless gray walls and unfurnished corners. A woman had come to her then, kind-spoken, with deft hands that loosened the chair restraints, long ears whose points peaked through waves of almost blond, and a face like old teak.

Kind-spoken though she was, the woman wanted everything, like him. Questions, questions, questions. From just beyond arm's length, with legs casually crossed, and fingers knitted before a face taut with concern.

"That gem. You know the one, pretty green like summer leaves. Where in all the world did you find it? Did someone give it to you?" the words were sweet syrup laced with poison.

Never tell. Never say a word.

The kind-spoken woman clicked her tongue. "It's quite important you humor us, my dear. We know you've hidden it, and we know it's in Dalkaldur. But that's a big place. Tell me how to find it, and we'll get the rest all sorted out."

When no answer came, the red lips flattened from concern to irritation, then relaxed. "As you will," she said. "Just remember. We know about the book, too. That's stolen property, my dear. And we can't let stolen property go unreported. It's not like you've kept some ordinary volume overlong. That one's a historical piece. The fines will be significant. Imprisonment maybe. Who's to say?" She tapped her fingers together. "Unless you tell us where you left it. Misplaced it, even, I'm sure. Yes, where did you last see it before you misplaced it?"

That was before the dark, before the cold, before the voice. When the kind-spoken woman went away, the light went with her. It wasn't so bad. Despite the restraints, sleep had come, until the voice woke her.

"Tell us!" it had screamed, shattering the silence. She gasped, heart hammering. From then on sleep was impossible. If her eyes closed, he woke her. Clanging steel bars, a nail against slate, a bucket of water. No more sleep.

When the trembling subsided, the chair felt different: hard, scratchy, and it creaked when she tested the restraints. The room smelled different: thick with the damp of mildewed floors and something moldering behind the walls. It was then she had begun to hear the rats.

Ticka-ticka-tick. Ticka-tick.

"A little light?" the voice asked again, scaring the rats away. The silence stretched, held its breath. She thought for a moment that he had gone. Then came the scrape of blade on whetstone, a gritty, shearing rhythm swollen with threat. She wanted to shout, to scream: *"You can't scare me! You won't hurt me!"* But in the dark she was no longer certain, and any word spoken was a broken promise to herself.

Light flickered into the room, leaving behind the shredded remains of a darkness his little candle could not clear. She glimpsed his hand as he set the light on a wooden shelf. In the soft space between his wrinkled knuckles and thumb, a faded shape blackened the skin: a teardrop. It hovered there for half a breath before the thick fingers evaporated with the rest of him into blackness.

On the shelf, an array of carefully aligned instruments glimmered: needle, physician's blade, baton, knife with twisted point, and a hook with a five-pointed star at the end. She squinted. Her eyes had grown weak in the room's perpetual darkness, and now even a candle seemed blinding.

He snuffed it.

"No," she gasped. *Mistake! Don't speak.*

"No?" crooned the voice. "I had begun to think we had struck you dumb." The flame sprang again to life, and the ragged shadows unfurled. "You tell me something, I leave your light."

No. She could control her mouth. That last word had simply escaped. One mistake would not become another. She licked the cracks along her lips and pressed them together. But it was so good to see again.

The man whose voice came from the darkness remained, shrouded in ghostly dancing shadows. Her eyes began to adjust, though for now everything was blurry and ill-defined. This was not the same room, nor the same chair—as she had suspected. The first room, burnished cleaner than any she had ever seen, and the first chair, soft and smooth, upholstery upon metal, were gone. Gray woodgrain ridges replaced them, a floor all dirt and stones, a chair that slipped splinters through her clothes and into her skin.

A cellar of some kind.

A guttural rumble issued from the shroud of black, and again the light went out. Her heart fluttered, but she bit down hard on her lip, refusing to let another plea break free. A door clicked open then banged against the frame. Eventually, she knew, they would break her. Wherever she was, it was far from where they had begun. Be it sound or sleeplessness, the dark or the light, something would give. If not, how far would they go? A table of sharp knives was one thing, but using them? *They wouldn't.*

Ticka-ticka-tick. Ticka-tick. She startled awake, twisted her head from side to side, listened. Where had he gone? Would they leave her there? She suppressed the urge to call out. The rats responded unbidden. *Ticka-ticka-tick. Ticka-tick.*

"Hello?" A new voice. A man's again, but not the raspy gravel of her tormentor. This one was lighter, frail even. Afraid.

She didn't answer.

"Where am I? They said I'd have a cellmate, that they didn't need me anymore. Hello?" A leather strap groaned and a chair squeaked in the dark.

Her mouth was parched. It felt like days since last they brought her water, and even then half of it had been used to douse her awake. Or maybe it had only been hours. Her tongue felt heavy and thick, and she tasted blood on her lips. Back in the clean room, the kind-spoken woman had escorted her to relieve herself. No such luxury here in the dark. The water washed some of that away. The smell lingered.

The door clicked open.

It was him. She could tell by the footfalls, the breathing.

"I'm supposed to have a cellmate," the other man's voice whined. "They said they didn't need me to answer any more questions, said they'd found someone else." His words accelerated as the heavy boots thudded over the doorframe and the latch snapped shut. He was squealing by the end. "There's no one in here. What are you going to do?"

"Hmm," rumbled the voice.

I'm here! Me! We're here together. Not alone, she wanted to say. But she knew what the man with the teardrop tattoo was planning. At least, she thought she did.

"He thinks he's alone," the deep voice called. "Are you so cruel? Answer him. Tell him who you are."

"Is someone here, truly? Hello?" called the second voice.

It took all her strength to remain silent.

And then the candle flamed once more. The shadows unfurled, her cellmate appearing in a flutter of orange and red and smoke. His eyes were wide and darting, blinded by the candle so close to his face. He was bare to the waist where his trousers, soiled like hers, covered him. Violently, he shivered as if whipped by a chill wind. But he could not move. The restraints saw to that.

"Is anyone there?" he called, his eyes flicking back and forth around the room. They alighted on her, and his mouth dropped open. "Oh," he said. And then a scream, like nothing she had ever heard, burst from his mouth, rattled his throat. He twisted against the restraints and wailed, staring into her eyes, pleading with his own. A five-pointed star erupted from the flesh near his shoulder, his wide eyes following the blood and metal as it wrenched his shoulder back against the chair.

"I'll tell you anything!" he shrieked.

"It's far too late for that," said the voice.

She clenched her eyes tight. *They can't do this,* she thought. But the writhing, howling man on the other side of her eyelids disagreed.

He bucked and struggled, his body thumping against the restraints. And she closed her eyes tighter.

Something heavy hit him, sending out all the air in a rush. For a moment he was still. Then with a shuddering gasp, he inhaled again. She clenched her jaw, forcing down the roiling nausea in her stomach. But it leapt up again, like the man in the chair.

He keened once more, flailing at his bonds, until no air remained in his lungs, the sound flat and dry and gagging at the end of each breath. For hours.

She felt better when he died.

✝ ✝ ✝

A rooster crowed somewhere in the distance. Shafts of dusty light peeked through the curtains, painting the western wall in pale gold. Out in the fields, the stalks grew long and green. Another six weeks and they would make quite the harvest. Thomas lifted a hand to his face, rubbing the sleep away. He'd gone to bed with the bracelet on his wrist again. It was the third time he'd dreamed the darkened cellar and the screaming man and the girl in the chair.

He lowered his hand and reached out with the other. Elise was not there. The bed was empty. He turned, rubbed the vacant space pointlessly. For a moment he feared, as he often did, that she had left him, gone away in the night. His eyes raked the room, and he found her at the small table across from the bed, her lean shoulders draped with a thin blanket and tangled black hair over all. And those eyes, so dark; sunlight never touched them.

"You shouted in your sleep," she said.

"I'm sorry. I didn't mean to wake you."

"It's not the first time, either." She shifted her weight on the chair, a bare leg escaping the blanket.

Thomas followed the leg until it disappeared back into the rumpled cloth. "It was only a dream."

"That's ridiculous," she said. Her eyes pinned him where he sat fumbling with the remaining covers. "You said 'Dalkaldur' and murmured about gems and books. I heard you say 'Askon' and 'Edward,' on both occasions, actually."

Thomas squirmed again, glancing about as the sunrise warmed their quarters with light. His wife sat still as stone, just as she'd stood at their small wedding before wrapping him in her arms, just as she'd stand for one of John's lectures before shouting him out of the room. He looked slowly to the table next to the bed. It was empty. Though he could not see it, he knew that she too wore a gemmed bracelet around her wrist somewhere under the blanket.

"Tell me what you saw," she said.

CHAPTER ONE

Decisions, Decisions

The wind curled a finger of dust around the little tree, its branches stretching toward the canopy above. Eventually it would tower over them all, but trees need not hurry to their destinies. Growth is growth and time is time. The dust swirled again, and a shadow followed.

More than a year had passed since the little pot in which the tree had lived its young life had been smashed against rough-hewn boards, since Askon had found the broken pieces and used one to replant the tree inside the powdery circle. Had anything ever been so white as the circle in front of the Tolarenz town hall? Perhaps the same substance on the floor inside, where Caled had fallen. Or possibly in the white that blanketed Apopsé's training grounds, where Líana had brought an end to Iramov's army of the dead, where Elise had brought an end to Iramov. If these had been whiter, he did not remember them so.

In Tolarenz, however, the circle once as vivid against the stones and brown earth as it was in his memory, had gone. Wind and rain and time had worn it away. All that remained was the little tree. Askon smiled at its progress, and a little at its lack of progress, remembering his father's words.

"This one has been scraggly from the very start. He came on in his own good time, waiting out the cold, choosing the right moment. He's not the prettier of the two, but he certainly has the best chance at filling out later on."

Askon's smile broadened. He hoped his father was right. And though for the moment it seemed unlikely, Askon knew better than to argue. He knew now the power of patience.

Above, the branches of the old oaks whispered to one another and to the wind. He breathed deeply and closed his eyes, recalling the moments above Dalkaldur, above the world, above the clouds, the endless blue sky, the brilliant sun. They were here too, clouds and sky and sun, muted and dull by comparison but beautiful still..

"Sir?" Leltan, his newly designated assistant stirred him from his reverie. For months Askon had resisted the idea. Tolarenz was his to govern now that Caled was gone. But, when Askon had forgotten to arrive for several scheduled meetings with townsfolk and had been woefully unprepared for the two he did attend, he had given up the fight. A city, a town, even a small one like Tolarenz could not be run by just one man. Most would complain that there wasn't enough time in the day, but Askon had no problem in that respect. In the months since Iramov's defeat, he had come to better understand the glowing green gem dangling from the chain around his neck. Late for an appointment? Slow the passing of time. Left something behind? Stop the sun in the sky to retrieve it.

Unfortunately, in those same months he found that the more he used the fragment, the more exhausted he was at the end of each day. Once, over the span of several weeks, he had fallen into an ever-worsening cycle: use the fragment, sleep too late, use it to catch up, sleep even later the next day, and on and on. For the better part of a month he had been all but bedridden. That was when he decided to give the Time fragment, and himself, a reprieve. As he breathed the smell of spring, he tried to recall the last time he had used it—and could not. Things were better this way.

Time may not have been an issue for Askon, but management and organization were. There were too many variables. Without someone else to make suggestions, answer questions, to see what Askon could not, all the time in the world made little difference. If he kept on without help, Tolarenz would soon be as empty as it was when Iramov and his men had ridden off through the pounding rain.

"Sir," Leltan said again. It wasn't a question this time.

Askon's eyes remained fixed on the little tree. "What?" he asked, with a bit more irritation than he intended.

Leltan went on, either unaware or unaffected by Askon's tone. "The granaries are in disarray. I have millers on one side, farmers on the other, pest infestations in the southern building, and a leaky roof in the northern one. Where would you like to begin?"

He was a small man, this new assistant, barely mature enough to call a man. He had narrow-set eyes of blue and green, though not like Askon's. Instead, flecks of each color mixed together like a shallow sea over white sand. Many of the South City half-elves shared the trait. Behind one pointed ear he kept a feathered quill. From time to time it would droop, and he would replace it absently then scratch at the bridge of his thin nose, a wedge always driving itself into Askon's business.

"Well?" Leltan insisted. "Where do you want to begin? Because after the granaries, there are meetings with the weavers and the herdsmen. There's been an incident between that new arrival, the huntsman, and the falconer."

Askon flinched at the last title, remembering Halan with his slow speeches and faraway gaze. And he thought too of Marten, the sable-gray merlin who had been Askon's constant companion. Months had passed since he had last seen the bird, or its new owner, Líana. "Anything else?"

Leltan lifted a bony finger above a volume he had produced from the satchel at his hip. "If you'll allow me to finish, the huntsman's dogs got into the mews and overset the whole place. Two birds died and one of the dogs lost an eye. Not to mention the damage to the structure and the detriment to the birds' training. Our falconer was none too pleased. Says they won't be ready for flying until spring."

"Convenient," Askon grunted. "They wouldn't have been ready before then anyway."

"I know that," Leltan said with a nod like a hen pecking at barnyard ants, "and you know that, but he doesn't."

Askon sighed. "That's because he's not actually a falconer. Not a proper one, anyway."

It was true. No amount of training would ever make Will Fernwood a falconer who could replace the one Tolarenz had lost in Halan. Certainly one day the birds would hunt and fly and return, the mews would be full, but Will had none of the talent Halan had used to connect bird and master, to help them understand one another until hoods and jesses and lures were no more than dead weight in one's pack.

Will claimed to have descended from the elves, though even he wouldn't venture any more than a distant relation. Some said he fabricated the whole story. In such cases, Will would trace his left ear, tapping a place where the cartilage folded into a slight angle. The right ear was as round as could be. However, none of the other South City refugees or straggling individuals who, like the new huntsman, had made their way to Tolarenz from other parts of the kingdom, seemed to have any inclination whatsoever for falconry. So, the task had fallen to Will.

"You may be right, sir," Leltan said. He chewed the inside of his cheek, unconsciously and steadily nibbling at his puckered lips, a habit that further irritated Askon. "But, he's all we've got if we want falcons."

"We do." The words were final. Askon's eyes were still locked on the tree he had planted in the powdered circle.

"There is one more thing," said Leltan. He relaxed the muscles in his mouth, rubbed his nose, and sniffed. "Your guests will be arriving soon. We'll need to finish our preparations."

As if woken from a sound sleep, Askon ratcheted his head around at his new assistant. His cloak shifted with the motion. "When?"

"A week," said Leltan, still rubbing his nose, twitching it back and forth, "a few days, it depends."

"Upon what?" Askon said, striding past the smaller man and into the woven tunnels of the garden. "They'll arrive whenever he said they would arrive. What was his estimation?"

"Their last communication would have them here in just short of a week, if they're being precise. And there are new letters as well. I've left them at your desk."

Askon smiled. "Then that's what we prepare for first. Send a carpenter to fix the leaky granary, and find someone who can deal with the pests. We can't afford to lose a quarter of our stores to vermin. Sift through it by hand if you have to. There are enough people lounging by the lakeside these days; put them to work."

"And the falcons?"

"To hell with the falcons if Will can't get them trained. Tell this new huntsman his dogs will be put down if it happens again. That should heighten his awareness."

Leltan lifted the quill from behind his ear, dipped it into the vial on his satchel's shoulder strap, and marked the page in his book several times. Whatever he had written, Askon cared little, as long as the incessant demands would settle for a while.

He left Leltan to his book and quill.

A shaft of yellow light splashed over the desk while Askon shifted in his seat. Out front the hall was dark. Every morning Leltan and one of the kitchen workers pulled the shades over the windows. If they didn't, Askon found the hall unbearable by mid-afternoon. Though the main chamber and the little room behind it were not the only places he spent his time, he found it impossible to work when it became too hot.

Askon moved the ledger into the light. Rows and rows of numbers, lists, and names blended together before his eyes. Who would be selling, who was buying, who needed materials, who needed travel supplies. How long before the storage would need to be restocked. What could they replace on their own; what would need outside assistance, and thus coin. It went on endlessly.

Askon laughed, an empty sound that jeered back at him off the stone walls. He stretched and brushed the ledger aside.

On the surface of the desk, several leaves of parchment remained. One was a map of Vladvir which Askon had drawn himself. It catalogued the path he had taken from Tolarenz to Austgæta and back, then to King's City, through Ellmed forest, across the plains to Grafmark, to Dalstone, and finally down the Grafdrek to the gates of South City. It wasn't the first parchment he had nearly worn through with scrawlings and erasures. He had done it so many times that this version almost seemed legible. Askon was no artist, but these days his quills often wore down to feathered nubs with sketching.

Beneath the map, at an awkward angle, lay another one. In the depiction, a ring of pointy mountains too narrow for their height encompassed a wide valley floor. On one side he had drawn a castle. He had meant for it to look ancient and mysterious, but the result was childish, the scale exaggerated. There was a lake in the center, and the word *Dalkaldur* writ large above it. He put it aside.

The desk was piled with such sketches, one over the other, some remade several times after scraping away the original from the parchment. He lifted one from the stack, intending it to be random. It wasn't.

There she was, staring back at him, her pointed ears and curtain of silken hair wrapped in that curious copper circlet. To anyone else, the drawing would have been even more unrecognizable than the others. He hadn't seen her face clearly. The nose, for instance, was all wrong. It protruded too far and sloped too steeply. Or was it too wide and placed too close to the eyes? The lips were too full, like those of a strange fish. But Askon's memory persisted despite the inaccuracies of his artwork. The hair, the ears, and the circlet. He tried to convince himself that those were the important details. It was as he had seen her with Edward and Thomas in the scrub grass of Dalkaldur.

Who was she? The circlet said "Alora," but that only made the vision more confusing. As far as he could ascertain from the books in Caled's library and from the Tolarenz townsfolk, the legendary Breaker of Hearts had never visited Dalkaldur. In fact, most of the histories called her time period "Before the Sky." Apparently, before the Tear first fell, the Vladvir plain had been an enormous lake, or sea. Dalkaldur—and Tolarenz, and King's City, and Grafmark, and all the rest—would have been under water.

Askon wondered which bits of land had stood above the waves in those days: the southern mountains, certainly, most likely those above Dalstone, and the plateau upon which Old Austgæta had stood before Iramov and the Lost burned it.

Askon smiled and looked back to the map of Vladvir. They had even camped briefly at the foot of Lover's Fall, a roaring torrent that shot out over the cliffside and plummeted a thousand feet into a grove of huge trees. At the time, he had thought little of it, still disbelieving Caled's claim that the Tear was real. Now, with the Time fragment hanging about his neck, Lover's Fall seemed all the more significant.

In the stories, it was where Alora and her lover, Heraphus, had jumped to their deaths. To hear some tell it, Alora's betrothed had kept the Tear when he found it on her pillow the morning that she jumped. Others said it was not shed until she approached the edge of the cliff, that it was discovered at the base of the falls by the Norill then lost in their squabble over who would control it. Still others said Alora had taken it with her when it fell upon the pillow in Telemicus' castle and while Alora was lifted up amongst the gods, the Tear continued on to the base of the falls.

For all of Askon's newfound power, station, and knowledge, the truth eluded him. He had been over every book, asked every villager, had his friends John and Edward question everyone in their own cities who might have additional knowledge. It was no use. Not even his memories of Caled and croaking old Morrowmen could help him. As many lifetimes as the two of them had seen, the events the common folk called "Before the Sky" had occurred long before either Caled's or Morrowmen's most distant ancestors entered the unfamiliar landscape of rugged islands and limitless, watery horizons.

Askon rubbed his eyes. It was slow and tedious work, running the daily affairs of Tolarenz, and his mind often wandered. When it did, his thoughts inevitably wound back to South City and Morrowmen, to the woman in the vision of Dalkaldur. He pushed aside the parchments; one fell with a rustle onto the rug. Two more lay before him, each rolled and bound with its author's seal. On one was the deep blue embossed stag of Edward, King of Vladvir. On the other was the tree and quarrel of the Darts of Grafmark which Eldred had adopted for Dalstone's official insignia. And though the former was bound with fine blue riband, the latter was wrapped with a beaded hempen string. Brâghda's work, no doubt.

He set aside the Dalstone missive, turning instead to the blue stag. His long, curved hunting knife sliced through seal and riband with a satisfying *snick*. The knife was a bit much for a letter-opener, but Askon refused to be parted from it. He unrolled the page; however, it was not Edward's hand he found written there.

Askon,

Our path has straightened since we last sent word. It seems that everywhere we turn, a new village has sprung up. Almost all of them require us to stop and eat and rest. A king's passage is slow, it would seem. And for every request there is yet another quiet, awkward meal where our hosts give too much from their stores and far too much of their formal manners for Edward's benefit.

If I have to sit through another meal primly picking at some woman's prize pig like some kind of exotic bird, I'll...

Never mind it. Give me a quail straight out of Marten's talons and a fire to throw it on, and I'd go a week between meals before I'd sit at another overwrought table listening to people, women mostly, babble themselves silly over my husband.

Luckily there should be no villages between the Greyarc and Tolarenz. Just have a bow and quiver ready when I get there and a cloak I can get dirty. We should be no more than a few days.

Líana

The smile upon his face broadened with every word. It was like she was sitting right there beside him. Over the course of the year, he had heard from her often, and most of the time her tone matched this newest letter. Though she adored Edward—and had no reservations or regrets in having married him—Líana's suitability for courtly life was something akin to loosing a coyote amongst one's chickens. No matter how well trained the intruder might be, disaster hung ever-present.

In King's City, she had been happy to explore the winding streets and to range widely under the leaves of Ellmed. But a queen, whatever her power and influence, cannot be absent at all times. And so, with constantly increasing reluctance, she appeared for meetings, briefings, disputes, and social events. The letters from the mornings after were always the best. Askon thought of

Leltan's tedious daily list of trifles and shook his head at the similarities between himself and his sister.

He added Líana's letter to the parchment pile and lifted the knife again. As he brought it down, he arrested it mid-stroke. Instead of slashing through the careful bead work, he set the knife on the desk and picked along the string until he found a tiny, precise piece of metal no Norill would have fashioned. He knew this type of work when he saw it: Thomas. When he unlinked the clasp, the rolled parchment popped the waxen seal and unfurled. The lettering was jagged and irregularly-spaced.

Couch-lounging Desk Captain,

Just thought I'd let ya know where we've been. Broke the tree line yesterday. Saw Edward. Thomas did, anyway, in that stone of his. Decided to race the crown hook to Tolarenz. Your bird saw us, I think. Be there soon.

John

Beneath, in a fine, graceful hand like that of the women whose lavishly-set tables so irritated Líana:

Askon,

John refused to let me send a letter without his express permission. Elise told him it was unnecessary, but he insisted. What he says above is true. The forest took more time to navigate than we had anticipated, and as per our previous communications, delayed our arrival by several days. Now that we have broken free of Grafmark, however, it is clear we should have almost no trouble reaching Tolarenz in the timeframe laid out by our fearless leader.

Indeed I did see Edward and Líana in the Sight fragment, though the image was blurry and unsteady. Progress is progress. When we sighted their party properly on the horizon, we knew my vision was correct. It seems juvenile to "race," as John would have us do, but as you know, he is quite intractable. Thus, we should be there shortly.

Thomas

By the look of them, the letters could not have been more than a day old. They had flown in on the birds that had been Leltan's suggestion. Askon would have preferred falcons, and had Halan still been alive to train them, would have used falcons. But in their absence, it was Leltan's pigeons that had secured him the position. Runners were more reliable, but the birds were much faster.

By rights, both parties should have been arriving any time, perhaps even that very afternoon. Askon looked at the stack of parchments, thought about the list of duties, and hoped to see them all sooner rather than later.

CHAPTER TWO
Old Friends

The next morning a dusty haze floated up from the narrow pass along the stream. Askon had woken with the sun, as the distant riders had as well, it seemed. He took his time, striding leisurely along the rows of houses, past the smithy that had once been Roland's, past the mill that had once belonged to Eric and would have passed to little Grace. Eventually, he approached the final crossroads. To his left the path wound through rows of tall, bare-branched trees past the mews. He did not look to his right.

On the hill, lonely and vacant, stood his childhood home. At his behest it remained unfurnished, uninhabited. For a while he made regular trips out to it so he could water the grove of tiny trees. Yet one by one, they began to wither and die. Askon wished he had asked his father more questions, about them, about every-thing.

After nearly a dozen turned slowly from green or red to sickly yellow and finally pale brown, he gave it up. Ironically, according to a recent report from Leltan, some of the trees had flourished since then, and thick ivy had begun gnawing at the house's bones.

By the time he reached the crossroads, the dust had thickened, drawing increasingly nearer. A willow hissed in the wind by the roadside. Askon waited beneath its shade.

Soon, roaring hoofbeats joined the silent cloud of dust. At first like thunder away over the mountaintops. Then, quickly the sound grew louder and louder until Askon wondered just how many his friends had brought along in their traveling parties. As they rounded the bend, he allowed the smooth, familiar tranquility of the Time fragment to pass over him, and he understood.

Four horses led the charge. The furthest away, and the largest, carried a man whose thick beard glistened with sweat and fine, sparkling dust. His mouth was twisted into a grimace as his mount flagged and horse and rider fell increasingly behind. John. Ahead in line was another man, tall and steady in the saddle. He rode with grace, but not with the speed of the leaders. He looked from side to side, as if waiting for something. Edward.

Out in front, the race was a dead heat. The poor animals had reached the end of their strength. The riders' eyes were steely and focused, unrelenting, thrilling in the speed and the freedom. And though the two could not have been more similar in purpose and determination, they could not have been more different in appearance. On the left, the rider was all black shadows and ash under a film of brown dust. Even the eyes were dark as night. Elise. But on the right, the momentary leader was a swirl of white linen, equally dusty, with a long golden braid bouncing along to the hoofbeats. Her eyes were blue and green, left to right, and Askon thought of his own, blue and green right to left. Líana.

They drew nearer to the rattling leaves of Askon's willow, and he tried to hail them. Líana's eyes snapped toward him, but in that instant Elise seized the opportunity and surged ahead. His sister's brows furrowed into a glare, and the horses pounded past. John came next, gritting his teeth, refusing to be beaten, though any hope he might have had at winning was long past.

But where was Edward? Askon looked back to investigate and saw the remainder of the party thundering up out of the haze, not so fast or determined as the leaders, but briskly nonetheless. He wondered if Tolarenz was prepared to house half a hundred tired guardsmen and attendants.

Out in front of the main column, maybe ten yards behind the racers, was a riderless horse. It was a magnificent beast, fit for a king. And then Askon knew. A grin broke out across his face as the horse galloped by, trying to keep up with its stablemates. With a shake of his head Askon closed his eyes and breathed deep. The hoofbeats and hissing leaves went silent; the dust froze midair, and the whole valley came to a halt.

Askon sprinted across the road, vaulting with a grunt into the saddle. He squinted, knitting his brows together, and the statue-still beast sprang to life. It galloped past John, whose face was still screwed up in hopeless denial. Then they passed Líana and Elise, again neck and neck with one another. He allowed the horse an additional hundred yards before releasing his hold on the Time fragment. The world again came alive, and he continued his blistering pace through the buildings and family gardens.

Out of breath and dizzy from the effort, he reigned up just outside the town hall garden. He slid, panting, out of the saddle and found Edward seated comfortably on a bench, a waterskin in his outstretched hand.

"Thirsty?" Edward said with a wink.

Askon snatched it away and gulped a few mouthfuls. Then he lifted his arm and brought it smashing down against the half-empty bag, spraying Edward full in the face.

With a splutter, the king looked up through soaking hair. "What was that for?" he asked, astonished.

Askon blasted him again. "To teach you not to cheat my sister."

Then Edward was gone. Askon felt strong hands drive into his back, and the earth rose up to meet him. The Time fragment glowed green. Askon put out his hands, righted himself, and looked around, but Edward was nowhere to be found.

With the fragment's power still coursing through him, Askon searched every corner of the garden. No Edward. When he felt he could hold his concentration no longer, and exhaustion threatened to overtake him, Askon relaxed. The world moved again as it should. He sat heaving on the bench when a wall of water splashed into his face, nearly choking him.

"I win," said Edward.

"When Elise and Líana figure out how we arrived here before them, neither of us will feel very much like a winner," Askon replied. He reached behind his head and shook a spray of droplets from his hood. Then, wringing a stream of water out of his hair, he tucked one side behind a pointed ear. "Here they come."

Up the hill the horses' hooves pounded, their mouths straining against the bit, their eyes glassy. Líana and Elise leapt from their saddles, almost as though they were rider and shadow. The horses slowed to a stop. Both women hit the ground running, but Líana lost a step when she saw Askon sitting on the bench and Edward standing by. She skidded to a halt, just inches behind Elise.

The shadow-half did not stop, however. She continued head-long toward the bench and without hesitation, slammed her open palms into Askon's chest. He tumbled backward into the grass. Elise rounded on Edward, her eyes smoldering, and thought better of assaulting the new-made king of Vladvir. Pivoting on her boot heel, she stalked off into the garden toward the town hall entrance.

Askon picked himself up and resumed his seat on the bench. He rubbed his lower back where a particularly sharp rock had gouged him. When he looked up, Líana had disappeared. His hood came down hard over his head. By the time he could react, the pathway stones met his nose and cheekbone. He rolled onto his back with a groan. Edward stood over him and gave an innocent shrug. A smirk appeared at one side of his mouth. Askon looked back toward the bench.

There stood his sister, all in dusty white but not in dress or gown. She was clad more as a man might be, in leggings and a linen shirt. Her braid had loosened a bit during the ride; it too was covered in dust. Her eyes were on Edward. One eyebrow inched slowly upward as if to ask, *"What are you smiling at?"* before she turned away without a word and followed Elise into the garden.

A few minutes later, Askon was seated again, rubbing his jaw where it had collided with the packed earth. Edward stood with arms folded, glancing nervously toward the garden, into which his wife had fled. For the first time since he had appeared out of the dust, the kingly posture and presence faded. He slouched a bit and peered nervously into the leaves, more fretful husband than confident ruler.

Hooves sounded once more along the path, though this time less frantic. Askon looked up. His sister's horse had wandered off with Elise's to nibble the garden grass. Leltan would be livid, but Askon shrugged it off. *Grass and flowers grow back*, he thought to himself. Down the path he saw a second pair drawing slowly near.

"What's the use of havin' a race when the two o' ya cheat like back-alley tavern wenches after I've had one-too-many pints?!" John was already out of the saddle, stumping heavily toward them. The second rider lifted a finger to his mouth, a sharp hiss issuing from behind it. John ignored him.

"Those women been half asleep for the last two days while I stood watch. They each got as good a horse as I do, but they're lighter and better rested. If that wasn't enough, now I've got you two usin' those fancy trinkets to beat me. What, Askon, you afraid of a little competition?"

Another hiss erupted from the second rider. Askon looked him over. A heavy cloak covered the face and body. His silhouette bulged awkwardly in front as though he carried something fragile. John turned back to look at him, grumbled something unintelligible, and flopped down on the bench beside Askon. The rider twisted slowly in his seat, lifting one leg over his horse and sliding gingerly to the ground. His hood fell from his head in an unshapely clump across his shoulders.

"Thomas!" Edward boomed warmly.

"*Shh!*" Thomas hissed back.

John laughed. "He's been doin' that all the way from Dalstone. I'm half tempted to go live in Vitæsta with the Norill when we get back. It'll be worth it if it brings an end to that gods damned sound." He leveled a huge paw at Edward. "Ya do know ya just shushed the king, don't ya Thomas?"

Edward rolled his eyes.

"I'd throw 'im in a dungeon somewhere, if it were me," John said with finality. He drew a knife from his belt and proceeded to run its point beneath each of his fingernails. Between fingers, he flicked the residue from the blade into the grass.

"And our dungeons would overflow with people who dared to annoy you," Edward replied.

Askon let them bicker, instead choosing to study Thomas. As though walking a path of broken glass, the younger man crept along carefully. The bulge beneath his cloak, he held perfectly still, though with one careful step he wobbled and nearly lost his balance. Back and forth his eyes searched, reluctantly alighting on John who was still carving dirt from beneath his nails. With no more sound than a deer bedding down in a thicket, Thomas circled around the bench and bumped John with an elbow. The bearded face looked up sullenly, then to his knife, then to the bulge. His face softened, and with a sigh, he rose and stood next to Edward. Thomas lowered himself steadily onto the bench.

He peeled back the folded cloak to reveal a round pink face. The little eyes, shut tight, squeezed tighter as the morning sun entered the cloak's cool shadows. Thrust up against the chin were eight delicate fingers curled around two tiny thumbs. One overzealous knuckle had driven itself into the puffy lips and soft red gums. The eyes scrunched again and the mouth wrinkled into a grimace. Thomas replaced the cloak, lifting a finger to his mouth.

"Yeah, we know," John said in an irritated whisper, "*Shh!*"

Thanks to Leltan's flying messengers, Askon already knew about the boy before his friends had even set foot outside of Dalstone. In fact, the first bird had arrived less than a week after he was born. Askon remembered his surprise at the timing. But that had been a few months ago. Now the boy was growing strong, though everything about him seemed tiny and soft.

Askon kept his voice low. "What is his name?"

Thomas shook his head. "Elise wanted to name him in Norill fashion, in honor of Brâghda," he said quietly. John shifted uncomfortably and made a noise of disapproval. "Oh I'm sorry, John. Do you have something to say, some advice for how I ought to name *my son?*"

John hesitated, and Askon thought to himself how much they had changed. No one would have been able to make John hesitate a year earlier. Commanders, generals, kings, a Norill chieftain in her own village, a madman who could summon an army back from the dead, none of them would have for a heartbeat cowed John of Dalstone. But today, Thomas did. And yet, it was only for a heartbeat.

"I do!" said John, risking the wrath of another shushing. "It's one thing to join forces with 'em. Hell, I've even made a friend or two with the twisted little bastards, but to take on their custom with your own blood? It ain't right Thomas; it just ain't right."

Thomas barely moved. He leaned ever so slightly toward John and Edward. "You want to take him for a day, John?" Thomas asked softly. "That would actually be a nice reprieve for me and Elise. I'll show you how to change hi—"

"Oh, forget it!" John barked. "Name him whatever ya want. Even if he does turn out to be a tunnel digging half-Norill."

A broad smile lay across Thomas's face. He settled back onto the bench. "Thank you, good sir, for being so kind as to let me make decisions for my own family," he said to John with a side-long glance at Askon.

Across from them Edward worried one of the pathway stones with the toe of his boot. He had worked it mostly loose, rocking it back and forth in the softened dirt. "So, what do you mean by 'Norill fashion'?"

The lumpy cloak shifted with the baby's movements, and with Thomas's adjustments to keep him comfortable. "It's quite simple, really," Thomas began.

"That's what you say about everything," John interrupted. The others ignored him.

Thomas continued: "The Norill name their children not on the day of their birth, as we do, but when the parents feel they have a name that suits the child they've begun to raise. Haven't you ever wondered what you might have been named if your parents had waited to see what you were like, what kind of person you would be?"

"Pain-in-the-ass," said John. "That's a terrible way to name a kid. By the time they're old enough to have a personality, they'd all be named Pain-in-the-ass."

The others went on ignoring him.

"At any rate, the Norill see this as the proper way to name a child, and we didn't have any names that seemed right when he was born, so we've decided to just let it happen as it will."

"The world is how it is," said Edward.

"You could'a named him John," said John.

Askon laughed.

When they found the women—or rather when the women allowed themselves to be found—they were seated at a wrought iron table in the depths of the garden. It had grown quite warm, and beads of condensation had gathered on the pitcher of water Elise and Líana shared. There were no chairs or cups for the men.

Above them in the trees, a pair—or an army—of cicadas buzzed noisily. The sound dominated the garden, drowning out even Askon's footsteps as he approached the table. Suddenly, the buzzing stopped. Líana rose from her seat and motioned to Thomas who sat gingerly across from his wife. Elise made no move to retrieve the baby.

Askon looked around, wondering what had happened to the overzealous insects. He soon found out. Like an arrow from a longbow, a shadow arced down from the sky and landed with a flutter at Líana's shoulder. She wore no leather guard as Askon once had. Instead, the deep purple jewel on her ring finger pulsed slightly brighter as Marten's talons pressed hard into her skin. They did not break the surface, though the bird's claws were as sharp as ever. He crunched the offending cicada in his beak and cocked his head, aiming one unblinking eye at Askon.

John rubbed his shoulder. "Never liked the way that bird stares at a person," said John. "Always felt like he was sizin' me up. Figurin' whether or not he could make a meal outta' me."

Elise thumped her cup onto the table, then pulled one knee to her chest. "Líana and I have decided on the price you two will pay for cheating," she said flatly. Líana turned away. Marten cranked his head around and trained the other eye on John.

"Oh?" said Edward. "And what is that price?"

Askon waved him off. "Don't negotiate with her," he said. "You can only lose." He stepped toward Elise. "We simply made use of the resources available to us."

"Really." Líana revolved slowly, and Marten snapped his head around again. "So, were we supposed to use our resources? The Life fragment would hardly be advantageous in a horse race."

Elise smiled, a dark smile unlike any Askon had ever seen on another. Somehow she had a talent for making even an expression of happiness seem grim and suspicious. "Perhaps he meant I should use mine," she said, more threat than suggestion. Her fragment, now set in the fine bracelet Thomas had fashioned, glowed red with her words. She tapped it with a fingernail.

"You wouldn't," said Edward.

"She might," said John.

Thomas sat perfectly still.

"A fair point then," Askon admitted. "Alright. What's the price?"

The dark smile broadened, and for a moment, Askon regretted his words. Then Líana stepped forward and placed her hands on the table.

"The price is that you tell us everything about Dalkaldur: the men, the chest, the fragments…the girl."

Askon shrugged. "It seems to me you know everything already. I wonder where you found such a knowledgeable informant."

Thomas sat perfectly still.

"It couldn't have been John," Askon began. He took a step toward the table. "In fact, if he were paying more attention to you now and less to Marten, he'd realize he has no idea what we're talking about."

They all looked at John, but Marten's gaze seemed almost to have hypnotized him. He moved from side to side, as though he might escape the bird's stare.

"And it wouldn't have been Edward. He has too much honor to—"

Líana grinned. "I wouldn't be so sure. I can be very persuasive."

That stopped Askon as effectively as Marten's stare had John. He rounded on Edward with a glare, but his friend's hands were in the air, one finger pointing to the ring on his left hand. The king shrugged. Askon turned the same glare on his sister who smirked with a shrug of her own.

"He didn't tell me anything," she said playfully. "But that calm, collected facade you present to the world is even more brittle than I might have guessed."

Askon spluttered something to himself. Edward finished for him. "And that leaves Thomas."

Thomas sat perfectly still.

"You can't hide from us," said Edward.

Thomas looked up, a *Shh!* forming at his lips.

"Oh, leave him be." Elise had pulled the other leg to her chest and now sat perched on the wrought iron chair with her arms about both knees. Her eyes narrowed. "It took me all of a breath and a tap at my wrist just now to intimidate the great Askon of Tolarenz and the rest of you four. You'll notice my husband hasn't spoken a word. Even four against two, you've lost miserably. Imagine Thomas on his own."

They all nodded over a slow laughter. Soon Askon was shaking his head while Edward moved to Líana's side. From beneath Thomas's cloak, a whimper escaped, which soon became a wail.

He handed the baby across the table to Elise, who proceeded to feed him. He and the other men, excluding Thomas, turned away.

"If it bothers you that much…" said Elise, covering herself and the boy with Thomas's cloak. "Three great warriors, one of them a king, and all afraid of a mother's breast. You'd think the lot of you weren't raised the same." She shifted the cloth until it was comfortable and waited for the men to face her. When they did, the dark smile had reappeared. "Now, tell us about Dalkaldur."

CHAPTER THREE
Meeting of the Minds

The hidden room at the back of the town hall felt smaller as each person stepped through the door. By the time all six had entered, the air was warm and thick. Askon sidled along the cool stone wall between Edward and Líana, indicating the four soft armchairs. Then he stepped out, snagging Thomas by a shirtsleeve on the way. The two returned shortly with a pair of stools. Outside the town hall, the two traveling companies took directions from Leltan, who sent the king's men to their lodgings and the handful of John's Darts along with them.

Back inside, Elise, seated already in one of the chairs, her knees again pulled up to her chest, worried the bracelet and Death fragment back and forth over her wrist. On the way in, Askon had introduced her to one of the hall servants selected specifically for the task of looking after the new baby. He feared now that the nurse's time with the child would be limited. Elise's black eyes wandered to the wall again and again, as though she might see through it to the child on the other side.

While the others situated themselves, Thomas flicked the clasp on his bracelet open, closed, then open again. He twisted the mechanism, which emanated a series of clicks nearly as piercing as the cicadas outside. Unfortunately, Marten could not eat this particular nuisance. With another twist, the bracelet produced an array of tiny tools; how Thomas had made them and what they were used for escaped Askon, though he remembered how helpful Thomas's mechanical acumen had been back in South City.

The bracelet rattled on as Thomas twisted and closed, opened and twisted. Finally, John grabbed the younger man's wrist. "If ya don't stop that racket, I'll snap this bony twig off at the shoulder and throw that contraption, stone and all, into the lake."

Thomas wrenched his arm away. Across from them Elise's eyes had left the wall and focused on the two men. The red glow at her wrist cast doubt on John's threat, however insincere it might have been.

Askon took a deep breath. Truly, the secret was not his to share, though the stack of sketches shoved into the corner told a different story. In fact, it was Edward who first revealed the untapped power the fragments could access when brought together. Why he had excluded the women and what might happen when their fragments were brought into the process, Askon did not know. But he had stalled long enough.

"I think it goes without saying," he said, "but anything you see or hear cannot leave this room."

They nodded.

"Edward, can you explain how it works?"

The king inclined his head. "Líana knows much of this already. My mother once told me a good king hides only what is necessary from his people, and nothing whatsoever from his wife."

"'Specially if she's saved yer life on more than one occasion," John interrupted.

Edward smiled. "Indeed."

He lifted his hand from his lap and removed the ring, placing the Space fragment on the little table. It pulsed a blue shadow onto the wooden surface. "The fragments of Alora's Tear can cancel the effects of one another," he began. "This much we all know. Some of us more than others." He looked to Askon. "I knew, or rather my father knew, that the stones can also work in tandem. All of Iramov's hopes were pinned on the possibility that the Tear could be reunited and controlled by one person. Whether that is true, I am not certain, but Askon, Thomas, and I have proven that the pieces can work together." He nodded to Askon and Thomas in turn, and they each removed their fragments, placing them softly upon the table.

"Morrowmen and Caled were both wise as well as clever," Edward continued, "and it seems to me they might have already known what my father considered to be a great secret of our house. Certainly, Caled worked alongside Morrowmen for long enough to encounter the tandem possibilities."

"However," Thomas interjected, "their relationship was often adversarial, as Morrowmen himself admitted. It's equally likely they went all those lifetimes without ever discovering more than the negation effects."

"And," added Askon, "we also know the fragments grant differing abilities to each possessor. Some have greater power than others, while some demonstrate altogether new phenomena, or none at all."

Elise released her knees and slid to the edge of her seat. She leaned forward, turned an eye on Líana, and nodded toward the table. Before the darker woman's gaze had settled again on the men, Líana's ring, and the Life fragment inside it, fell to the table with a *clack*. The Death fragment, and Elise's bracelet, were last, completing the circle.

"Alright," John growled. "Now that all the jewelry's out, can a man get some answers? The fragments work together. I get it. What does that have to do with Dalkaldur?"

Edward moved to continue his explanation, but Thomas could not resist.

"Sight, Space, and Time," he blurted. "It's really that simple. Well, at least to me it seems so." He turned to Edward. "Do you mind?"

Edward shook his head. "Would it matter if I did?"

"You see," said Thomas. "Time controls the when, Space the where, and Sight, well…"

"What ya see," John offered.

"Right." Thomas nodded, his eyes alight with giddy excitement. "The thing is, we don't know what when we were watching from where or whom it was we watched."

John's face went blank, his head cocked slightly to one side as he struggled to understand.

"Maybe this will help," Askon said, rising from his stool and collecting the stack of sketches from the desk. He leafed through them with each step, frowning at his inability to convey even a fraction of what he perceived when he and his friends had watched the girl stumble through the brush.

One by one, he handed the drawings around the table. John chuckled at the girl with the too-large nose and puffy lips. "What's this supposed to be?"

Askon pressed his hands against his face and ran them slowly into his hair. He tucked both sides behind his ears. "It's supposed to show you how important what we saw was. It's all I can think about." He leveled a finger at John. "And it's more than just the girl."

So he told them, about the sky and the clouds that went on forever, about the castle and central lake, about the girl scrabbling through the bushes in her desperate escape, and finally about the book and the chest and the fragments that lay inside. When there was nothing left to tell, and after Thomas and Edward had added details of their own, Askon let his head fall again into his hands. The five fragments pulsed together, completely synchronized, the glow like a slow deep breath.

"So what you're sayin' is that it's about the girl," said John. He thumped Askon on the arm, jostling him enough that he had to steady himself on the stool.

Askon looked annoyed. "Didn't I say that it wasn't?"

John laughed. "O' course you said that. I'm not deaf. But I'm not dumb either. This parchment's thin as a bad dice player's bluff. You've had this ugly woman scratched onto it a dozen times already. And I'd bet there's more'n just one parchment. Prob'ly had five or six of 'em in the fire, like as not." He scratched at the long black hairs beneath his cheekbone.

"I may not know a thousand names and places, rites o' polite manners and the like—the way our man Edward does—and I might not be able to puzzle out the clatterbox contraptions that Thomas seems to love so much, but I know 'bout as good as anyone what a soldier looks like when he's struck by the right girl." He smiled and sucked his teeth. "Well, more often than not it's just bein' struck by any girl. So maybe it's just that?"

Though his sister's earlier remarks had made him uncomfortable, John's jabs did little to unsettle Askon. He waved the comment away and shook his head.

Elise, however, wasn't finished extracting details. "I think it's pretty clear that whatever Askon's obsession with this girl—"

"Alora," Askon interrupted. "That's what it said on the circlet. Alora."

"See?" John added with a gesture that suggested they all congratulate him.

"She is important," Elise said heavily. "If any of you could allow a person to finish a sentence, we might actually make some conclusions about what you saw."

Thomas apparently felt that her sentence had finished. "She has the circlet, which could mean anything," he said hurriedly. "It doesn't necessarily mean her name is Alora."

"Then why wear it?" Edward asked.

"I don't know. But she somehow has, had, or will have access to the fragments. And, they're the same fragments, well the same vessels, as ours."

Líana, who had remained quiet through Askon's story, scooted to the edge of her seat and stared into the multicolored ring of pulsing light on the table. Her long braid tumbled off one shoulder as she leaned forward. Soon, all eyes were upon her. She seemed entranced by the glow. Then her features pinched together in disgust, and her eyes looked up from beneath her brows. "Maybe, since we're not in the vision, this isn't our problem to solve. Something about all this just doesn't seem right. It might be better left alone."

Askon wasn't convinced. He plucked the Time fragment from the table, holding it between his forefinger and thumb. Its emerald glow lit his face in livid shadows, and for a moment, the gem eclipsed his one green eye.

"It's calling to us," he said, lowering the stone. "These fragments came to us; it is our responsibility to make use of them. We are meant for more than sitting around, hiding in rooms full of ledgers and lists."

The others glanced knowingly, nervously at each other. Askon, in his plea, did not see them.

"This girl, this Alora, if what her circlet says is true, is in danger," he continued.

"Or will be," Thomas corrected. "She can't have a book that isn't even written yet or fragments that we can see plain as day before us."

"Yes, yes. Fine," said Askon. But he wasn't finished. "She has the fragments, whenever these events take place. Most importantly, it seems that someone else wants them. Isn't it our duty to protect them, and her, in whatever way we can? Why else would the fragments show us this vision?"

John shrugged. "Random chance."

Askon's voice grew slightly louder. "If it was so random, we might have seen anything: an old boot lying in the gutter, an owl in a tree—"

"A proper woman swimming naked in a lake," John suggested with a smirk.

"Do you have to make a joke out of everything?" Askon glanced back at John, who had produced the knife again, its point carving grime from beneath his nails.

"Stop that!" Askon barked. "Do you know what Leltan would say? We don't have enough cleaning workers to take care of your leavings. They've all been reallocated to repair the granaries, or to tend the gardens, or help my useless excuse for a falconer."

Suddenly, Askon was acutely aware that all of his friends were sitting, and he was standing; for a heartbeat, the green gem glowed brighter, pulsed faster. His thoughts tangled around one another like feet in a forest of creepers.

"So much for the virtue of patience," said John. He didn't even bother to look up from his nails.

Askon cracked the gem down onto the table with the others and lowered himself onto the stool. It creaked under his weight.

Edward put a hand on his shoulder. "I understand, Askon. These things are not easy. I had the luxury of a royal grooming and education. Even so, the day-after-day tedium wears a person down. You've done the right thing by getting Leltan to help you."

"Caled didn't need a Leltan," Askon grumbled.

"No?" Edward asked. "Maybe you just never saw him. Caled governed this community for half our lives."

"More than that," said Askon.

"Well, he did so for a great deal longer than you have. Give yourself a chance. It will settle in. Soon, Leltan will seem unnecessary, and you'll be as strong a leader as Caled was." Edward let his hand fall.

"He doesn't want to."

The voice was soft, separate from the others, distant. It swept the room like a sun-shower. They all turned their eyes to her again.

"I'm right, aren't I, Askon?" said Líana. "All this," she gestured around the room, "it's what you've wanted as long as I can remember. Though I admit, I don't remember as far back as all of you." Her face flushed pink. In the time since her transformation at the hands of Morrowmen and the Life fragment, age had become a subject she avoided. She went on. "But now, you don't want it, and I think I know why.

"When we rode in, even as fast as we did, I could tell right away. This isn't our Tolarenz. The birds don't fly the same, the gardens don't grow the same, even the sun doesn't seem to shine as it once did. Edward's right. You might someday be a leader as Caled was, but that isn't what you wanted. You wanted to lead *our* people."

"Our people are gone," Askon said with a ragged breath. "And who will lead this squabbling husk of a village if not me?"

"They will," said Líana. "You can't make this into the Tolarenz we knew, but they can make it their own."

"And then what would I do?" Askon spluttered. "Where would I go?"

John smiled. "You could come sit in the tavern with me. Dalstone's none too lively these days, what with Brâghda on our side and the Lost scattered from hell to breakfast. At least we'd have a good time."

"Maybe." Askon sounded doubtful. "What about Caled, Morrowmen, Mother, Father, everyone? This is what they left to me."

"No," said Líana. "This is what they left in your care."

"What's the difference?"

John set the knife on the table. The gleaming steel and leather-wrapped handle seemed crude alongside the finely set gems; the glowing light painted a sickly rainbow over the blade. "Even I can see that," John said. "It's like Thomas's kid out there." He pointed toward the hallway. "Today, he needs Elise's, uh—"

"Breast?" Elise suggested.

"I was going to say, 'help'. But yeah," said John. "That."

"You were saying?" Elise coaxed while John stared.

"I was sayin'... I was sayin' that it's like the kid. Right now he needs all the help he can get. Can't protect himself, can't clean himself, can't feed himself, the whole works. In a few years, he'll still need Thomas and Elise, but it'll just be less and less. Then one day he'll be old enough to figure they've got it all wrong. By then it'll be too late for 'em to teach him anything else. He'll have to figure it out by himself." John grinned. "Just like your little town, here."

Askon shook his head. "But then what do I do? Where do I go?"

Still so proud of himself he seemed like to burst, John slapped him on the back. "You're Askon! You've earned a rest. Come to Dalstone or go spend some time with your new relations in King's City. Hell, go live in the forest and hunt the Lost along the borders. I'd steer clear o' the South Kingdom, though. I don't think Apopsé's too fond these days."

"Or..." It was the voice like water again. He'd known she'd come to it sooner or later. "You could tell us what you've really wanted to say this whole time."

She had him cornered, as she so often had them all cornered. Despite her lacking years, Askon's little sister seemed to understand them all more clearly than they did themselves. He wondered if the ability stemmed from the Life fragment. His own perception grew more acute under the effects of the Time fragment, but Líana's intuition was different, almost as though she felt what they did rather than simply seeing more clearly.

Askon's eyes flitted from face to face, waiting for one of them, any of them to interject, to keep him from admitting what Líana already knew. But they didn't. John went on picking at his nails. Edward and Thomas waited quietly. Líana stared at the glowing lights. If anyone would speak, Askon knew it would be Elise. She was impatient, demanding, and all too curious about what the others had seen, perhaps even jealous that they had seen it. Yet even she stayed silent.

Askon considered using the Time fragment. John could joke about patience, but Askon was no longer out for revenge, no longer so easily tipped into anger's void. He could slip under the fragment's power, read their movements, see their intent. Or he could escape, wait them out, accelerate time until their patience ran out. They would never even be aware that he had done it. But somehow, he was certain, Líana would know. She might keep it secret, but it would not matter. She would know, and he would know that she knew. He gave up.

"Alright," Askon said, curling the cuff of his shirtsleeve until it reached his elbow. "Líana's right. When you first contacted me, I made sure everyone would be here at the same time. I wanted to see each of you, and the new baby, of course, but I also hoped for something more.

"Since the wedding, I've spent so much time thinking about Dalkaldur and Alora and the fragments in the chest that I can hardly do anything else. Not to mention my failings in organizing Tolarenz. I knew Líana and Elise would want to know more about our discovery, and I knew that Edward wouldn't, and Thomas couldn't, keep them in the dark."

"And what about me?" John wondered aloud. "Am I just extra baggage?"

"Of course not," Askon said. "You may not have a piece of the Tear, but you're as much a part of this as any of us. I wanted you here, too."

"Heartwarming," John said.

Askon took a breath. He'd waited long enough, planned long enough, worried enough. "I want to go back, wherever or whenever it is. That woman needs help, and the fragments could never be safe in such a place. If nothing else, we need to look again, to try to understand who or what she's running from and why they want the fragments."

"And what if you're wrong?" asked Elise. Her eyes were cinder-black in the shadows of the little room. "Not too long ago you misjudged me, based your opinion on what you saw, fragment or no. What if you've done the same with this distressed damsel? Maybe it's us that she's running from."

Askon sighed. Elise was right. He knew nothing whatsoever about the woman in the vision. "We'll never know unless we look."

Elise smiled that same dark unsettling smile. "At least on that point, we agree."

CHAPTER FOUR

Circlets and Seekers

"So, do it!" Elise ordered. She glanced again at the wall, thinking of her son on the other side.

Edward nodded to Askon and Thomas. They stood, and Thomas moved so that all three were side by side. Sun rays filtered through the hidden room's skylight and glinted off the bits of silver and gemstones before them. The pulsing colors of the fragments slowed in unison.

"Wait," Thomas said, his voice low and uncertain. He plucked the ring with the purple stone and the bracelet with the red from the table, then handed them to the women. "We don't know how the other pieces will react when added to the process. It's possible that any number of negative outcomes could arise." He shook his head. "No. They need to go. It would be best to use only the fragments that were present before. The effect will be more predictable that way."

Líana looked worried. "We can't just leave them behind or send them with one of the guards."

Askon held out his hands, moving them slightly to indicate that Elise and Líana should give him their fragments. His sister dropped the ring into his palm with no hesitation; Elise, however, moved more slowly, guarding the bracelet, covering it with her opposite hand until finally relinquishing it into Askon's care.

The effect was immediate, like a hammer blow to the ribs. His vision blurred until he could hardly discern Líana's form from Elise's, only the black and the white made any difference. He stumbled, and a shower of sparks erupted before his eyes. His stomach, still reeling from the initial impact turned and sloshed as though he might retch. His nose was overwhelmed with the smell of blood and rot mixed horribly with spring flowers.

He grimaced against it, squinting and struggling to remember why he had taken the fragments in the first place. With an effort greater than he might have imagined, he reached out to the Time fragment and the world came nearly to a stop.

The feeling, however, did not dissipate; it grew stronger. He lumbered across the room to a wall hanging and pulled it aside. A nauseous wave curdled his insides, and he doubled over, releasing the Time fragment's effect. With his vision full of stars and his other senses reeling, he pried a stone from the wall and jammed bracelet and ring into a small alcove. As quickly as it had come, the feeling was gone. He stood for a moment, trying to recover, then replaced the missing stone. Sweat beaded his brow.

"Those things heavier than they look?" asked John.

Askon did not respond. He crossed back to Edward and Thomas.

Líana stared at the wall hanging then glanced around the room. Several of the intricately woven tapestries hung at intervals on all sides.

Askon pointed at two of them. "There are compartments behind some but not others. I found them one day by accident. One was empty, and one held some kind of documentation concerning the founding of Tolarenz. Leltan has it now. He's trying to figure out if it is important. I doubt it will be. The third had several notes concerning the Time fragment. I hoped that I'd learn something new, but it was only information that we've already discovered on our own.

"It makes no matter. Our concern now is to see the events of Dalkaldur. Morrowmen used to carry the Life fragment in a stone case. I saw him use the fragment with the case and without, but it seemed he only removed it when he needed the effect to be stronger. A thick building stone like the one that conceals these alcoves should reduce the effects even further. As long as Líana and Elise don't try to use them, I think we'll be safe."

One by one they gathered around the table, the men on one side, the women on the other, and the three remaining fragments aglow on its surface. Time and Space cast their rays across the room, painting the surrounding faces in deep blue and green. Sight, however, shone dim and steady. Askon wondered how much Thomas had trained himself to see through the sky blue gem.

In unison, they reached down to grasp the fragments. And as before, the respective colors spilled out between their fingers, casting beams of blue and green all around the room. Askon drew himself to his full height, breathed slowly, and watched as wall, chairs, and carpeted floor vanished behind Líana's expectant face.

Then recognition dawned in her eyes. The six of them floated—entirely still—above a field of purest white. Over their heads a sky bluer than the clearest day spread out to infinity around a golden sun. No fog shrouded the image this time, a product of Thomas's newfound control of the Sight fragment, Askon assumed. Then just as before, they were falling.

Through the cloud bank they went, a total whiteout through which they could no longer see even their nearest companion until they emerged on the other side. The whiteness pulled away above them and the ground rushed up: first, the mountaintops, then the foothills, then the valley floor, and last, the great glassy lake.

With no more impact than a feather alighting upon a pillowcase, they found themselves on the ground amongst tufted grass and patchy brush. Nearby, the vegetation grew thicker, blended with the outliers of spruce and fir, and vanished into a dark evergreen forest that smothered the surrounding hills.

And then, there she was, all red-brown skin and chestnut hair, even the pointed ears, which Askon had not noticed until much later when they observed her before. With a breath, he reached out to the Time fragment and her steps slowed, the image of her face drawing nearer. He began at the circlet, which clearly read "Alora" as it had before. But again the face which he had sketched and sketched and sketched was unclear. He let his eyes wander across her whole form, shoulders, chest, waist…

"Askon!"

He looked up, away from the girl stumbling through the brush. Elise was glaring at him.

"It's probably an effect of the fragments. But your agonizing study of every curve and bump on her body, we see that too."

Her voice sounded distant, as though she were calling to him from under water. Askon glanced around the circle. Líana looked embarrassed and Thomas just as awkward. Edward seemed un-moved.

"Didn't bother me none," laughed John's voice from some-where far away. Askon could see him sitting there, just as he had been in the room at the back of the hall. His eyes were trained on the image before them.

With an effort, and more than a little embarrassment, Askon tried to think about the larger picture. He had spent so much time thinking about the girl and now here she stood. Askon pushed the image back and saw again the shifting brush and looming trees. The woman stumbled into motion once more and scratched through the grass, searching.

"Now she'll go for the chest. It's buried right over there," said Thomas. He pointed to their left. The lake shimmered beyond his outstretched finger.

"Shh!" Elise hissed. "We'll see it for ourselves, if you don't mind."

As before, the girl with the copper circlet tore through the grass with both hands until she found what she was looking for. Beneath a thick layer of sod, a hole opened in the ground and light spilled out. Askon fought the urge to simply watch her work, and instead helped the others to see the book as it went into the underground chest.

"*The Book of the Tear*," Elise said quietly. Askon could barely hear her, though she stood only a few feet away. "By Thomas of Dalstone."

John chuckled. "Thinkin' of puttin' down that baby an' pickin' up a quill?"

"In fact," said Thomas, "I began work on it as soon as we returned from the wedding." He shuffled a foot across the grass. "It's mostly notes and bits and pieces of our journey. I actually started with the—"

"Shh!" Elise pointed back at the girl. She had produced another object in addition to the book. With a furtive eye on the forest, she dropped the silver chain identical to Askon's into the chest. The Time fragment's deep green added to the red and blue that already bathed the inner panels with light. She slammed the lid down.

"That's all we saw," said Askon. He waited for the image to dissipate as it had before, but the girl in the copper circlet persisted. In the time since they had arrived, their little circle had drifted slightly, positioning them between her and the forest from which she had emerged. Now, she rose and stared directly at them.

She wore a man's clothes, deep blue-gray like a lake under an overcast sky. Cut more closely than Askon's own, or those of any man he had encountered, only the leather armor that Líana and Elise wore in battle fit as tight. The style made it difficult to discern where shirt ended and trousers began. If not for a thin belt, he might have thought it a single top-to-bottom garment.

Askon could almost feel her eyes upon him. But it was not for him that she searched. In the forest beyond, branches shivered as the girl's pursuers drew nearer.

Askon swiveled around, peering into the trees. A trio of forms appeared slowly, disentangling themselves, batting at limbs and breathing hard. More fought through the forest somewhere behind them, but how many, Askon could not yet count. The three leaders brushed sticky needles from their uniforms and scanned the area.

"They're soldiers of some kind," said Thomas.

"Not from any company I've ever met," John grumbled back.

Their clothing did match, but Askon had never seen its like before either. Like the girl, their gear was the same top and bottom, making the transition between pieces vague, but where hers was blue-gray, theirs was black. Heavy belts girded their waists, about which hung an array of pouches and strange scabbards short and wide in comparison to even the broadest daggers Askon had encountered. Upon their heads, smooth helms framed oddly reflective eyepieces.

"What kind of fool wears glass in their helm?" John grunted. "End up with shards in yer eyes. Don't get any ideas, Thomas."

Thomas would have answered, but the men sprang into motion all at once. Behind them several more burst through the tree line, all wearing the shimmering black uniforms and strange helms.

The soldiers bolted across the grass, snapping brush and bracken as they went. They were shouting.

Again Askon rotated, fearing for the girl's safety, uncertain of her pursuers in spite of having seen them clearly. But when his eyes fell upon the hidden chest, she was gone.

"Where is she?" Askon shouted frantically. "She can't outrun that many."

Elise was unconvinced. "Who's to say we don't want them to catch her? And how do you know she can't outrun them? Her clothing seemed much lighter than those uniforms. And she doesn't have a helm and eyepiece to contend with."

"She's exhausted. You saw her trip and fall. More than once." Askon turned to Edward. "Can you move us?"

Edward watched calmly in that slow, ponderous thought process of his. He inclined his head. Suddenly, they were within a village, somewhere further along the bank. The girl spilled out of a wild rosebush, thorn scrapes red across her cheeks and chin. Her knees buckled as she turned an ankle against a stone. With a grimace, she lifted herself out of the rocky pathway between the shacks and limped along for several yards, panting, struggling to round the corner of the first building.

Perhaps, Askon thought, *she's hoping to lose them amid the townspeople.* But the paths were empty. Not a single person seemed to inhabit the village, just old empty houses with poorly thatched roofs and doors hanging crooked on the hinges.

Then the rosebush erupted in a blurred shower of petals and dust. The lead soldier thumped heavily through while the second trampled the bush flat behind them, clearing the way for the others. Fifteen feet ahead, the girl still struggled to gain the corner, but her ankle could no longer support even a limp. Askon thought he heard her cry out.

Off came the lead soldier's strange smooth helm, and the eye-piece too, revealing slick dark hair matted with sweat. A circlet, like the one the girl wore only in dull black, laced itself through the flat damp curls. A word was printed on the band, but Askon could not read it.

The soldier's hand dropped to his scabbard and lifted again to indicate the girl, as a commander might point a sword when his unit charges into battle. But this was not a command to the troops who filed in behind him over the demolished rosebush, and it was no sword in his hand. He held his arm still, still as a...

One more faltering step and the girl fell twitching onto the stony path. In all his time spent in King Codard's service, Askon had never seen anything like it. Her face grew red, her jaw clenched. The shuddering continued. As the soldiers gathered around her, they further obstructed Askon's view. Soon, only her ankles were visible beyond the swarm of figures in black. Her feet twitched jerkily, then intermittently, then one last time before they hung limp.

The leader collected his helm and gestured to the rest of his men. With a half-hearted kick, he reached down, plucked something from the girl's body, and pressed it onto the end of his weapon before jamming it back into the scabbard. He was shouting, his face flushed, his mouth wide and wet. A portion of the unit tromped back over the rosebush toward the hidden chest. The others followed him deeper into the village. The last two scooped up the girl, her arms and legs dangling lifelessly, and dragged her along behind the leader.

Thomas gasped. "Askon! She's still breathing."

In the hidden room at the back of the Tolarenz town hall, the air had grown warm. Now so thick and damp that every breath seemed a labor, the six of them headed for the door as one. Askon hit it first and burst onto the other side, gasping as though he had just risen from a lake bottom. He didn't stop until he heard the chirruping birds and whispering oaks of the garden. He filled his lungs with fresh air as the others appeared behind him, one after the other, until they all stood panting on the town hall doorstep.

Elise's black eyes raked over Askon and fell upon Thomas. "That's not what you told me you saw," she said. All at once, the others turned to face him.

"I—I thought," he stammered, "that we would see it. But it was—it is—after that."

Askon drew back. It was unlike Thomas to hide anything from him.

"What do you mean, *after that?*" said Askon.

Thomas looked out over the garden and into the sunlit sky. Beads of sweat trickled down his cheeks and nose. They might have been tears.

"I've seen where they're taking her," he said. "It's dark. They torture people there. And I think they're looking for us—for these." He held up his wrist where the Sight fragment lay enclosed in its mechanical casing. He tapped it with a finger. And told them the rest.

CHAPTER FIVE

Determinations

The day's last light cast the room in silver and cool blue. Edward sat, unfastening his boots. He ripped at the first buckle with a clatter as the strap slipped his grasp. After a breath he ran a thumb over his brow and down into his eye. He was tired. His hand moved slowly from his face back to the boot, and the buckle came free. With his eyes on a warped board in the floor, he flicked the laces back and forth with a series of soft pops, pulled the boot from his foot, and dropped it heavily next to the chair.

Líana rose from her seat at the foot of the bed, scooped up the tinderbox from the side table, and set a thick candle alight. Oily smoke rose from the wick, filling her nose with its charred scent before swirling into the rafters. She used the first candle to light another and another.

"Circlets and teardrop tattoos, torturers and places no one has been for hundreds of years, and fragments, fragments, fragments," Edward muttered to himself. He wasn't looking at her. She wondered if he would hear her if she chose to speak.

In a few light-footed steps, she had the tinderbox back on the bedside table and the riding clothes in a puddle about her feet. That would surely get his attention. But it didn't. He went on staring at the floorboard and murmuring about Dalkaldur, his strong face lined with worry. A few of those lines, she knew, had begun to remain on his face even as he smiled, even when they were alone.

She stood by the bed for a moment in nothing but candlelight, her long braid looped playfully over her shoulder and down her chest, before finally pulling a shift over her head and past her waist where it hung loosely above her knees. The Tolarenz town hall servants had prepared the house for them days ago, but Leltan had followed them down the path and filled a basin with water from the central well. He had left it only a few moments ago.

She would have done it herself, but she couldn't be in the square anymore. Too much fire and ash. Too many old voices.

A woman's face looked back at her from the still basin water. Her eyes were there, one green, one blue, the opposite of her brother's, and her nose, yes, that was the same too, just bigger and a bit more slender. But the rest, the rest was still foreign, even after a year. It had all happened so fast. She looked again at her husband, her king. Sometimes she wished she was still a little girl swinging sticks at trees and sneaking up on her brother in the garden.

She plunged her hands into the basin and splashed her face, rubbing away the grit from the ride. A few splashes more, and it was gone. When she looked up, Edward's other boot sat toppled next to the first. The chair held only his cloak, deep blue with his father's stag in silver. He sat down and peeled his own riding gear from his chest and shoulders, the muscles taut against the warm orange candle flames. His head fell into his hands.

The bed frame creaked as she knelt behind him and pressed her thumbs into the ridges of muscle. Round and round they went, tracing the shoulder blades and spine, her other fingers following in a loose ripple. After a slow breath, he straightened, gently removed her hands and faced her. "I can't follow him," he said.

It was there in his face. He felt like a betrayer, as though Askon had asked too great a favor. She would have known it in the dark because she could feel it too. The weariness, the indecision, the powerlessness all seemed to radiate off him in waves. With the others, she could feel the sensation, like heat or light. With Edward it was different. The waves became her own thoughts, her own feelings, and if she let them, they blotted out the Líana inside her, leaving only Edward's sadness or stress or frustration.

Back in King's City, the only remedy had been to give something, to find what he needed and provide it. Sometimes she cast the feelings out with only words, words upon words for hours. Other times, it was her body he needed, and she gave it freely, eagerly. It had been food, once or twice. That had made her laugh. Whatever the solution was on this night, she had yet to find it. Instead, she smiled weakly and kissed him, though she knew it would not be enough. He carried the weight of a kingdom and shouldered the burden of loyalty. Kisses and bodies in the dark could not bear such troubles away.

Her head hit the pillow first. Edward's followed. He shifted restlessly, but the discomfort came from within. They both knew it. When she rose to snuff out the candles, she felt Edward's doubt and exasperation lift, and a bit more of herself peeked through those dreary clouds. Then the inner curtain fell away. She was herself again. Edward had fallen into a sound sleep.

As the first candle went out, she watched the purple light of the fragment pulse in time with her husband's breathing. When the second went out, she felt just how tired she was from not only the morning's ride, but from everything: King's City and its endless parade of courtiers, a husband she loved but who often had cares and responsibilities beyond those of his wife, a brother whose dream had turned out to be little more than a tedious prison sentence, and herself—her desires not only physical but for freedom to be the woman she had dreamed on nights spent camped under the stars, waiting for a brother she wished she could stand shoulder to shoulder with on his adventures.

She blew out the third candle, and knew what she had to give.

✛ ✛ ✛

The baby was crying again. He wailed and squirmed, a face with a wide dark gap of a mouth and inside all pink gums and tongue. He had nursed only a few minutes before, content for a moment. Then the cries began, mounting slowly, softly, grating against the nerves. In the crook of her arm, his face grew redder and redder. She bounced and rocked, swayed and paced, whispered soft questions and soothing words, she even hummed a bit of song she'd heard Thomas sing on long nights. Nothing worked.

Moonlight spilled over the little red face; she had lit no candles. What good would they do? If anything, they would make it harder for Thomas to rest. He'd been given the first watch (as they'd taken to calling their nights with the sleepless child) and had done his best to keep the room quiet and dark for her. It was one of the reasons she chose him in the first place. From the moment they met in the cramped corridors of Vitæsta, he had been more considerate to her than anyone save Brâghda. And he'd eclipsed that consideration easily on their journey with Askon and in the months since the battle of South City.

Unlike their half-elven leader, Thomas was motivated by the desire to help, to make the lives of his friends better, easier, more enjoyable. As a husband, he had done exactly that, and what had she done?

When the boy was born, they told her to stay in bed, so she did. For days. They pampered her with fresh linens and whatever culinary requests she could devise; the baby had stirred a creativity of cravings she had never before felt. And for every one, Thomas was there. How he did it, she could not say. John most likely had a hand in it, though he would never admit it.

After that, it had been his constant presence and watchful eye. Just before the baby had frustrated her to the end of her wits, Thomas would scoop him up and carry him off to some other corner of their quarters or out onto the porch or into Dalstone's trackless paths for a walk. And he smiled through it all, taking it in stride as though he had been born to the task.

Then it had been, as it was on this night, his ease at caring for the child when the cries were the loudest, the nights the longest, the exhaustion the greatest. For hours he would rock and sing, place the boy in the bed they kept at the foot of their own, only to rise again shortly thereafter and do it all again.

But he could not do it forever, and now it was her turn. She hummed again, louder this time, watching as the baby's eyelids relaxed and scrunched, relaxed and scrunched, each time lengthening the period of peaceful rest. On her wrist, the Death fragment pulsed red. She hated that they called it that: the Death fragment. There was so much more to it than simply the end of life. Within it thrummed the power to take life, yes, but also it whispered of a world without life's joys, and so emphasized just how precious the little man in her arms was, how beautiful her husband's sacrifice and care was, how valuable her friends were, and how important it was to protect them—at all costs.

"Your father will want to go," she whispered to the sleeping little face. "But how can I let him?"

The boy went on sleeping. Thomas pulled the bed covers tighter around his head. She watched as he did so, hoping she hadn't woken him.

"Who will look out for you if we aren't here?" she went on. "Who will look out for *him* if I don't go?" The baby squirmed, his eyes clenching again. She loosened her hold. "It's his arms that let you sleep, that let *us* sleep. It's his voice that quiets your cries, that quiets me when the cracks begin to widen. A mother gives her child what it needs to be safe and happy. With me, you will always be safe, but with him, you'll be happy. And then, I'll be safe."

Askon would surely claim that he could defend Thomas, that he could protect the man who had given her this child, the man she had chosen to keep by her side. But Askon had made such claims before, and what had those promises come to? It was not Askon of Tolarenz who had brought Lord Iramov to an end. Nor was it the beautiful, golden sister who had all but risen from the dead to wipe away an army that truly had risen from the dead.

"It was *my* sword that ended it," she said. The baby stirred, and she bounced him lightly again. "I saved them all. I protected your father and Askon, stopped Iramov from killing Líana, saved even the king himself."

She smiled, that slow dark smile only she could conjure, but no one saw it. Not her son, not her husband, not the keeper of the Time fragment, or the king. Gently, she lay the baby into the cradle and slipped under the blankets next to Thomas. She laced her arms around him, drawing him closer.

Someone has to do more than promise to protect them, she thought. And in a heartbeat, she was fast asleep.

+ + +

The dice beat the table like a hailstorm.

"Bones and stones!" John boomed. "Drink."

It had been a bad business from the start, for the loser. The fool half-sprite might be able to rub his little necklace to make sure he was on time for an appointment, but time's got nothing to do with luck, and only a little to do with strategy. John watched as his friend poured a clumsy finger or two of brown liquid into the glass.

"So much for that clear sight o' yours," John laughed as Askon tipped the bottle upright and splashed the table with liquor. "The rule isn't 'pour'," he went on thickly, "it's 'drink.'"

An unbidden laugh climbed up from inside him and burst from his lips. After all, even a handsome man lucky as himself couldn't win *every* dice roll. But Askon was a sight worse for the wear. Those two-toned eyes of his seemed more than half crossed as he lifted the glass again to his face. It hovered there for a time, then fell to the table with a *clack* and a liquid splatter.

"You win," said the half-elf. "I don't know how you do it, but those dice fall in your favor far more often than they should."

The words were approximations, all *f*'s and *s*'s, but John got the point. He leaned back in his chair, tipping the legs an inch or two off the floor. "Ah. Now there's no sport in a sore loser," he said. "I'm not sayin' I'd never cheat. You know, make 'em tumble the way I want 'em, so to speak. But why rig the game when it's so easy to beat you?" He thumped the chair back against the floor. Askon wobbled visibly and brought his elbows down on the table.

"We all have our skill set," Askon mumbled. His eyelids drooped like dead leaves on a pond, unsure whether they ought to float or sink.

When Askon had given them the speech, John was onboard before his friend had even truly begun. It had been hours ago, but it felt like days. Around the fire in the main hall, they had sat: Líana with her pretty braid and prettier body, a ghost in white linen and fire shadows; Edward, stoic and stern, too much a king already and not nearly enough the prince who'd once lost a similar dice game in the foggy forests near Vestgæta; Thomas, the fool, though a fool John couldn't help but call friend, with his unnamed baby asleep in a swaddling blanket; Elise, dark and dangerous, and all the more attractive because of it; and of course, Askon up in front of them all making his case.

"I know you have responsibilities," Askon had said. "And I don't expect that you'll all join me, though I hope you'll at least consider it."

He'd been pacing. That meant he was unsure of what he was about to do next. John had seen it time and time again: in the tunnels under Austgæta, on the field in the battle of Dalstone, in King Codard's chambers, and on and on. What the fool didn't know was that he would always end up choosing the most drastic and heroic course. John had seen that too. It was how they ended up at Iramov's tent, surrounded by guards, and how Askon had ended up in a swarming Norill camp all by himself with only a half-crazed, half-starved prince to help him escape. And here he was about to do it again with this woman he'd only ever seen in those fancy stones.

"I'm going to Dalkaldur," Askon had continued, to the surprise of no one. "The elves came through to our world in that place. You all remember the story. Morrowmen told us everything while—"

"Yeah. Not me," John had offered. "If ya recall, I was busy actually doing something to help the war effort. While you all sat and had a nice dainty dinner, complete with story time, my Darts and Brâghda's warriors were cuttin' down Iramov's men only to have 'em get back up the next day."

They had all looked at him then. It was how they always looked at him, like he was stupid, or nothing more than an over-grown child. Truth was, humor had always seemed a better alter-native than all their dour seriousness. A wisecrack had never stopped him from driving a spearpoint through an enemy's breastplate.

"Well, you've heard it since then," Askon said. He clearly wasn't in the mood for John's commentary, which had only made John want to comment all the more.

"Don't worry," he said. "I won't make ya tell it again. It's not gonna change what ya want from us anyway."

Askon had shrugged his shoulders at that, an old habit he'd kept up since his bird had flown the coop to live with Líana. John couldn't blame Marten's choice.

"It's simple," said Askon. "I want to go to Dalkaldur and in-vestigate what we keep seeing with the fragments. There's a reason the Tear is showing her to us. I think we're supposed to help her."

"And what if we're meant to stop her?" said Elise in that harpy screech she used when trying to get her way. She'd brought the damned idea up enough times. John hoped Askon would just give her a straight answer.

There was a long pause. "Then we stop her," Askon said. But he didn't mean it. Not a single breath of that was true. Of course, Askon hadn't known it, though John could see it clear as day.

Edward sighed. "What about our responsibilities? You have them. I have them. John has the Darts. Elise and Thomas, the baby."

John was already a step ahead. This wouldn't go over well with the king's little blond wife. Especially considering how quick she could be with blade in hand. A person with the power to mend even the most life-threatening wounds could certainly wring more than a little pain out of another.

But she didn't say anything about it. For all his experience reading the actions and inactions of soldiers, John's predictions concerning women were strikingly inaccurate. When he thought they'd attack, they'd retreat into themselves. When he figured they'd throw themselves at him, they usually threw their drinks in his face instead. Sometimes he wondered if he could understand them simply by predicting the opposite of his gut feelings about them.

Askon had finished his speech, and the others had gone to their rooms shortly thereafter. None of them gave an answer. John had patted his friend on the back then.

"They'll come around," he'd said, uncertain whether or not it were true. "Ya got me on one condition."

"Do I?" Askon said. "And what condition is that?"

That's when John had lifted the little leather bag he carried. Inside were the polished bone dice that had lost him plenty of pay and earned him many a night's worth of escape from the toils of battle. They'd won him the eye of many a tavern girl, though they were always better looking right after a dice game than in the morning. And they'd won him food, and sometimes trinkets, or a bed in the street while he sobered up. But tonight, he simply figured they'd win him a laugh at his friend's expense. It would be more than enough payment to follow Askon to a place no sane person even believed was actually real. And by the look in Askon's eyes, he needed a drink—or a dozen.

Now, with his face hanging low above the table, his eyes glassy and unfocused, Askon said it again. "You win."

John laughed. "Of course, I win. You're always too busy pushin' parchments around your stuffy back room to have any fun. Ya gotta get acclimated to a life as enjoyable as mine."

"Well I'm not going to!" Askon shouted. Nothing would come of it, John knew, but the few times Askon had actually had this much to drink, his old anger tended to surface in his voice, whether he truly was angry or not. Then a little more calmly, he said, "She's in trouble, John, or will be. I'm supposed to help her. I know it."

"Yeah. I figured you'd say that." John snatched Askon's glass from the table and held it up. "I never told you the stakes of the game."

Askon looked tired, confused. "What? If I win, you go with me? You win…"

John tipped back the glass. "I go with you."

CHAPTER SIX

A Secret Revealed

His tongue felt like he had slept through the night with a mouthful of sand, and his eyes, swollen and puffy, squinted against the half-light. At least Leltan hadn't thrown open the curtains. Where was Leltan anyway? Askon sat up slowly, and nearly toppled back into bed. Inside his head, something sloshed around painfully. When he reached up to stop it, his cheeks felt hot against his tingling fingers. He let out a ragged breath.

"Damn it, John," he grumbled to the empty room.

At least the drinking match had done some good. If nothing else, now he knew that his trip to Dalkaldur wouldn't be a solitary one. The thought of saddling a horse and riding alone into the southern mountains seemed to him foolish at best, and improved only slightly with added company.

Unfortunately, having John along didn't help matters much. To accomplish his aim, Askon needed the others. A pang of guilt roiled through his stomach. Or was that the remains of the drink? Whatever it was, the guilt lingered. He hadn't asked them the hardest question the night before. It was easier to simply request that they all follow him to Dalkaldur, but if his plan were to succeed, what he really needed were the fragments.

With an effort, and another significant wobble, he made his way across the room to the basin. It was a small room, really only large enough for the bed, the dresser upon which he had placed the basin, and a small desk and chair for nights when he could not sleep. Like the larger desk in the back room of the hall, this one too was covered with sketches and speculation about Dalkaldur and the girl, though in total there were only a handful of parchments in his sleeping quarters, compared to the dozens in the larger room.

After a splash of cold water, he felt more himself, but the drumbeat of drink throbbed along unabated. He tried to shut it out. Fumbling along the dresser, he found a towel and dried his face and hands. He wondered again where Leltan was, assuming his new assistant had found him in his defeated state and elected to begin the day's business on his own.

At least he had proven himself good for something.

Askon rested his hands on the dresser for a moment, then opened the drawers and pulled on some loose-fitting riding clothes, laced up his boots, and lifted his cloak from the hook by the door. He folded it over one arm and reached for the handle. With a sharp intake of breath, his hand snapped to his chest and felt for the Time fragment. It wasn't there.

He turned back toward the bed, over-rotated, and had to catch himself on the dresser. There, hanging from the corner of the mirror, the Time fragment pulsed green. Little flecks of its light rippled off the basin water. Askon pressed his fingers to his temples and scolded himself for being so careless. At least they had been in Tolarenz where threats were unlikely. Had they been on the road or in a tavern somewhere, John's little game could have become an unforgivable mistake.

With his panic and his balance once again in check, Askon looped the silver chain around his neck and dropped the stone beneath his shirt. It was cold against his chest, like a heavy chunk of ice. He stepped through the door into the hallway that led to the main chamber.

They were waiting for him, each and every one. Around the table they had seated themselves, the remnants of a breakfast at the center. The rest of the hall was empty and most of the shades, thankfully, still drawn tight. At the far end near the door, light peeked through the windows. Askon averted his eyes, shielding them with the cloak draped about his arm. Through squinting lids, he peered up at them.

Pang!

Every head turned toward the sound. John stood at the table's foot with a cast-iron pan in each hand, grinning through his black beard. Edward only rolled his eyes, as did Líana. Thomas looked ready to strike a blow, but his hands were full with the baby boy who cooed and murmured, seemingly undisturbed by the racket. Elise, satisfied that John had not upset the child, eyed Askon through a curtain of dark hair. She pushed it aside.

"The hero returns," she said dryly.

Pang! John beat the pans together once again. This time Elise rounded on him.

"Once is enough of your childish game," she snapped. "It's your fault he's in this state to begin with." John lowered the pans. "You've had your fun."

"Yes, you have," Askon added.

John dropped the pans to the floor with a deliberate clatter. He flopped into the chair and slid heavily to an elbow, one boot clicking rhythmically against the table leg. He breathed in as if to say something but thought better of it and exhaled audibly.

"I apologize," Askon began.

"Well, you shouldn't." It was Thomas. He held the boy in one arm and a piece of bread in the other. "Everyone needs a chance to relax. You most of all, maybe. We all know you've been looking forward to our arrival. And anyway, it seems like your man Leltan has everything under control."

Askon laughed. It hurt. "I'm sure he does. It's likely he'd rather every morning started this way."

"He is a very organized little fellow," said Edward.

For several minutes the others talked about Leltan and his various ticks and tendencies. Askon simply tried to breathe. He poured a glass of water from a pitcher, drank it in one long draught and then poured another. He was halfway through the third when the others acknowledged him again.

"Are you alright?" Líana asked. She looked concerned. "You know, I've never tried it, but I bet the Life fragment could help you."

Askon shook his head. "I don't think that's necessary. I'm feeling better. I just need a little time." He laughed quietly to himself, *time*.

"Actually," he began again, "let's not talk about fragments or visions or any of it this morning. You're all here for more than that. We can discuss it later. Give me a few moments and we'll go find Leltan. Maybe there's something we can help him with. Besides, you've hardly seen what's been done with Tolarenz since the wedding. I think after a walk and a little work, we'll all feel better."

John scooted the chair back. "Speak for yerself. Work's about the last thing I'm interested in. Though I do recall seeing a few faces on the way in that I'd like to get to know a little better." He laughed, a boom that rumbled from deep within his chest. "Maybe I'll have work to do after all."

"Doesn't it seem a bit early for that?" Edward said.

"Never too early for that kind o' work, if ya ask me," John replied.

Edward rapped his ring against the table, drawing John's attention to the significant looks all around.

"Right," John corrected. "Probably best to tend to that later."

Outside the sun shone bright, and Askon felt the sharp tug of regret. At least inside the town hall there had been shade and water and food. Under the unflinching sun, John's drinking game felt all the more foolish. Askon showed them everything he could think to show in the little town, every change, every difference. A new smith was forging where Roland had once cheerily beaten out tongs and shovels and the occasional sword. The mill ground flour again, its wide sails trundling along with the wind. Will Fernwood's falcons circled above the lake, though not so numerous or so free as Halan's had been.

And then it came to it. In the early afternoon, the party had seen all that Tolarenz had to offer, and they reached the end of the path. Askon turned sharply on one heel, headed back to the hall, but Líana stopped him. She pulled on his shirtsleeve, and he almost reached down to pat her on the head, to ruffle the little blond curls. But when he turned to look, he remembered Líana the woman, the *queen*, and laughed to himself.

It was in their eyes as well: Edward, Elise, John, Thomas, all of them. With a sigh, Askon stared up the grassy slope to his childhood home. Líana wanted to go, so they would go.

Along the pathway his father's trees had taken root. Not all, naturally, but enough to make him smile. They were tough, and outside of their little pots, almost impossible to kill. Elsewhere, weeds and wildflowers filled the empty spaces. And from foundation to eaves, the house had sprouted thick ivy that hung like a rich green winter coat, shaggy and tangled.

Líana approached the door, but Askon stopped her.

"Wait," he said. "I haven't been entirely honest with all of you."

Askon released Liana's hand and shook his head. "I can't stand it here. Everywhere I look, I see another reminder of what Tolarenz used to be, *who* it used to be. I've tried to replace them. I've sorted the bickering, settled the disputes, assigned and reassigned everyone." A scowl crawled across his face. "It's just not the same."

Líana drew closer. "Of course it isn't," she began.

"You'd a' had to tell me twice, if I'm bein' honest," interrupted John. "Ask me, this place is about as un-different as it could be."

"He's right," Thomas agreed. "Though I never came here before we met, Tolarenz seems as ordinary as any small village in the kingdom. To return to such conditions after the devastation this place saw, it's remarkable."

Elise narrowed her eyes. She had spent most of the morning in silence, glancing back toward the hall where her son was sleeping in peace. "You should be happy for what you have. What is the alternative, an empty valley where all the houses look like this one?" She ran her fingers through the ivy. "At least there's life here. The world is—"

"I know," Askon barked. And immediately realizing his mistake, bowed his head. "I'm sorry. It's just, I'd hoped for so much here. Now, all I can think about is a place or time that makes no sense and a girl who might not even be real. I need to go there. I need you to come with me. And there's still something I haven't told you."

Edward smiled, but it was not an expression of mirth. His face was grim, dark, as though a storm cloud had settled somewhere behind his eyes. "Then two of us have left something unsaid, and we are not so unalike." He motioned them to the door. Líana opened it, and they all stepped inside.

They sat on the floor. The furniture was gone, fuel for Iramov's fire. The house felt as dead as a skeleton left to bleach white in the summer sun. John shifted uncomfortably.

"Well get on with it, you two!" he ordered.

Askon, with a nod, deferred to Edward who, perplexed at such a formal gesture, returned the favor to his friend.

"I'm not wearing a crown. I haven't brought any guards. Don't treat me as though I'm anything but your friend. That is all I am today, for now at least."

Again Askon gave a nod, but this time he began slowly. "I've thought this through a bit more than I let on yesterday." He brushed a lock of hair away from his face. "I do need as many of you as are willing to come with me to Dalkaldur—"

"You know what you're sayin' don't ya?" John asked. "It's not just like we hop on a pony for a quick ride to that place. We don't even know where it is."

Elise leveled a glare at him, and though John did not quaver under her gaze, his eyes betrayed him and he was silent. "I want to hear what he still isn't telling us," she said.

She brought her fist down against the floor to punctuate the point. It produced a satisfying *thump*, and she looked across at Askon.

Thump. The same sound again. But no one had moved.

Askon's head flicked toward the ceiling; all eyes turned upward. His hand dropped reflexively to his right hip, but the sword hilt he expected to feel was not there. With a shake of his head, he muttered a curse and rose from the floor. His desk-bound months had cultivated a habit of leaving his sword in his quarters. As the leader of Tolarenz, he was no warrior and thus did not need such a weapon with him at all times. At his other hip, however, was the long hunting knife he refused to part with. He found the hilt and popped the clasp.

The others stared quietly. Edward stood now, as did Thomas and both women. John remained seated.

"Probably just a kid rummagin' through. Or, considering the state of this place, could be a squirrel or raccoon," he said. A huge yawn escaped his mouth, and he scratched his ear. "By all means, go hunt it down."

They left him there, though Askon couldn't help but smile to himself. Even after nearly a year, the old reflexes persisted. He let his hand fall to his side but left the clasp open. Above, the floorboards creaked. Another *thump* issued from the rooms at the top of the staircase.

"Hello?" Askon called. "You shouldn't be in here. Do you know who is speaking?"

No answer.

He cupped a hand to one side of his mouth. "It is Askon. This is my family's home. Show some respect and leave it be. It is no place to play!"

Another creak of the floorboards.

John laughed. "Would *you* answer? I know what I'd be doin'. Tryin' to hide or climb out a window." He shook his head. "Probably did that more'n a few times back in Dalstone as a kid."

"Whoever it is shouldn't be here," Askon snapped. He turned a glare on John and took the stairs two-at-a-time to the top.

His feet hit the landing, and he realized what his actions might look like to his friends or to the intruder—if the intruder happened to be one of the younger children simply caught in a place where they shouldn't have been. With a breath Askon checked his speed, assuming again the posture and temperament he had witnessed so often in Caled.

He went left first, toward the space that had been his own room. It was empty, as empty as it had been the day he met Morrowmen, the day he had received the Time fragment. Next was Líana's room, also empty. She was at the foot of the stairs looking up when he passed the landing again.

Thump.

He lengthened his stride, covering the distance to his parents' room in only a few steps. The door stood ajar. Behind it, the room glowed with sunlight. Applying his best stern look of disapproval, he pushed the door aside. The light came through the windows stronger than he had expected, and a brilliant glare shone against the still-broken glass that he and Iramov's soldier had shattered in their struggle. He raised a hand to shield his eyes and, through the throb of headache, sidled along the edge of the room until the glare darkened. He lowered his hand.

Across from him, only a few steps from the window stood an adult Norill. Its eyes moved sluggishly, as if confused or disoriented. When they alighted on Askon, the creature cocked its head to one side. It took a step forward.

Askon put up his hands, palms outward, and looked into the Norill's face. "Are you Grafmark Norill?" he asked softly. "We know Brâghda. Do you come from Vitæsta?"

The Norill took another step forward. The names, and the words in general, seemed to have no meaning to it. It stepped forward again.

"*Sors?*" it asked. The tone was flat, hollow somehow, as if the creature had asked the same question a thousand times.

Askon shook his head. "I do not speak the Norill tongue, though I know someone who can." He gestured to the door. "I am Askon." He pointed to his chest where the Time fragment rested at the end of its chain.

As if a flame had kindled behind the creature's eyes, its face came suddenly to life. "*Sors?*" it wondered again.

"This?" Askon lifted the chain. "Maybe that's how Brâghda told you to recognize me." The fragment pulsed along with his measured breathing.

"*Sors!*" the Norill said, louder this time. It stepped forward, now only a few feet from Askon. "*Sors.*" A click rattled low in its throat. Another step. "*Sors,*" it said, as though admiring its beauty and power.

With his palms still outstretched, Askon backed further toward the door. The creature followed with sluggish eyes, muttering the word over and over. Then, just as Askon passed through the door frame, it stopped and emitted another click. Without warning, the creature's legs bent, flexed, and it launched itself at Askon. The hunting knife clattered away as they both went down. Askon's head bounced off the floorboards, and a burst of white light filled his eyes. He lifted his hands, fending off blow after blow.

The Norill snarled and spat as it tore wildly at Askon's wrists, trying desperately to pry them away. All the while its eyes stared at the glowing gem. In a wild rush, it batted Askon's hands away, and brought both its fists down on his forehead.

When his vision returned, Askon found his hands curled tightly around the fragment. The Norill reared back, something silver glinting in its hand. The knife.

The blade flashed down and halted with a *pop* only an inch from Askon's face. Then the knife retracted, and the creature screamed in rage and pain as its forearm snapped. The knife dropped to the floor. With another snarl and a frothing screech, the creature turned on its assailant just in time to see the sole of John's boot collide with its cheek and jaw. It tumbled into the corner limply. The boot came down again. A crunch told Askon that it would not rise.

CHAPTER SEVEN

A King's Troubles

"It wanted the fragment," Askon said a quarter of an hour later. While he regained his wits, John and the others had combed the house and surrounding property. All evidence suggested the Norill had been alone. Now, they sat together before the empty hearth. Askon nodded to Elise. "What does that word mean, *sors*?"

She shook her head. "It has more in common with what we would consider a word part. It applies to actions and when they take place. It wouldn't make any sense on its own, like calling something a *pre* or a *'tion*." She shook her head again and a strand of black fell over her eye.

"So it isn't a Norill word," said Thomas. He was twisting the mechanism on the bracelet again, opening, closing, opening. "Maybe it's another dialect or another language altogether? Surely there are other Norill tribes besides Grafmark and the Lost."

Edward stood. He pulled his shoulders back and looked down at them with stern gray eyes. Askon's fragment pulsed and he saw clearly the new king's intent: a crinkle of the brow here, pupils changing size, a glance at Líana.

"Regardless of the language, it wasn't acting alone," Edward said.

John looked up, his legs stretched straight across the floor. He lifted one foot and crossed the other at the ankle. "Now, I just searched this place high and low, an' you're tellin' me that our intruder's brought more than himself along?" He tapped his toes together. "Seems unlikely."

"That's not what I meant," said Edward, an edge creeping into his voice. His eyes narrowed, then closed, and he rubbed his forehead slowly. "Not here. The others aren't in Tolarenz."

"Others?" wondered Thomas.

"Yes," Edward continued. "It started weeks ago. At first we took them for isolated attacks by the Lost or some other tribe as yet unknown to us. For a time, we thought perhaps the Lost had splintered, some of them retreating to the north while other factions remained in Vladvir to cause mischief in the smaller villages. Messages came from all around the kingdom."

"Not from Dalstone, they didn't," piped John. He clicked his boots again to emphasize the point.

Edward sighed. "You're right. There weren no reports from Dalstone, but every other area where my scouts keep watch have at least heard stories of Norill attacks. And they are all eerily similar to what we've seen here today."

Askon watched Edward closely, his face suddenly worn and tired. Whatever these incidents and their frequency, his friend had been troubled by them more than he let on, maybe more than he recognized himself. With the fragment's help, Askon knew the right question to ask. "You've heard that word before, haven't you? *Sors.* What does it mean?"

Edward dropped the hand from his forehead. "I think I know, but cannot yet be sure."

John gave a tremendous snort. "Well, that's a great deal of no help at all," he laughed. "Every bit as useful as nothin', though I don't suppose sittin' in your tower's done a lot o' good in discoverin' anythi—"

"That is enough! I am the king of Vladvir. And I'll not be spoken to in such a way on matters of my kingdom's security!" Edward shouted. It was so unlike him that they all sat back, or gasped, or blanched. All except John.

"Hm," he mumbled. "Seems I struck a nerve on that." A smile spread through his thick beard. "Now don't take offense. I just figured I ought to test how serious you are about all this."

With little more than a rustle of the cobwebs, Líana was at Edward's side, holding his shoulder tightly. "Very serious," she said. "Imagine if you will, being a farmhand or a baker or a weaver at the loom. A creature out of your darkest fears appears in your house or at the roadside demanding something you can't give. It is aggressive, murderous even, and altogether uncommunicative."

Thomas nudged John with an elbow. "It means no matter what you say, they won't understand it, and no matter what they say, you won't understand it."

John glowered, but Askon knew. Thomas had been right to explain.

Edward put his hand over Líana's and nodded. "And now imagine the same story occurring a dozen times across a kingdom. There's no way of knowing when or where they will strike, but it's frightening the people. They'd likely stay in their houses, if their houses were safe. They'd likely seek out the attackers, if they didn't seem to appear out of thin air. There is no solution. None, at least that I or my advisors have been able to uncover. And now it's happened here."

"Thomas," Elise barked. "The baby." Her face went dark, and she began to lift herself from the floor. The Death fragment glowed red at her wrist.

Líana, who was standing next to her, placed her other hand on Elise's shoulder. "It's alright," she said in that steady way that told them nothing could be more true. "These incidents only happen once at a given location. It is always some time before the same village reports another."

Elise stood anyway but did not leave. Her eyes darted to the door, then back to Líana. Thomas had begun dragging a finger through the dust. To the others it looked like an idle motion. Then it became clear. He was drawing a crude map of Vladvir. Grafmark forest on the left, the great river Estelle down the center, the forest of Ellmed on the right, and the wide Vladvir plain between.

"Where have the attacks taken place?" he asked Edward.

John puffed a loud sigh. "Didn't you listen to anything? He said they were all over the kingdom."

Askon thought he saw a glimmer of blue flash through the Sight fragment. Thomas shook his head. "No. I heard the generalities. I want specifics. Your Highness—"

"Don't do that," said Edward with a smile. "I overreacted with John. I'll have no titles from any of you."

"Right then," Thomas continued. "Edward. Where exactly have the reports come from?"

Edward knelt beside Thomas and pointed. "It started near the Austgæta reconstruction. We thought nothing of it at first. Of course the Norill would return to that area. It was only later that we realized the Austgæta attack was related to the others."

Thomas put his finger in the dust, leaving a smudge behind on the floorboard. "And?" he coaxed.

The king's finger moved south. "Then in Shale. There have actually been multiple incidents there, but each one is days apart from the last."

Thomas marked his hometown with three dots.

Edward continued. "We've had several in King's City, though with the larger population it is difficult to tell which are real encounters and which are rumor."

Three dots for King's City.

"One was reported at Greyarc, one on the road near the borders of Grafmark, at least three in Vilmar and the surrounding area—"

John laughed. "How is Iramov's ol' stomping ground anyway? I thought about headin' up there to see for myself a time or two."

With a sigh, Edward began to speak, but Líana cut him off. "The people are confused and scared that outsiders will come for them. Iramov controlled the area, but that does not mean he was supported in his efforts. You saw his army. Can you blame those who went along with his wishes?"

"I might," said John. But everyone knew there would be no more discussion of Vilmar or its people.

Clearly irritated at the interruption, Thomas thumped his hand against the floor. "Were there more attacks?"

"I have rumors of similar sightings in the South Kingdom. But of course, that's all I have from them these days. Apopsé has not openly challenged me or the kingdom, but that conflict will need attention in its time as well."

"Is that all of them?" asked Thomas.

Edward gestured expansively to the house. "And now Tolarenz. But yes, that is all I am aware of at this point."

The younger man scratched absently behind his ear, looked about the room and back down at the floor. He twisted the mechanism on his bracelet back and forth, and again Askon thought he saw a flash of blue course over the gem inside. The moment lengthened. Thomas counted the dots, then recounted, his hand hovering here and there over the map.

"None in Reed?" he asked.

"No."

"Vestgæta? Norogæta?"

"None in Vestgæta, and we haven't begun rebuilding Norogæta yet."

Thomas rubbed his palms together and stared down at the floor. The rhythmic swish continued for another long moment while Thomas breathed softly, deep in thought. Then the swishing stopped, and the room was suddenly silent. He lowered his finger, drawing a line from Tolarenz to Austgæta to King's City to Shale, then to the Greyarc and to Grafmark, down the Grafdrek and into the South Kingdom. When he reached South City, he flopped back into a seated position. His hand went to his forehead.

"Look familiar to anyone?" he asked. "Askon?"

To another onlooker, the swirls in the dusty floor would've been nothing more than that. But to those gathered around Thomas's makeshift drawing, the lines and dots meant a great deal more. Askon circled around the image and knelt on Thomas's other side. The path was perfectly clear, as it would be, Askon assumed, to all of them. It was his path through the kingdom from the moment he set out from Tolarenz to Iramov's end at South City.

"It follows our footsteps almost exactly," Askon said softly.

Thomas turned to face his friends. "I don't think it does."

Edward followed the line with his finger. Once, twice, three times. He shook his head. "What do you mean? Of course it does. Well, some of us weren't at each of the points. For instance, Elise didn't come along until Dalstone. But it is Askon's path, and eventually all of ours."

"Not all," said John. "I took quite a different route much of the time. Look." He pointed at Grafmark on the map. "No sightings in Grafmark, and I was up and down that place while you all took your sweet time gettin' to South City."

Thomas nodded. "It's possible that Norill encounters have gone unnoticed in Grafmark, mistaken perhaps for Brâghda's people."

"The alternative," said Elise darkly, "is that we just haven't heard the stories yet. Maybe the attacks have been more successful in Grafmark. Maybe the victims are dead and no one was there to see it."

A silence hung over the group for a time. Thomas broke it.

"No. The path we're seeing here isn't our own, not precisely. It's the fragments'. They're showing up everywhere that the pieces of Alora's Tear were used."

CHAPTER EIGHT

Punctures

Metal hissed against metal. He was back again. The man whose voice menaced in the darkness. For what seemed to her like days, he had berated and demanded, shouted and spat. Sometimes mentally, sometimes physically, he tried and tried again. There had been no more light.

"Are you ready to tell us yet?" he asked over the dry rasp of steel on stone.

The little dance always began this way. He would ask. She would resist. He would rage, shout, hit her. But it went no farther. He threatened, oh yes, he often threatened. Something, however, stopped him every time.

She thought now of those other times. A bucket of icy water to the face. How did he enter the room so silently? A hard slap out of the quiet darkness. The bruise still hot and tight on her cheek. The chair beneath her yanked out to send her crashing to the floor. Yet it was never more than bruises.

And the food. They'd taken it from her, dumped it inches from her chair where the smell wafted up to her nose; fed her moldy bread; and once gave her something she could not identify in the dark but devoured so quickly she hardly noticed. This time, though, there'd be no food. She'd already eaten—ravenously—and several hours ago, she guessed.

He had laughed.

"How many times must we do this?" he wondered aloud. The metal grated to a stop. "Soon *she* won't tell me to stop. She'll let me cut, cut, cut." He chuckled. It turned her stomach. "Pretty ones, not pretty ones, men, it doesn't matter. Eventually she lets me. And they all scream." The scraping began again. "*She's* the one that stops me, you know? Tells me to take it easy. Once she's mad? Then I get my way."

Another empty threat, the same as a half-dozen others? No. This time, something was different. Every sentence leapt gleefully from his lips, a chilling child's inflection in a man's intonation. The scraping stopped again. His boots thumped closer. In the dark each step thundered. It had been so long since there was any light. Only the sounds told her where she was, where *he* was. And the sounds grew louder, clearer, closer.

Then the door clicked shut.

She listened, waiting for him to speak, to run the steel against the stone, to try again to scare her. When he didn't, she could still sense him. She closed her eyes. Or were they already closed? It was hard to tell anymore. Then she heard it. On the other side of the door. Voices, muffled and soft, but her time here made muffled and soft seem clear as church bells in winter. It was the kind-spoken woman and the man.

"We've opened several more today." The woman. "No. Of course they don't come back. And who would care? We see what they see. Until they're dead, that is."

Then the man. But even with her heightened hearing it was too soft, too far away.

"Yes. We need more time." The woman again. "No. Not a hole. Not a door. A quick puncture that we can sew up just as quickly. And if we can't sew it up? Well, we don't yet know."

A long pause.

"We don't know about the others either. Sight is here. That's for certain. We saw her with it. If we find it, we'll find the rest."

The door clicked again, swung open, then shut. His steps crossed the room. She counted them. *One, two, three, four.*

His breath warmed her cheek, and she expected it to be sour and foul. Instead it smelled of sweetened mint, and beyond that, a musky spice like crushed tea leaves. He didn't touch her, but she could feel him moving around the chair, one thumping step at a time.

"One more chance?" he rumbled from somewhere behind her.

No. No more mistakes. She breathed deep. Listened for him. Shivered.

Now the steps thudded around the other side, almost a complete circle from where he had started. Then, a shuffle.

"Easy. Start with something easy, she told me. How about a name?" The voice came from below, near to the floor.

They know that already. Why ask my name? They've known since it began. Since they started following us. Since I first met—

A lance of pain spiked through her foot, searing, burning as though lit afire from the inside. The dull *thunk* of metal on wood reached her ear a split second later.

She screamed.

"That's not a name!" he shouted over her. Then his hand was on her knee. He pulled it left, right, grabbed the blade lodged in her foot, wrenched it loose, drove it down again.

"Alora!" she shrieked as her leg twitched and shuddered. "My name is Alora!"

"I know," he said flatly. "What a wonderful start. Except there's no cliff for you to jump off, and it's just ordinary tears and snot running down your face. I doubt you even look the part after being in here. But I want the other names." He pulled the blade free and drove it down a third time.

Again she screamed. And told him all the names.

✝✝✝

A fierce afternoon sun blazed down, warming their faces and backs only moments after dragging Thomas out of the house. Elise knelt in front of him on the stairs, her pale hands flashing up to his face, down to his hands, and back again. The gem at her wrist glowed red, and she murmured something to him. John, above them by the door, stared down with hardened eyes, but it had been John who dragged the young man from the musty sitting room into the daylight.

"He's not hurt," said Líana softly. She lay her hand on Elise's shoulder.

The dark woman's head snapped around, every bit as keen and deadly as a striking snake. Her eyes were black against the shadowy frame of her hair, and Líana recoiled ever so slightly.

"You'll let me be the judge of that," she hissed. It was the cold command that gave no room for debate, no option but compliance. "If there's nothing you can do to help him, then get away from us!"

Líana took a step back, and Edward's arms caught her. She pressed her face against his chest. "He'll wake up," she whispered. Edward nodded and let his chin rest on her head. Her fingers twisted into her long blond braid as she watched them, Thomas shifting and fitful on his back, Elise hovering over him.

Askon watched them too, watched them all. Above them on the peaked window of the second floor Marten was also watching. Askon felt a sense of standing outside the image his friends composed: king and queen wrapped in each other's arms; a father lying unconscious before his wife and the baby somewhere in the hands of a stranger; a gruff man, equal parts bristle, gristle, and irreverence; and above them all, the intelligent—inhuman—gaze of the falcon. Marten loved them as Askon loved them, would protect them as Askon would protect them, had done so, but could never be one of them. And all of it painted against the backdrop of a village brought to life from the brink of death.

Thomas sat bolt upright. "Alora!" he shouted.

Elise wrapped her arms around him, but he hardly moved. His eyes, wild, almost frantic, scanned the gathered faces and alighted on Askon.

"Her name is Alora."

The Sight fragment flickered blue. Then it went dead. Thomas slumped against Elise, his breathing ragged. He stared past her to the ground where one of the little trees had twisted its roots around an overturned pot and back into the earth. "He's hurting her. Hurting her until she tells him."

"Tells him what?" Edward wondered.

Thomas looked up into the stern gray eyes. "About us."

Had the breeze not rushed over the hills, they might have heard the deep green cloak stir. Elise rose from where she knelt at the front of the house. She rounded on Askon, red gem glowing, black hair streaming. But whatever she had hoped to say, she never said, because he was already gone.

CHAPTER NINE

Departure

Leltan,

It is with heavy heart and burdened mind that I write these words. Never in my farthest imaginings did I expect anything less from myself than full devotion to our cause. When Iramov's army fell and Apopsé was revealed as a traitor to our people, I would have gone beyond the edge of the world. Would have walked, climbed, swam to where the sea meets the sky in order to rebuild Tolarenz. And so we have.

But now I must go. For so long I have known it, and now I must act. An errand beckons me. It is one I must choose either to answer or to lose myself in the madness of its call. I cannot tell you where I will go, as I myself am not yet certain, though it is possible I shall not return.

And so I leave you as Steward of Tolarenz in my absence. Protect it and guide our people. You have already done so much. Perhaps they needed me only to begin. Now they will need themselves—and you—to continue.

With unequal parts regret and hope,

Askon

Askon's fingers trembled as he flicked the final stroke over the paper. He folded it gently and ran a slow crease across its length. Repeating the process, he reached for the wax which had only just begun to melt over the flame at the edge of the desk. He pulled it nearer, poured a bit onto the fold, and pressed down the seal. As it cooled he busied himself with the final preparations. His pack had already been set aside, long before his friends had even arrived. His sword was sharp and wrapped for travel, his armor oiled and fitted. The town hall kitchen had supplied food: dried meats and fruit, root vegetables, nuts, and the like. He hadn't told them why.

Now it was only a matter of gathering the maps and sketches. Though no self-respecting cartographer would have given them a second look, Askon knew that in either their smudged lines or pale spaces lay the secret to finding his destination. Somewhere in those details was the valley of white flowers. Somewhere in the snows of the Southern Mountains, he'd find Dalkaldur.

And that would only be the first step. John, he'd convinced already, but the others remained uncertain. When Thomas had awoken shouting the girl's name, Askon knew. If they were going to follow, he would have to leave, to lead. After all, it had been Askon who set out for the South Kingdom when Edward's father branded him a deserter. Thomas and Edward had followed him then, and though he did not know it at the time, so had John. In their time and place, so did Elise, Líana, and eventually South City's half-elves. Even Brâghda, leader of the Grafmark Norill, had followed in her own way.

CHAPTER 9 | DEPARTURE

If what Thomas said was true—and what reason did Askon have to doubt him?—they were all connected to the girl somehow. But Askon already knew how. They all did. In the little buried chest by Dalkaldur's lake lay some, or all, of the fragments of Alora's Tear. They lay next to a book which, until that morning, only two people knew existed. And someone was looking for them, someone with clothing, weapons, armor the like of which neither Askon nor his friends had ever seen.

He slid the parchments into the pack and shouldered it heavily. On the desk the wax had cooled, his farewell note ready. He picked it up and blew out the candle. For now, at least, he'd have the luxury of a horse. One journey across Vladvir on foot was more than enough. With a lingering glance into the crosshatched skylight, he turned from the hidden room and slid open the panel that led to the rear passage of the Tolarenz town hall.

There, on the other side of the door, stood Edward.

"Where are you going?" he asked.

Askon adjusted the pack on his shoulder. He looked up, the eyes of blue and green meeting the gray. "You know where I'm going."

Edward smiled. "I know where you want to go. And though you think they are the same, there's a great deal of difference."

"You sound like Morrowmen," Askon mumbled. He tried to make his way around Edward, but his friend simply sidestepped and blocked his path again.

"I take that as a compliment. He always was very wise."

Askon moved again, and again Edward stepped in front of him.

"I find it frustrating," Askon said retreating slightly. "Too many riddles and never a direct piece of advice. Why would you want to follow questions with more questions? By definition, you'd never find any answers!"

From somewhere in the main hall came the clatter of dishes. Askon watched as shadows flitted over the walls and floor at the end of the passage. "Where are the others?"

Edward turned to look, and Askon made another move toward the main hall. Edward's open hand met his chest, stopping him again. "They're headed this way," said the king. "Of course, they'll be much longer than I was." He tapped the ring on his left hand where the Space fragment glowed steadily.

Askon pushed his friend's hand away. "I have to leave. I have to find Dalkaldur."

"And there it is," said Edward, nodding. "Have you considered that perhaps you shouldn't go looking?"

"Yes," Askon replied, shifting the weight of the pack. "I have. But tell me this. Could you ignore something that keeps you awake at night, and when you do sleep, finds its way into your dreams?"

Edward laughed. It was a laugh of little mirth and much recognition. He folded his arms. "You mean something similar to, say, violent non-communicative creatures appearing out of thin air to harass and murder townspeople? I suppose if one were a governing official that *would* be distressing." He shrugged. "I might even think a person would call upon their friends to help with such a problem. And perhaps expect more from them than running off in search of a mythical valley that for all we know could be buried under thirty feet of snow and ice!"

Askon took a breath and raised a finger in an attempt at a counterpoint. Edward waved him off.

"And I know there's a good chance that it *does* exist, and that you might even reach it, but it's no certainty. These attacks, these people who fear to sleep in their own houses are more than a certainty. They're dozens of certainties. How am I supposed to leave them?"

Again behind Edward, from the tables in the main hall, plates and cups clanked and scraped. The shadows danced along the walls.

"You won't have to," said Askon. He gestured toward the end of the passage. "Now will you let me pass? We can speak to the others when they arrive. Until then, there's food. But be certain, I *am* going to Dalkaldur."

Askon shifted the pack again and rounded the corner into the main chamber. A line of food had once again been spread over the tables there. This time, however, there were no place settings or glasses, only the dishes themselves. It was a serving line. Leltan had apparently decided the best way to feed their guests was by opening the town hall, providing a veritable feast, and sending the men on their way after they had taken their portion. The front entrance already stood ajar. Leltan was there, along with a gathering of soldiers. He spoke to them calmly while Askon and Edward approached.

"Sirs!" Leltan chirped. "As you can see, I've taken the responsibility of organizing some provisions for your men. It shouldn't be long until the cooking staff have everything ready. There should be plenty for all. Will the two of you be joining them? And what of the lady Líana, and our Dalstone guests?"

"No," said Askon.

"Yes," said Edward.

They spoke in unison. Leltan looked from one to the other, confused.

"Which will it be then?" he asked tentatively.

After a heavy sigh, Edward waved vaguely to Leltan. "We'll be sharing in tonight's meal, but I'm afraid there's news that will take Líana and I elsewhere at first light tomorrow."

Askon shook his head. "Edward, you don't have to—"

"Yes, we do," Edward interrupted. He nodded to Leltan. "Thank you. We will return shortly with the others."

Leltan nodded back, then cast a curious look at Askon.

Askon handed him the letter and followed Edward out into the garden where half a hundred men waited their turn to partake in Tolarenz's hospitality. Edward addressed some of them as they walked, and finally pulled one aside.

"I'm needed elsewhere," Edward said.

The soldier smoothed a bewildered look from his face, then nodded.

"My wife and I leave tomorrow."

Again, the soldier nodded, more confidently this time. "I'll inform the men. We'll be ready at—"

Edward cut him off. "No, you won't." He shook his head. "You'll stay here for a few more days. I'll leave instructions. The details will explain enough of my plans that you should be able to take them back to King's City and continue operations until my return."

The confused look returned. "But Your Majesty, I can't just watch you leave. My assignment is to tend to your safety and the safety of the queen."

"Then don't watch," said Askon with a laugh. The soldier did not share the amusement.

Edward placed a hand on the man's shoulder. "Listen to Askon, my friend. We will return after this errand is complete. And though we brought you along for this visit to Tolarenz, our next destination needs to remain secret for the time being."

"As you wish," the man said.

"Thank you," said Edward.

With that, they continued through the garden and down the hill until the voices of the soldiers were only a quiet murmur amongst the leaves.

By the time the murmur subsided, Askon and Edward were clear of the town square, nearing the quarters that had been arranged for the king. Down the central path, the others were making their way back once again. Thomas had an arm around Elise but seemed to be walking mostly of his own accord. John walked on the other side, feigning indifference, his eyes returning to Thomas every few steps. Líana led them, her white clothes bright in the sunlit afternoon.

As they approached, Edward led them into the house where he and Líana had stayed the night before. "It's time to decide," he said to them all.

"I'm going," said Líana brusquely. The door had hardly closed behind her before the words came tumbling out. "I've weighed the options, and there is little any of you could do or say that would change my mind." And as though the room were empty, she pulled off the linen shirt and flung it to the floor. Standing there, half covered by the garments she wore beneath, she gave a terse flick of her wrist, indicating that they turn away.

"I can count on one hand the number of times I've been of use at the court—besides as an accessory to Edward's wardrobe." They heard a trunk click and groan as she opened it. Then a shuffle and a clatter.

"Oh of course Edward makes my presence known. He tries his best to include me, to give me a say. But they don't. They just want to see me. And always in white. It's as though they want to be sure I haven't been outside, as if my clothes will do the reporting."

John rotated his head slowly back in Líana's direction. Askon jabbed him hard in the shoulder. He averted his eyes again, gesturing to Elise who had remained facing the queen, as though that gave him permission to do the same. Líana went on unabated.

"Well, I've seen enough of dinner tables. Talked enough of children. And if I ever cared which nobles are marrying into which families, or the romantic histories of the court's latest arrivals or which current engagement will end in scandal, gods strike me dead where I stand!" The trunk closed with a bang. Another shuffle, and then the distinct sound of creaking leather. Askon watched as a smile spread across Elise's face. No one said a word.

A clatter issued from behind them, followed by a cold hiss and a solid click. After a series of pops which Askon assumed to be boot laces, Líana gave an explosive sigh. "You can turn back around," she said.

They did. And there she was, wrapped tightly in the leather garb that had once signified Morrowmen's agents. The long blond braid hung over her chest, curled slightly as though it were tensed for the spring. Behind her, the purple hood lay shapeless between her shoulder blades. Glowering in the shadowed interior, her breathing slowed. At her hip she had sheathed the thin sloping sword given to her by her former mentor. Her right hand came to rest against the hilt.

"I'm going," she said again with finality.

Askon smiled. They all smiled. This Líana was just what Askon had hoped for. In the white linens and at endless court dinners, his sister had lost something of herself. If he wanted any of their help in reaching Dalkaldur, he needed the Líana that now stood before them. Needed her to toss the queen aside and be again the fearless girl with a clever blade that had once handily outmaneuvered his own.

"Well that makes two of us," John added. "I mean, I was already decided, but this makes the choice even easier."

Elise's smile faded, her mind elsewhere. Askon watched as she glanced back toward the town hall where her baby slept soundly under the servant's care. Then the dark eyes moved to Thomas, and finally to Askon himself. She remained silent.

"You two have the hardest choice of all," Askon began. "If you go with me, either of you, I can't guarantee that you will return."

Elise nodded, her eyes still far away.

"But without me, *you* have little chance of coming back at all," said Thomas. He clicked open the bracelet on his wrist. "I've seen where she is, and I see more than you can, even when we bring the fragments together."

"Yes," Askon replied. "Without the Sight fragment, I'm afraid we'll be hopelessly lost in the Southern Mountain snows. Codard couldn't find Dalkaldur, and his command of the Space fragment granted him the ability to move large groups of men at great distance. We need to be able to see where we're going, and hopefully use that sight to find the path that will lead us there."

Edward sat on the edge of the bed. He placed his hand on the blanket next to him and gave a nod to his wife. Líana took a step, then changed her mind. She crossed the narrow room and stood with Elise. "What about you?" she asked.

As if a bell had rung somewhere inside her head, Elise turned to Líana. She blinked and pushed a black tendril of hair behind her ear. "Askon knows I can't just let Thomas go. He knows that with my son here, I can't leave. And yet he asks anyway."

"The Sight fragment…" Thomas began.

"And what of it?" Elsie snapped. "It is no sure thing, no certainty you will find that place. Sometimes you can't even summon the fragment's power. Sometimes, an hour ago, for instance, it puts out the lights in your eyes, and you leave us, leave me." Her voice cracked and faltered with those words, and Thomas moved closer, wrapping an arm about her shoulders. Líana paced back and sat on the bed next to Edward.

Thomas watched them for a moment. Watched their hands entwine, the fingers moving slowly into place. Then he looked up. "Edward could send you back if something went wrong—if you came with us."

"So you've already decided," Elise muttered. She started to pull away but leaned into him instead.

"No—well, perhaps—I just—"

"'Course he has," John barked. He had found a comfortable seat in the low chair at the room's entryway. His feet, crossed casually at the ankles, had found the other chair. "Our boy Askon says 'Jump!' and this one here says, 'What distance? How many times? And with what facial expression?'"

Elise glared at him through the curtain of dark hair. "Didn't you jump first?"

"You're damn right I jumped first. But I jump for all sorts o' reasons, none o' which make any sense half the time."

"Well that *is* a certainty," Elise said.

"Either way," John continued. "Thomas has made up his mind, so that makes three. And you're gonna go whether ya know it yet or not. I can see it glowin' in that stone o' yours. The boy's keepin' ya though."

The Death fragment had indeed begun to glow sometime after John had declared Thomas a member of the expedition and within a few heartbeats of him telling Elise what she would do. Thomas pulled her closer, but the fragment only glowed more brightly.

"Like I was saying," Thomas offered, "the Space fragment could help us a great deal. If Edward—"

"I shouldn't," said the king, and the whole room turned to him.

"You all saw it for yourselves. All across the kingdom, aggressive Norill are appearing and attacking villagers and townspeople. If I don't see to it that they are dealt with, who will?"

"Seems the townsfolk already are dealin' with 'em." John adjusted his feet, rotating one at the ankle. "As I see it, they'll more or less sort out their own problems. That is unless—"

"Unless the Norill start appearing in greater numbers," Edward interrupted, resuming what had originally been his own explanation. "For now, these mumbling Norill are easy targets and always alone. But how long will that last? Wherever they're coming from, it doesn't seem likely they will continue on indefinitely one at a time."

"Perhaps Brâghda knows something of these creatures," offered Thomas.

"No," replied Elise. "Brâghda wouldn't allow them to behave this way if they were under her control; therefore, they must be acting independently."

Askon, who had tried to remain silent while his friends made their decisions, turned to the king. "There was something wrong with the Norill in my family's home. It didn't speak normally, or behave as we have seen other Norill—friend or foe—behave. We may be seeing the strategy of a new player. Maybe we're looking in the wrong places." He ran a hand over the stubble on his chin. "Apopsé's been quiet."

John laughed. "That cod-liver snake?! I'd have my doubts." He shook his head slowly. "No. Our king Edward here might not have heard from old Apopsé in a while, but the Darts have been keepin' an eye. He's holed up in his palace with no more fragment to tell him what's what. Got enough on his hands sortin' out trade agreements and holdin' together the busted pieces of South City. I don't think he'll be botherin' anybody any time soon."

Edward sighed. "The details don't matter at this moment. The point is, I shouldn't follow Askon, not while Vladvir is under attack."

"Small attack," said John with a smirk.

"Tell that to the families whose fathers or mothers or children are frightened, maimed, dead!" Edward snapped.

"Maybe the two are connected," Thomas suggested. He had released Elise and moved to sit on the arm of the chair where John's feet rested. "We can't predict where the Norill will appear. We don't know how they are sneaking into the villages and towns, even inside buildings, as happened here. What if the vision of Dalkaldur, and the Norill attacks are part of the same mystery? While I was—" he paused, "—away earlier, I saw, well heard, something new in the room where they torture the girl."

"Alora," said Askon softly.

"Yes," Thomas went on. "The people in charge—a woman, and a man with a teardrop tattoo on his hand—were talking outside the room where Alora is kept. It was muffled, difficult to hear. But it sounded like they were arranging some kind of attack. It could be anywhere and on anyone. Wherever they are, they're looking for us, and they're looking for the fragments. These Norill only appear where the fragments have been, and most frequently where the fragments have been *used*."

"So you have to go, Edward," John chuckled. He pulled his feet slowly from the chair, bringing the boots down with a thump. "If the two problems are the same, a good king would have to investigate. It'd only be proper."

Edward hesitated.

John stood. "It's not like you've got any better ideas. Might as well give it a chance. After all, you could always use that shiny stone o' yours to send yourself back to King's City if things go sideways."

He ran a hand through his thick beard and grinned. "So that's everybody."

"So it is," said Askon.

CHAPTER TEN

Another Day

It was raining again. The city was quieter for it, quieter in the way she liked best. Curtain after raindrop curtain pelted down while rays of light glimmered along the street. There had been only a minute to spare when she stepped outside, and she had been both surprised and not surprised. Always it was so, the storm would roll in all thunder, flicker, flash, then the cool rain would drown the sounds of the city. It reminded her of the stories she'd read, of what it must be like where trees grew thick, or where winds hissed through seas of twisting grass, where one could listen for hours to a cataract in a clear stream. She cherished these moments, the ones in the rain, because without them her world was little more than stone and steel.

Stone and steel. He was sharpening again. Sharpening, sharpening, sharpening. Had she passed out? How long had he been there, waiting for her to awaken? She tried to move, to stretch her legs, but pain lanced up, and she sucked a hiss of air through clenched teeth. She put the foot back down and it throbbed liquidly, sending a shudder through her body. She gagged, coughed, spat.

"Ah. You're awake then," said the voice. "It hurts, I know. But that's the game now. She told me I could. I hurt. You talk." He gave a tremendous, mucosal snort, then cleared his throat. "You know what they say. 'When it rains…'"

She blacked out.

The thunder had passed, hurried along by the quickening wind. Even the shadows of cloud had rumbled off away to the west. Down the long row of buildings she saw the horizon, half sky and half storm. Her immediate errands were finished, and her father wouldn't expect her back home for hours. So she rounded the corner, letting the rain speckle her face between the eaves and awnings of the street. The city had all gone aground, even the vendors whose shelter she had appropriated for herself sat sullen and wordless, biding their time until the storm passed.

Another bend, another long stretch of overhangs, and she'd found what she was looking for. A half-filled carriage sat waiting. She batted the loose droplets from her clothes and leapt inside, the other passengers wordlessly making room. A rivulet of rainwater trickled from her damp hair, past her circlet, to forehead, to nose, and there waited. She rubbed it away with her hand.

He held her hand, pinching, squeezing the fleshy area between index finger and thumb. It didn't hurt so much as it irritated, an odd mixture of nausea, dull ache, and revulsion. Her head lolled, and she blinked in the darkness.

"Too sleepy now," he said, then struck her hard with the back of his fist. Something began to run down her face. Blood? Tears? She didn't know.

"Too much hurt does no good," he said. "Then you'll just go dumb. I think there's enough left in this foot to get what we need." He paused, and the silence swallowed her. "Shall we see?"

His boot came down, and she started to scream, but the sound and the pain fluttered, faded.

"Do you know how long I've been waiting here?" Daeron's voice came muffled and weak from somewhere behind the desk. Outside, the rain droned away at the glass. Its quiet pattering had drummed the carriage the whole way in.

She smiled. "As long as always," she said, straightening her circlet and lingering in the entryway. Spacious was the word she would've used to describe the hall, spacious and quiet. Daeron asserted that the domed ceiling created the effect, that the room wasn't really all that large, and she went along with it for the sake of argument. With Daeron there was always an argument.

A muted *bang* rattled the contents of the desk that wrapped a deep mahogany semicircle around a tall slab of shelves. Its corners, hardly corners at all, flowed smoothly from side to surface and down again like a wood-grained bar of soap or tumbled river stone.

Daeron emerged, his face deep brown as the expansive desk, his brow squinting and pinched in concentration. When he saw her looking at him, he smoothed his dark hair and rubbed the back of his head, assuming an expression somewhere between nervous wince and winning grin. "Well, you're the only one who comes here besides the occasional dozen academy children plus customarily frazzled instructor. So, yeah, I've always been waiting a long time."

"Oh, there's more than that. You just remember the school tours better because they leave *you* frazzled. And as for the wait, it depends on how you define 'a long time'," she said, approaching the desk. "Imagine how long it's been since the ink dried on some of these pages. Imagine how long it's been since the first foundation stones were set in the temple or the first beams were sawn in the village." She closed her eyes, as if doing so would bring the history closer. When she opened them, Daeron rested an elbow on the desk, the heel of his hand pressed against his cheekbone. His smile was genuine, his eyes dreamily half-lidded. She knew that look.

She waved a hand in front of his face. "Aren't you going to ask me if I'm looking for something?" she asked, leaning against the desk, which met her at the ribcage.

He straightened with an awkward gasp and his dark skin reddened a bit at the cheeks and thin, pointed ears. "Uh, well, are you?" He stood and took a step back.

With another little smile that she knew he'd misinterpret, she ran a finger along one of the papers on the desk's surface. "*The Book of the Tear*," she said.

"Again?" he wondered. "What do you need with that? It makes no sense. Everybody knows the story of the Tear. And this isn't it, despite the title. Why not *Filion's History*? Or *Darkened Times*, or even *Before the Sky*, though that one is more religion than history. You'd be as well-served with *The Candied Castle* or *The Changeling Beast* as with *The Book of the Tear*."

And there it was, the arguing. At least when his hackles were up like this, he forgot to look at her that way. Even his appearance became a better version of itself once she'd set him off: his eyes a little more aquamarine than just blue, his thin, bird-like features more dignified than frail. His skin was rich brown, though not from physical labor or even lounging in the sun. It simply *was*, like most of Daeron. A generous two inches made him shorter than her, but not awkwardly so, and on no account of her own height which was similar to any number of young women in the city.

He turned to her and extended a wiry arm. In his hand was *The Book of the Tear*, somehow dusty, though she'd been reading it only two days before. It smelled of leather and a world no one remembered, that probably hadn't existed at all.

"Waste of your time if you ask me," Daeron huffed. "I could show you whole stacks of books that—"

She took the volume from him, inadvertently brushing his fingertips with her own. "Thanks," she said quickly and left him mid-sentence. As she walked away, she hadn't seen him look briefly at the fingers she had touched, move his thumb across them, and slowly—sadly—close the hand against his chest. Instead, she'd hurried through a side exit, out onto the steel-framed patio, and into the garden area beyond, already knowing he would find a signal in the accidental contact that wasn't there.

"You've got it wrong!" She shouted, tears running again down her face. How could there be any tears left? Everything was dry and cracked, yet somehow still damp and musty.

"Have I?" said the voice. "Why don't you set it right?"

She hesitated.

He twisted his boot heel against her injured foot. She cried out, but it came choked and rattling from her throat. "There's nothing in the book you don't already know," she managed.

"But. Where. Are. The. Pieces!" he thundered, each word a drumbeat against her foot. The pain seared and throbbed.

"They call them *Fragments*," she said with a whimper.

"It's getting late," Daeron murmured quietly from somewhere behind her. She looked up, and sure enough, hours had passed since she had met him at the front desk. The quiet garden could do that to her, did that to her often, in fact. Sometimes she wondered whether the books or the place itself drew her here. Today it had been both. And the rain. Sometimes it was the rain.

"Alora?" He said the name softly, as though it might break were it not handled with care. "I have to close up. You should get home."

Past the garden and the distant rainclouds, the sun had set some time ago. A lazy moon rose to take its place, yellow and fat. It hovered between whorls of rosebush thorns as if trying to shake off a heavy-lidded sleep.

Her cheeks flushed red in the pale light. It was well past time for Daeron to close the doors, well past time that they both should have been home. He had let her stay beyond, significantly beyond, what the rules allowed. The consequences if his superiors found out would be more than she cared to shoulder. With the clumsy flourishes of embarrassment, she marked the page she'd been reading and gathered up the pen and notebook she'd filled with little sketched imaginings. One hand rested on the line where she'd stopped in *The Book of the Tear*. "Caled, Knight of Vladvir," it read. Her other hand lay on the notebook next to a sketch of a tall man in armor with a long, straight sword and flowing cape. Beneath the image, she'd sketched the name "Caled" and for brevity's sake, the letters "KoV."

She scooped the items up to her chest and, without meeting his eyes, handed the book to Daeron. "I'm sorry," she said. "I didn't mean to be here this long. I know you're supposed to lock the doors by—"

"Oh, they'll never know the difference," he interrupted. "If they actually cared about this place, they'd do a lot more than staff it with one person at the desk and a handful of groundskeepers."

"Still," she said, her hands fumbling to place the pen and notebook back into the small leather bag she'd slung over her shoulder, "I'm sorry." She didn't look up.

"Don't be," he replied as she slipped back through the main hall and out the front entrance. He looked again at the dusty old book and smiled. "Just come back soon."

"Come back," the voice singsonged in the dark. She felt his thick fingers tap the side of her face. "Come back," he cooed again.

She breathed deeply, an acrid, chemical odor burning her lungs and nose. The chair thumped beneath her in the dark as her body spasmed against the bindings. Her eyelids, puffy and raw, were rimmed again with tears.

"Just some salts to wake you up," said the voice. "They're unpleasant, sure, but not deadly. She doesn't want you dead. Not yet, anyway."

Something hard contacted the table, and she listened to his boots clump across the floor. Closer. Closer.

"It's good you've decided to cooperate," he began. Had she? There had been so many awakenings and so much darkness. She couldn't remember.

"*The Book of the Tear* tells things the way they were. Nobody knows that. Well, I do, and now you do, but by and large, nobody knows. And nobody cares." He clapped a heavy hand on her shoulder and paced behind the chair. "But you still won't say where you've hidden the fragments. Now that they're here, we need them. Think of the power. Think of what we'll be able to make, to do!" He continued his circle, starting with the left shoulder and moving slowly around the right. She sensed his face only inches from hers, smelled his breath, then spat.

But there was nothing left. Only enough to dampen her own lips. He laughed, long and booming, then sniffed and spat back at her. He pressed his palm against her face, and drove the chair backwards to the ground. Her head bounced off the floor in a burst of glittering stars.

The stars were out, and the faltering lanterns masked fewer than they had only a fortnight earlier. She counted: ten, twenty, all the way to two-hundred before she sighed and gripped the door handle. Above her, faintly in the night sky, the Mender and the Breaker reached out to one another. Alora, her namesake, and Heraphus the hero locked ever at arm's length. She turned the handle and stepped inside.

"Well aren't you just the studious researcher today?" her father said without looking up from the scattered mass of papers before him. The thin metal table legs screeched against the floor—a dog-whistle sound she'd always hated. It reminded her of the bats that fluttered in the dark above the library gardens. "What did you find out?" he asked. Then without missing a beat, "I think I've discovered the thread that could unravel all of this." He reached up and swung the flimsy arm of the desk lamp into place. Its light pulsed weakly over a few mismatched pages. "Motivations, locations, accomplices, agendas, it's a treasure trove!"

She slung the leather bag over a hook by the door, pulled the circlet through her hair, and placed it on another hook next to the bag. Her father's hung there already, iron not copper, the continuous loop severed so they "couldn't track him." When she came to the desk, he put his arm around her and pointed with the opposite hand at the overlapping pages. Without the circlet, she couldn't read them, but she humored him anyway.

"The clerks came through with the documentation." A smile spread slowly over his face, and he turned to look at her. "People want to know," he said, "and as long as we can trust them, they're willing to take risks for us."

"You take too many risks!" the voice shouted. She lay on her back, still tied to the chair, which she was now certain had broken beneath her when he pushed it over. Something sharp prodded her lower back. The more she moved, the sharper it felt.

"I could've killed you by now! No one would care. No one would know. You'd just disappear like any other leech in this city. Dead? Alive? Who would notice?" He punctuated the last with a kick that jabbed the broken chair against her spine.

A whimper escaped. He drew her—and the mangled remains of the chair—up from the floor, stomped across the room, and slammed the door behind him.

Daeron would notice. Daeron, and her father, and the others. They would notice, if they were still alive.

CHAPTER ELEVEN

The Road

The heat had come on fast, and lingered. They'd tried cloaks and layers, thin shirts and shirtless, but nothing lessened the sun's sting. Overhead, Marten circled, a tiny speck of black against unending blue. If there were clouds, they were beyond Askon's far-seeing eyes. Below, yellow waves of grass and stick-brown thistle spread as wide as the open sky. Askon, sweating under the shadow of his cloak, batted a fly from his face for what might have been the thousandth time. At the head of the group, Edward did the same. His close-cropped hair, almost black with the damp of sweat, glinted in the blistering sun. The others fidgeted uncomfortably in the saddle. Askon hoped for a breeze, but none came.

"Askon the Great, hero of Vladvir, and all around worst navigator since Thane Kelden led that hunting party into a box canyon and lost a third of his men," John grumbled. "Tell me again why we didn't take the quickest route to the river?"

With a shrug, Askon billowed his cloak in an attempt to move the air around him, anything to feel a bit cooler, if only for a moment. "We're taking the quickest way to the Southern Mountains," he said. "It's late enough in the season that we'll need to outrun the first winter snows if we're unlucky in our search for Dalkaldur." He batted another fly.

Elise scoffed audibly. "As unusual as it might sound, I agree with John. What did you save us? A day? A half-day? And for it we swelter under this heat with the journey only just beginning." She shook her head. "Winter snows. Perhaps we should turn back now if this is the sort of leadership we can expect."

"Feel free," Askon grumbled. "We can carry the Death fragment to Dalkaldur, and you can go back to Tolarenz with your family. We've been gone less than two days. He'll hardly know you've been away."

She checked the horse, drawing level with Askon. "And what would you know about it?" she snapped. "You have no son, no daughter. What would you know about leaving family behind? Your sister's here, isn't she?" Elise's eyes grew dark. "I'll not let Thomas stumble along on your quest without someone to protect him, to bring a father back to his son. And I'll carry this fragment across all of Vladvir if it means keeping them both safe. I don't like it. And yes, I'd be happy to turn back. But we both know there's more to the visions, that there must be a reason we're seeing them—seeing her."

While Elise lectured, Thomas rode up beside them. He reached out and placed a hand on her arm. "We made this choice together. The baby is safe in Tolarenz, as safe as if he were with us. There are children in the hall and around the town. He'll be happier there, for a while at least."

She slapped his hand away, as Askon had the flies. "Do you think that helps? That I feel better about it?" She glared at Askon through a black fringe of hair. "You had better hope nothing happens to him. To either of them. Or you'll answer to me." She spurred the horse and galloped ahead. Askon thought he saw the gem at her wrist pulse a little brighter.

In truth, his decision to avoid the river and make a straighter path southward had been a mistake. Now, after only a day-and-a-half they were tired, overheated, and irritable. The miles they had traveled to stop Iramov had been motivated by necessity. Elise, for one, had needed to escape Grafmark—and the past that haunted her there. Happy as she might have been, without the victory against Iramov, she and Thomas would have been forced to remain in Vitæsta with the Grafmark Norill, outsiders no matter how accepting Brâghda and her people tried to be.

They all had similar reasons to pursue the cause and follow the path to South City, but now it was a request that put them again on the road and away from the comforts of home. Askon reminded himself that though his new position as chief handler of all petty squabbles in Tolarenz was tiresome and not at all what he had expected, the others had put aside joys, interests, duties, and responsibilities in order to follow him. Some, like Edward's investigation of the mysterious Norill appearances, continued as they went, or would continue as soon as they reached another settlement, but others, like Elise and Thomas's son, were simply put on hold until Askon's errand was complete. He kicked himself for not valuing the gift, and their agreement, more than he had.

Marten swooped down, alighting with a flutter at Líana's shoulder. She brushed back the purple hood and leaned in as the falcon folded his wings and bobbed his head. Then she turned to the others.

"We're nearly within sight of the Æsten Ridge," she called. "By tomorrow we could be traveling along the river and perhaps even in the shade of the ridge for a few hours."

When no one responded, she shrugged and rocked forward, repositioning herself in the saddle. "And let's hope you're all happier for it. Dalkaldur will be a long journey indeed, if you're all so dreary."

Edward laughed. "Well, I don't know if everyone is quite as happy as you are to be on the road again. While you might be escaping, others are sacrificing."

"Not me," said John. "I got nothin' to give up but a cartload of green recruits. If you tell 'em to fletch an arrow, they throw it for one of the dogs!"

Thomas smiled. "Oh, they're not that bad."

John sat up in the saddle, incredulous. "What? You think I'd joke about somethin' like this?"

"You joke about everything," said Edward.

"Well," John began, nonplussed, "that may be true, but I'll shave my beard—hell—my whole damn head if not a day before we left I didn't ask one of the recruits to fletch an arrow and he threw the shaft across the yard. O' course none o' the dogs chased it. They're at least trained well enough. So he had to go fetch his own arrow before he could fletch it." He chuckled. "Sometimes that particular sort o' simple just flat astounds me."

The afternoon wore on as the sun beat down. Sweating and grumbling beneath their cloaks, all save Líana who rode on cheerily despite the heat, they drew within sight of the Æsten Ridge, and below its towering cliff face, the river Estelle. When the sun faded to little more than a thin haze of blue at the edge of a darkening world, even Líana's tolerance for the day's warmth had been exhausted.

"We can set camp on the riverside. After today we could all stand for a washing before the road calls again in the morning," she said. Her hood lay draped down her back, the long braid curling beneath it almost to her waist. Mopping her forehead with an already damp sleeve, she eased her horse to a trot as the first stars flickered to life in the east.

With the sky darkening further, they crossed the last stretch of grass to the waiting river, still distant enough from the ridge to see the whole of its shape silhouetted against the sun's fading light. John was the first off his horse and onto his knees, splashing cool water over his face and arms. The others followed one by one, each with the same vigorous splashes and contented sighs. Soon, they all sat around a small campfire, river water drying in their hair.

With the horses staked and hobbled for the night, Askon peered out of the firelight toward the ridge. To the others the sun's fleeting presence was little more than a silver line, but to Askon's eyes the entire slope shone in cool gray. Behind him an unlucky pair of partridges hung sizzling over the flames while the group murmured something about John's recent tavern exploits.

Wonders like the ridge were easy enough to locate in an expanse like the Vladvir plain, but Askon worried that Dalkaldur would prove far more difficult. The Æsten Ridge stood hundreds of feet high in the middle of a flattened grassland; Dalkaldur hunkered in its hiding place atop a single peak in a sea of peaks. He hoped the fragments would give them some clue before they began the search in earnest. If no clue came, their efforts could very well be for naught. His thoughts and eyes wandered over the great cliff's shape, tracing the outline from river to base to slope to pinnacle. And his worries began to dissolve.

Was it the shape he noticed first, or the color? Whichever it was, something along the ridge line had moved. No. Not moved, changed. While he pondered the group's next step, the air and light on the Æsten Ridge had shifted. He first guessed that a group of pilgrims still lingered, waiting for some sign from the gods. Perhaps a priest had climbed the rock in order to receive his blessing or cast himself into the river below. Whatever had happened, the shift in light was no fire. Askon had seen fires and torches at a distance often as a scout in Codard's army, had seen them when they meant not to be seen, even. This was different. And somehow still familiar. He shifted his position, focusing more intently this time. Again, he saw it: a ripple in the air and a strange color cast across the ridge. He considered calling to the others but knew they would see only the faintest sliver of twilight. Then he remembered.

"Líana!" he called. "Come over here."

His sister picked greedily over a partridge breast, popping strips of meat into her mouth and licking her fingers. "Can it wait?" she asked through a mouthful. "I'm starving."

"Bring it with you, then. Unless you're trying to remember what it's like to eat at a noble's table."

She giggled, handing the remaining portion of the bird to Edward, though not before tearing off a healthy portion for herself. "No. I am not."

The others perked up at Askon's request, but he waved them off and led Líana out of the firelight. Now certain of what he was looking for, Askon saw it clearly: a shimmer and wavering purple glow all along the ridge, even as the night grew darker. He pointed into the distance.

"Look right there," he said quietly. "Do you see it?"

She wiped her mouth with the back of her hand and followed his outstretched arm. "See what? What am I looking for?"

"The ridge top. Tell me what you see."

A few moments went by and Líana, like Askon before her, shifted and squinted in the half light. After taking a few steps further from the flicker of their own campfire, she turned to her brother.

"It's not a fire," she began. "It's the wrong color, and the light isn't moving like flames. It's more purple than orange or red. And there's something else about it."

"The air," Askon finished. "It's the air, shimmering like a heatwave."

"The sun's been down for quite a while. Could it be warm enough up there for something like that at this time of night?"

He shook his head and stepped closer to the faraway ridge. "Maybe the shimmer…"

It was then that Askon knew why the shifting air looked familiar. He had seen it before from a hilltop outside the small village of Shale. There, Codard had used the Space fragment to transport a group of soldiers in pursuit of Askon and his friends.

The others by now were standing and looking out into the night toward the Æsten Ridge. John, clearly eavesdropping on the whispers of Askon and his sister had already started toward them when Askon called out.

"Edward! Everyone! Douse the fire and come out here. There's something I want you to try to see."

While Thomas and Elise tended the fire, John and Edward made their way to Askon and Líana. "I don't see nothin'," John mumbled. "Dark as the folds in a bartender's belly out there. What are we supposed to be lookin' for?"

Askon grabbed Edward and pointed into the darkness. "On the ridge a moment ago, Líana and I both saw it, the air is shifting like I've only seen once before. It's the way the air bends for the Space fragment."

A crease formed on the new king's brow. "I don't understand. I've only ever seen it with the fragment as well. How could that be? Maybe it's some sort of illusion."

Finished with the last of the embers, Thomas and Elise came up behind them. "Water and heat often create such illusions," Thomas said matter-of-factly.

"And do they also fill a hundred-foot space with purple light?" Askon asked pointedly.

Edward put out a hand. "What did you say?"

"He said there's a purple light up there," Líana interjected. "I saw it, too."

Her husband peered again into the darkness. "You're sure," he said, more statement than question.

"Yes," Askon and Líana said together.

A slow weariness crept over Edward's face, and he leaned forward until his forehead met the palm of his hand. It rested there for a moment before he looked up.

"I've yet to see it myself," he said tiredly, "but we have received reports claiming that witnesses saw strange lights where the hostile Norill have appeared. My instincts and my information are aligned on this. If we climb that ridge, we'll find one of those Norill."

For the better part of an hour, the six of them had crept their way across the mile or so to the base of the ridge. As plains turf transitioned to sharp stones, the darkness and uneven ground slowed their going. At intervals the peak glowed purple before them, though several times they had lost sight of it, further hindering their progress. Halfway to the top, slabs of rock jutted up like enormous headstones. Askon was glad for the cover. They flitted from one to the next until only a third of the slope remained. Purple faded to black.

Another few minutes passed, then a quarter-hour, then a half-hour; but the light did not return. Huddled with their backs against one of the boulders, they waited for the glow to appear again. Askon peered around the edge of their shelter into the moonless night. "There's something up there," he whispered. "I don't suppose any of you can see it?"

John emitted a scoff. Líana crept to the opposite edge and leaned around the rock. After a moment she slid back down and sat with the others. "If there's anything to see, I can't tell whether they're people, animals, or just more of these stones." She thumped a fist against the slab. "It's too dark now, and too far."

"We could light a torch," John suggested.

Edward nodded slowly. "Yes, we could. But that would reveal us to whoever or whatever is up there. For now at least, it seems, we have gone undetected."

"What about Askon and Líana?" Thomas asked. "They could scout ahead for us."

Elise shook her head. "And lead us like blind beggars through the dark? I think not."

Thomas smiled. "Not completely dark." With a flick of his wrist, and a quiet series of clicks, he opened the bracelet that held the Sight fragment. Its faint blue pulse couldn't illuminate the entire hillside as had the light they followed this far. However, it did reveal a few dim feet of grass and rock ahead of him.

"If we cover them up," he said waving his wrist along the ground. "They won't give us away. And even in the open, they'd be difficult to see at any distance."

Askon laughed quietly, remembering the clumsy young soldier who had fallen from his horse at their first meeting.

"Alright," Elise agreed. "We're already up here. We might as well try."

CHAPTER TWELVE
The Æsten Ridge

Green. Red. Blue like morning sky. Blue like evening sky. A color-less shadow. And purple like the light that led them up the slope. One by one they flitted further and further ahead. Stone by stone they came nearer and nearer the edge of the cliff. Overhead—quiet, cold, and distant—the stars did little to brighten their path.

Askon led the way, though he sensed Elise's footsteps mere inches behind his own. Had she the sharpened eyes of a half-elf, he knew, it would have been the Death fragment and not Time that chose their course. As it was he moved silently, and she followed. Thomas and Edward came after, lighting the way for John, then Líana who crept cautiously, peering into the night behind them, watchful and wary.

Soon they pressed themselves against another huge stone, their feet crunching softly against the gravel and dust that had overtaken the whispering grass. Once more, Askon leaned out from their hiding place and surveyed the remainder of the ridge top, his fingers catching along the cold surface where countless visitors had etched layer upon layer of shapes, images, words. He paused for a moment, waiting, watching, then crouched in front of the others.

"Three of these stones remain," he said, gesturing at the ground before him. "Here, here, and here." Looking up at the group, he pointed first to Thomas and Elise. "You two take the right." He drew an invisible line from them to their destination. Then he pointed to Edward and Líana. "You go to the left." He drew another invisible line.

"John and I will take the center."

Elise shifted against the rock, her eyes narrowing. "And why divide us? It seems with our lack of light, we should stick together."

John lowered himself to Askon's level. "And I thought you said you 'always go left'?"

Askon sighed. "I do, but each edge needs two lights. If we encounter resistance, it will be easier to converge on the center than to cover one flank with only a single light."

"Then why not put yourself and Líana on either side?" Elise demanded. "Both of you see well enough in the dark, especially with the fragments."

"I suppose you're right," Askon said with a sarcastic sigh. "And then you can be paired with John."

Edward put out a hand. "Lower your voices!" he whispered. "Bickering about the details won't help us. Askon is in command here. It is his errand, and this is but the first part. We take his orders now and debate them later."

"If we're still alive," Elise mumbled.

"If we're still alive," Edward echoed.

Under the faint starlight, the final span spread out before them. Askon and John positioned themselves against the center stone and waited for the others. When all six were ready, Askon revealed the Time fragment's light, casting eerie shadows over his face and deepening the green of his hood. Red, purple, and the two blues came to life as Askon gave the signal.

In the center of the ring, a half-dozen forms stood sleepily. They stared out over the edge of the cliff, long arms swaying gently and without intent. Askon drew nearer, noting the telltale signs that confirmed his suspicions. All six of the shadowy figures were Norill. He nodded to the others, their swords already rippling with the multi-colored light from the fragments. A sharp *pop* shattered the silence. Thomas drew back a step, and the Norill turned together to face them.

"*Sors?*" said one, its crooked posture straightening, its head swiveling toward the sound.

Askon covered the Time fragment with his fist, and the others followed suit. Motionless they waited, six shadows still as the stone slabs behind them.

Another Norill stepped forward limply. It too angled its head toward Thomas. "*Sors?*" it queried into the silence.

Now came the decision. For the moment, the Norill seemed blind to Askon and his friends. They gazed vacantly down the slope, past the headstone boulders and beyond into the night. At six and six, and seemingly with the element of surprise, Askon and the others would make short work of the Norill. However, killing without hesitation was the sort of mistake Askon indulged before the tragedy at Tolarenz and before his failures against Iramov. He held up a hand to stay the others.

The Norill looked out over the slope for another moment, then turned back to the cliff's edge. Askon stole a glance at Thomas, noting his young friend's expression, anticipating the debate over why the Norill had not seen them. Even on such a dark night, and with the fragments covered, the distance should not have been enough to conceal them. Nonetheless the Norill turned their empty-eyed attention to the wide plain and thundering river a thousand feet below.

Askon waved the group ahead. They advanced, though Thomas more slowly and carefully than before. At the space of a yard, Askon halted them again.

"Vladvir," said the Norill at the center, clear as if it had spoken the word every day of its life. And then the syllable they had all grown uncomfortably familiar with: "*Sors.*"

The other five shuffled toward the cliff's edge, their arms swaying loosely. "Vladvir *sors*," they echoed.

Close enough now to reach out and touch the creature nearest him, Askon signaled the attack for the four on the outside edge. With his fist closed tightly around his sword hilt, he gestured to John, bringing the pommel down in a pantomime signal to subdue the two at the center rather than kill them. John gave a terse nod.

"*Sors.* Vladvir *sors*," the creatures chanted.

On Askon's mark, his friends executed the commands flaw-lessly. Thrust, retract, hard downward cut to the base of the neck. The four outside forms fell. Edward's target flailed and screeched in the dust before a final stroke silenced it. Thomas gripped the handle of his weapon and pulled. The blade, lodged firmly in the creature's shoulder, came free with a squelch. Carried by the mo-mentum, Thomas regained his footing with a clatter and a heavy, sliding step. The women had turned already to the remaining two, closing in until they, along with Askon and John, formed a semi-circle around their enemies. The cliff's edge completed the ring.

"Vladvir *sors*," the Norill said to the darkness as though they didn't realize their comrades had already been dispatched.

John snaked a thick arm around the nearest Norill's neck. Askon did the same. On contact, the creatures jolted to life, scrab-bling and twisting, fighting to break free. Askon felt the bony fin-gers clawing, grasping for its belt. As he struggled to keep it still, he brought his sword pommel down hard. The creature went limp, and Askon adjusted to its shifting weight. But the Norill pivoted, drawing a slender blade no longer than a butcher's knife, its eyes darting and awake now, flicking left and right in their sunken sock-ets. It took a faltering step back.

John wrestled his captive to the ground, clubbing it unceru-moniously with the hilt of his sword as one might pound a rising loaf of bread. When it ceased to struggle, he gripped it tightly for a moment. Then with a shredded strip of cloth torn from one of the dead, he bound its hands and feet.

The others warily ringed the last Norill, closing in slowly, backing it toward the cliff. Hissing and spitting, brandishing the glinting knife, it leapt forward, slashing at the five of them. The blade's reach was far too short to be a threat, though Askon had known soldiers who could bury a dagger inches deep in a tree at fifteen paces. Those feats, however, were highly dependent upon countless repetitions at predictable distances and a great deal of focus and concentration. This Norill seemed to have neither, but Askon readied himself against the creature's desperation nonetheless.

"Vladvir *sors*?" it wondered at them.

"What does that mean?" Askon shouted, his voice echoing across the ridge top. The Norill's head swiveled to its left, eyeing the bound form of its captured comrade. Then it swiveled right to the forms that lay there, dead. Its expression shifted. The eyes softened, and the brows knitted thoughtfully; the face grew concerned, fearful.

"*Sors*?" it pleaded. "Vladvir *sors*?"

Askon took a step forward. "Tell us what that means."

The Norill retreated, and the knife quivered then dipped, almost falling from the trembling fingers. With a keening cry, the creature shook its head, the knife rising again. In the darkness, Askon thought he saw tears stripe the gray cheeks.

"*Sors!*" it begged.

Again, Askon stepped forward.

Whimpering, the Norill eyed its outstretched wrist. The blade rotated until the point faced not its attackers but itself. Air rushed into the Norill's lungs in a ragged gasp. Then it backed away again, only inches from the edge. A feral wail, half rage and half sorrow, leapt out into the night, and it drove the knife into its chest, wrenched it free, and opened a wide gash across its own neck. It coughed once, blood flecking its lips, and fell bouncing against the cliffside into darkness and the rushing Estelle.

"Vladvir *sors*," came the chant again, and they turned to the ridge top. John grabbed the bound captive by the hair, lifting its head, but the creature was unconscious.

Among the headstone slabs, purple lights flickered then faded. The chant grew. "Vladvir *sors*." A breath of silence. "Vladvir *sors*." Another. "Vladvir *sors*!"

With each repetition the volume of the words grew. Slowly, from behind the boulders, Norill after Norill appeared in the open space at the peak of the Æsten Ridge: five, ten, a dozen. Askon lost count.

"Conceal the fragments!" he whispered. "And stay close to me."

The chanting continued, growing stronger with each iteration, even after the purple lights ceased.

Askon put his hand out, placing it on Edward's shoulder. "How many of us can you move?"

Edward shook his head. "I'm not sure. Myself and Líana. Maybe a third, but then not very far."

"Far enough to run?"

"Yes."

They drew closer together as the chanting Norill line advanced. Elise pushed Thomas toward Edward. "Thomas, then!"

she hissed. Get him and—" Her hand slipped from the bracelet, revealing the Death fragment's deep red glow. A brittle silence fell.

"*Sors!*" The word echoed with finality.

Slender blades flashed in the night across the Norill line as a hundred eyes kindled to a frenzy.

"Take him!" Elise shouted.

Líana stepped away from her husband and toward her brother. "I'm staying," she said. There would be neither time nor room for argument. "Take John."

Jostling for position, the Norill swarmed up the hillside, shoving and tripping over each other in their frantic dash toward the Death fragment. Edward hesitated, looked to Líana, then to Askon.

"Go!" Askon said.

And then they were gone, the air shimmering and fluid in their place.

The remaining three drew close to one another, their backs facing the cliff's edge. On Elise's wrist the Death fragment glowed brightly, her eyes wild with it. Like a puppet cut from its strings, the Norill leading the charge fell to the earth. The lifeless body contorted itself awkwardly on contact with the rocky ground. Askon looked again to Elise. She shifted her weight to the next oncoming Norill, waiting with sword ready. A moment later it too crumpled, boneless, to the earth.

Askon breathed deep and felt the Time fragment's power course through him. In his heightened awareness, he sensed a slight change in Elise's posture. Unlike her first aggressive shift in stance, this difference suggested a weakening, a lessening, though certainly not in her resolve.

Another Norill's life leapt away, leaving its body behind; but now the group had caught up with its most zealous members. One among them fell, instantly dead. Then another. And another. When the seventh Norill fell, Elise shuddered and collapsed next to Askon.

"Hold onto me he barked at Líana. "Don't let go."

Breathing deep again, he watched as the Norill slowed, their wild eyes glaring, their yellow-fanged mouths salivating at the sight of the glowing stone on Elise's wrist. One more breath and they came to a stop. Concentrating hard, Askon lowered himself and wrapped one of Elise's arms about his shoulder. Líana did the same on the other side, careful to keep contact between them.

"Hurry," Askon said. And they dragged Elise through a gap in the Norill line. Vicious, hungry grimaces raced by, every one twisted toward where Askon and the women had been.

Halfway through the line, Askon counted greater than a score. Far greater. Dozens of furious, chanting creatures dotted the Æsten Ridge, and Askon's strength was flagging. His concentration wavered, and the creatures moved again, still unaware of their escape. Another hundred feet and he was through the mass of attackers. Askon stumbled, fell.

Suddenly, Líana's hand grew warm. The sensation traveled through his arm into his chest, and from there radiated outward. The fragment's power held, and they limped, all three exhausted and with Elise barely conscious, to the first of the huge stone slabs. A moment later, John appeared, Edward slung like a potato sack over his shoulder. He flopped the king down with a grunt behind the stone.

"He was out already when we got back," John panted. "Had to carry 'im through the last row o' stones."

Elise sat bolt upright. "Where's Thomas?"

John looked back up the hill where they could hear the Norill clamoring far away.

"Where is he?!" Elise snapped.

With a muffled thump, the last of the six tumbled down the hill and into the shadow of the stone.

John let loose a long sigh. Whether it was at Thomas's clumsiness or that his friend was alive, he would never say. Elise's arms were around her husband in an instant, the glow of the Death fragment receding.

Askon fished his own fragment from where it lay against his chest. The heartbeat rhythm pulsed slowly, but the gem's inner light seemed somehow fainter, weaker. His body felt much the same.

They helped each other to their feet. Edward, still unresponsive, hung limply over John's shoulder as they plodded back to the riverside camp.

CHAPTER THIRTEEN

A Cold Camp

Silver starlight chased the shadows from Edward's face, a halo of grass fringing his dark hair. Not far away the Estelle roared steadily, masking the chirp-and-clatter night sounds of the plain. The horses, awake and nervous, stamped and snorted, ready to bolt. On the distant ridge no light had glowed since Askon and the others emerged on the opposite side of the strange Norill force who for now seemed confined to the ridge top, planning or waiting, Askon could not decide which.

Crossing the distance from the ridge to their camp had taken a greater toll than any of them expected. Elise dragged herself alongside Thomas, reaching the river through a combination of his support and sheer force of will. John, strong as he was and believing himself a great deal stronger, lay panting and tired next to the water. Edward, John claimed, was heavier than one might guess by looking. Askon himself could barely put one foot in front of the other by the time they reached the campfire's smothered ashes. And though he could guess at why they were so exhausted, he dared not entertain the thought, even had he the energy to do so. He sat, sweating and numb, next to Edward.

Líana and Thomas were less affected by the flight from the ridge. Thomas had aided Elise while Líana kept watch behind them, guarding against any intrepid Norill who might discover and follow their trail. None did, and by the time they had drawn close to the river, Líana assisted the others however she could as their burdens grew heavier. Now she knelt beside her husband.

With a deliberate gesture, she waved the Life fragment over Edward's forehead and face, then slowly down to his chest where her hand hovered for a moment above his heart. Closing her eyes, she rotated the ring until the stone faced downward and, breathing deeply, covered stone and ring and one hand with the other. She lowered her overlapping palms, darkening the fragment's light. Through the barrier of her hands, it glowed like the embers of a strange violet fire, beating there for several moments before Edward pulled in a gasping breath and awoke as if startled from a dream.

Líana smiled, warmly, tiredly, her eyes half-lidded. Edward tried to sit up, but she only shook her head. He lay back into the pillow of grass, gazing up at her and to the stars beyond. Her head dipped; her eyes closed; her cheek fell softly against him, the long braid tumbling down. Neither could recall falling asleep, nor could the others. Thomas watched over them all.

+ + +

The minutiae of the road can fill a not-insignificant portion of a night's watch. Horses need tending, supplies need checking, perimeters need patrolling, and in cases like the night under the shadow of Æsten's Ridge (though the others stubbornly insisted on using the commonplace and incorrect *Æsten* Ridge) friends and fellow soldiers need careful observation.

Elise was first, or at least the first that he saw. So unlike her to be asleep so soon, and his bias meant he watched her closest. John had followed. A longtime veteran and self-proclaimed man of the moon, John's candidacy for such extreme tiredness was equally unlikely. By the time Askon lay curled up in the long grass, Thomas had expected it, and had already begun forming several theories as to why his friends were so singularly susceptible to sleep this night. Something weighed on Askon that Thomas could not yet identify, but it seemed tied (as everything did) to the fragments. When Líana and Edward slept soundly together, after yet another revival by Líana and the Life fragment, Thomas's mind wandered to other matters.

In truth their escape had been narrow, and only an escape at all on account of the fragments and their powers. Now, a hostile Norill force large enough to cause systematic destruction throughout the kingdom roamed unchecked in the night. If these creatures had designs or orders to attack any number of villages in Vladvir, wreckage would be all that remained. Most communities, like Shale, where Thomas had been raised, were woefully under-prepared for any kind of assault, especially after the devastation Iramov and his armies had wrought. Shale itself was an exception, of course, after the attack and defense more than a year before. Whatever the case, not only had the six of them barely made it out, it was clear that the sudden appearance of hostile Norill with a penchant for a certain syllable would only grow more frequent.

Hours passed, and although no light grew yet in the east, Thomas sensed the coming of morning. Several times since his watch began, he had considered waking them. With the Norill free to pursue their as yet unknown goals, it seemed he and his friends should move to counteract them. Each time he resolved to rouse the group and be on their way, something stayed his hand: a peaceful expression, a reminder of their trial on the Ridge, a pang of guilt at the sleepless demands of parenthood. But with sunrise tingling at the edge of the world, the memory of the previous day's blistering heat and his nagging worries concerning the Norill threat tipped the scales of decision. He woke John first.

The snarl of black beard opened in a gaping yawn, and John stretched each of his thick arms before sitting up, resting his weight on his elbows. His mouth clicked wetly and a grunt escaped.

"Are you awake?" Thomas asked.

"*Hrm,*" John grumbled in assent. "Why'd ya have to wake me up first?"

Thomas grinned. "Because," he said lightly, "it's what you would've done." He raised John's already-filled waterskin. "Only you would've been much less polite about it."

John's eyebrows lifted the slightest of degrees. "Oh?" He tried to look nonchalant. "Well, have at it then."

Thomas shook his head. "Another day maybe. I've spent most of the night readying our supplies and gear. We need to break camp and head off those Norill."

John rolled to his side, shifting to one elbow. "What makes you think they didn't just lie down and go to sleep like it seems we all did? I figure if that's the case, we've got a head start rather than ground to gain."

It was a scenario Thomas hadn't considered. Not, certainly, that the Norill had fallen asleep, but that the enemy force had simply stayed where it was on the ridge. Their behavior *had* been strange, as had the behavior of all the Norill intruders throughout the kingdom. If their orders merely commanded them to gather, or even to wait for further reinforcements, they might still be looking pointlessly out over the cliff.

"That's not an altogether terrible idea," Thomas said.

"The hell it ain't," sputtered John. "Go wake the others. O' course we've got work and some hard riding to do, probably even before the sun properly rises. If that knot o' crazy bastard Norill's still up there, we have to at least let Edward figure out what he wants to do about it. The man's got a bit more responsibility than back in his pampered princely days." John stopped, stared at Thomas, tilted his head. "You heard me. Get on with it and wake 'em!"

Scrabbling to his feet, Thomas saw the first hint of morning's light bloom at the edge of the night sky. They would need to move quickly. Edward, when he woke, would need to decide quickly. And Askon's plans might need to adapt quickly. It was unlikely either would be happy, whatever the decision.

The others rose easily. It seemed the hard sleep had done them all a significant bit of good. Askon awoke in his usual grim mood, his eyes fixed—even upon first waking—on some point in the southern sky. Thomas wondered if such fascination, like Askon's for finding Dalkaldur, would prove itself more dangerous obsession than harmless fixation in the end. Líana and Elise were their usual paradoxically friendly opposites in their discussion of the previous night. His wife quiet and controlled, even somewhat ashamed at the battle and her use of the Death fragment, while Askon's sister (and the queen, he reminded himself yet again) thrilled in the chance for combat, the near-miss escape, and even the revival of her husband after they had cleared themselves of the ridge.

Edward himself was a somewhat different story. Though not entirely exhausted, he awoke with an enduring tiredness and dimness of spirit that Thomas found more than a bit unusual. The king had an innate ability to appear unaffected in the face of hardship, social awkwardness, the heat of argument, or a darkened battlefield. On this morning the gray eyes, more colorless than sterling, reminded Thomas of the glazed and glassy Norill atop the ridge, and though he would never say so aloud—the eyes of Iramov's dead army brought back to life.

Thomas shared neither the refreshed energy of the majority nor the warmed-over doggedness of the king. He was simply tired. Too many hours without sleep, and too much exertion in the battle, and the flight, and the watch, and the preparations to leave at first light had taxed the young father beyond his limits. His son's face lingered before his drooping eyelids as he dropped off to sleep in the saddle.

✝ ✝ ✝

"I can hardly sit back and watch as my kingdom burns to the ground around me!" Edward was shouting, his face ragged.

"I'm not asking for you to 'sit back and watch'," Askon fired back. "There's an army, and militia, and guard posts all over Vladvir. Let them deal with these Norill. We have more important things to worry about."

"More important than my duty to my people?!" Sleep had clearly fended off the king's breaking point, but only just.

Askon sighed loudly. "Perhaps. We've been over this. The fragments could do more damage than any amount of Norill if they were to fall into the wrong hands. And then there's—"

"Oh, not the damn girl again!" Edward shook his head and leveled a finger at Askon. "You'd drag the king of Vladvir into the mountains while an enemy force runs rampant through towns, villages, the whole countryside. You'd put all of us at risk to see that woman again."

Askon felt the muscles of his shoulder flex, a precursor to slapping Edward's hand away, but then he felt something else, a familiar sensation that the world was moving faster than he was, that time was outrunning his thoughts. He breathed deeply and knew that time indeed outstripped not only his thinking but every-thing about him. Though he could harness the Time fragment's power, had done many times since the battle with Iramov, this was the first moment he could recall feeling its negative effects in more than a year's time.

"I—" he stammered.

"Find a girl in the usual way!" Edward snapped. "It's your own fault, staying locked in your study for weeks at a time poring over maps and scribblings like half a madman. It's time—"

"Call me half a man again!" Askon roared. "Your horse isn't high enough that I can't knock you into the—"

"That's enough," Líana said riding between them. "Fighting with each other does us no good. Not to mention it places me in a difficult position. You're both too tired to think clearly. That's ob-vious to us all. Unfortunately that's also exactly what we need to do. We can't decide anything with the two of you trying to shout the other into submission. Edward, what happened to following Askon's lead?"

Edward jerked the reins and spurred his horse, turning point-edly away from her. Askon smoldered beneath his hood and tried to convince himself that he was angry at his friend for slighting his sister, while his eyes still stared southward. Líana looked after her husband, her eyes narrow, mouth pursed, and looking more than a little like her older brother.

When Edward and his horse had widened the gap between them to shouting range, he turned broadside to face them. "We make for the Greyarc!" he commanded. "By then I will have made my choice." He spurred the horse again and separated himself even further from the group.

Thomas, fully awake after his time dozing in the saddle, drew closer to John. "So much for Edward's unflappable temperament," he said in a stage whisper.

John laughed, so loudly that though Edward would not have heard it, everyone else certainly did. "Oh, you just haven't seen these two at it before. Though, I'll say it's usually Askon who rides out shoutin' curses to no one but himself. Edward takin' off is somethin' new at least. I figure it's good entertainment for the road. They'll be thick as thieves again by nightfall."

Askon, sullen and sulking, rode heavily at the head of the group, while Edward cantered ahead, apart from the rest. Thomas looked after them, unconvinced by John's explanation. "Whatever you say," he began, then paused. The silence filled with the unsteady rhythm of clopping hooves. "Something is different today, though. I might know what it is, but I'm not ready to say anything to either of them yet."

A puff of air rushed out of the black beard. "You're gods damned right 'whatever I say'! I'll tell ya' what won't do any good, pestering them with one of your overcooked theories. Just let 'em be for a couple hours. They'll cool off. I've seen it more times than I can count."

"So at least as many as you have fingers?" Elise offered. She had ridden quietly next to them throughout the conversation, watching the others, forming her own dark thoughts, remembering the son she'd left in Tolarenz. "Your experience may be greater than both of ours collected, but your record is, let's say *mathematically imprecise*."

"Bah!" John huffed. "You been shacked up with this fool husband o' yours too long, a Dalstone girl like you, stringin' words together like some noble's son tryin' his luck with poetry instead o' real work. I'm as accurate as I need to be. Mark my words."

"Oh, they've been marked," Elise retorted. "And not all Dalstone 'girls' need to construct a sentence like a half-drunk innkeep angling for coin."

John glanced sidelong at her. "Are you accusin' me o' being' half-drunk? We're barely past sunrise."

"We know," Thomas interrupted. "You've," he dropped his voice and soured his facial expression, "'usu'lly had enough the night afore tuh be more'n two-thirds drunk by sunrise.'" He grinned at his little impersonation. Elise laughed softly, and John turned away to hide the smile spreading over his face.

CHAPTER FOURTEEN
White

A clatter erupted in the alleyway, startling one of the city's feral cats. Whether it was only one—or five—a person could never be certain. One could be as irritating as ten, so five didn't seem like much of a stretch. Whatever their number, they'd knocked over some sheet metal or a wood frame. The sound rang out against the paving stones, triggering a cascade of yowls from here to forever. She looked up at the ceiling—grimy and water-stained as it had been the day before, and the day before that—and released a dramatic sigh.

"A few days more," her father had told her a week ago, "then our trail will be cold. You'll be safe to go back and read your books." Now they were going around it again.

"Just one book, really." She thumped a fist absently against the bed frame. "I don't see why it makes any difference. It's not like they're looking for me. As far as we know, they aren't even looking for you."

He turned from his work at the desk, the crook of a halfhearted smile showing over his shoulder. "Always the optimist," he said. "But I suppose you're right, though I'd emphasize *as far as we know*." He turned back to the papers spread before him and adjusted the arm of the lamp. "The alternative, of course, is that they *do* know. And if they do, isn't it in their best interest to make sure we don't know that they know?"

She shrugged, despite the fact he wasn't looking at her. Optimist that she might have been, he was just as prone—if not more so—to circular thoughts like the ones he was about to indulge. *But what if they know that we know that they know? And what if they know that we know that they know that we know?* It would go on until he could no longer track how many *knows* all of these shadowy characters *knew* or until he realized she wasn't listening anymore. She curled up and faced the wall.

They'd been forced to move again. To "relocate" as her father put it. And it wasn't as if they had been in the previous place long enough to call it home. The move was one more in an ever growing string of places she used to live. Her father meant well, as always. Protective to the last, like any father really, though more often than she liked, protective to a fault. She was well aware of the dangers they faced, the risks that he took. In fact, she'd considered simply leaving. Most of her former friends had left home after their schooling was complete. But she couldn't. Her father had already gotten himself into trouble by then. When they had been three instead of two, it would have been easier. Before her mother had passed, she might have been able to leave, to find her own way. And so it was that four years had gone by. Someone had to protect *him* while he was so busy protecting her.

She picked at a flaking bit of paint on the wall next to the bed, thinking about Dalkaldur and the Knight of Vladvir and *The Book of the Tear*, for the thousandth time wishing there to be another copy or a more lenient lending policy for precious volumes. She hooked a fingernail under the paint and pulled, then retracted the hand with a yelp, sucking air through her teeth and sticking the finger in her mouth. After a moment she pulled it away to examine the damage. A tiny bead of blood welled beneath the nail.

"What's wrong?" her father wondered without looking up.

She curled herself tighter against the wall and pulled a blanket around her shoulders, thumbing the nail to apply some pressure. "Nothing. Just pricked my finger is all. It hurts."

"It hurts!" she screamed. Sitting bolt upright, she gasped, her heart hammering against her chest. A bright light surrounded her, her eyes struggling to focus. For a moment she sat panting, whimpering at the remnants of the nightmare as the fear faded.

A soft white sheet clung cool against her body, and she suddenly felt the sensation of being completely exposed, as in a dream where the people and place are ordinary enough until something shifts and the eyes well with laughter as she'd realize she was naked. Or even more eerie, having the realization first while those in the dream responded as if everything were completely normal. Such dreams where she'd think, *Can't they see? Shouldn't they notice? Should I hide? Cover up? They don't seem to care.*

Should I? and go on with whatever mundane task the dream presented wearing nothing but her own skin. No, this time the lights and the room, and the bed beneath her, the pillow and the white walls, and the cool white sheet were all too real. It was no dream.

She pulled the sheet up to her chin, her eyes bleary with the light. The tiniest of laughs escaped her mouth. Had they found her? Rescued her? Taken her away? Taken her home? A numbness crept along her right leg. With an effort and a repositioning of the linens, she ran her hand down past the knee to the ankle where she discovered that she was not entirely unclothed. A thick bandage encircled her foot. She pulled the sheet back, revealing a blurry smudge of pink that she took to be her toes; the bandage was clean, skillfully applied, and white, like everything else.

She found a bedside table to her left and a small cup of viscous liquid, hardly more than a few thimblefuls. Below it lay an illegible note, and next to it, her circlet. They'd taken it from her in the dark room where *he* was. She fumbled for it, her fingers slipping over the smear of shapes, and set it carefully on her head. Running her fingers through her hair, smelling lavender and wildflowers, feeling its smoothness and startling cleanliness, she waited.

And then her vision cleared. The note came into focus. In a tidy hand it commanded, "Drink when you can read these words." Wherever she'd been taken, it was certainly an improvement upon the dark room. She considered the note, considered it a moment too long as a dull ache warmed her bandaged foot. Quickly it erupted into real pain. Her legs clenched, her knees coiling nearly to her chest. She hissed a breath through clenched teeth.

Wrapping the sheet around her body and under her arms, she reached for the cup, gulping the thick liquid. It burned pleasantly, like the mint leaf oil her mother had kept in the cabinet with the crushed basil leaves, sage, and garlic cloves. The effect was immediate. Her foot, which she'd swung over the edge of the bed, pulsed a handful of times along with her heartbeat, each time lessening the pain until it was gone, replaced again by the cool numbness she had felt when she first awoke.

Opposite the bed stood a glass-paneled cabinet and chest of drawers made of the same polished white metal as the bed frame. Inside the cabinet hung a set of plain white clothes, apparently to match the decor. She wondered if they'd fit. Even if they didn't, she determined, they would be better than the clumsily wrapped sheet. Half hopping, half limping, she made her way from the foot of the bed to the cabinet. Standing with one foot raised in an awkward parody of the pose she'd been taught by her health instructors, she reached for the cabinet knobs and pulled. When nothing happened, she bent a bit at the knee, ever so slightly resting her injured foot against the cool floor tiles and pulled, harder this time. The doors came free.

The sheet dropped, pooling onto the floor, and she felt first a pang of concern at the dust and dirt it might collect there before becoming pointedly aware that nothing remained to cover her. After a reflexive crossing of her arms, she smiled to herself and surveyed the empty room. There was no one to hide from. She grabbed the glass doors and pushed them back, producing a soft click as the hinges fully opened. Then, another heavier click sounded and she was no longer alone.

Cover up? Turn away? Reach down and gather the sheet? Her mind froze with the decision. She simply stood there, stark naked except for the bandage, one foot raised as if interrupted during a balancing exercise. Her eyes darted and she reached for the clothes in the dresser, grabbed them, and felt her weight shift; but there was no foot to catch her, or rather there might as well have been none as she fell to the floor, clothes in hand, and banged her elbow against the tiles.

"Oh now, let's not be too worried about all that." It was the voice of the kind-spoken woman. No rescue, then. "Are you all right? There's little need for concern about prying eyes. We both have the same..." she hesitated, searching for a polite term, "... equipment? No. Too sterile. How about anatomy? Hmm. Too scientific. Well, you take my meaning, I'm sure."

Meanwhile Alora had scrambled back into the sheet, still gripping the set of clothes in her free hand. Her elbow throbbed now along with her foot. But she was still on the floor, the tile clammy and cold.

"Go ahead," continued the kind-spoken woman. "Get up and into those clothes. That's what they're here for, of course. You don't think we'd have you lying about in here without a stitch to wear?"

Though the woman's tone sounded sincere, memories of a darkened room, tortured screams, and days of filth suggested otherwise. What had she said that convinced them to bring her back into the light? Where had the man with the voice full of threat gone? And what mistakes would bring him back?

The woman reached down to her and, when she didn't reach back, pulled the sheet from the floor and held it up between them. "Fine," she said. "If you're so worried I'll see something I've seen every day in the mirror since I was born, off you go." Her voice was almost cheery. "I'll even close my eyes."

For a fraction of a breath, a daring escape flashed through Alora's mind. Knock the woman down while she wasn't looking. Make for the open door. And then what? Bare as she was, and with a foot that couldn't support her weight, the scenario shifted quickly from dramatic to ridiculous. She pushed herself up from the cold floor and, using the dresser for balance, slipped into the clothes.

"There," said the woman. "That's better, I'm sure." She turned and snapped the sheet out before her where it floated, weightless for a moment. Then she tugged lightly, bringing it back to rest on the bed. With practiced precision, she tucked the corners, folded her hands, and looked up at Alora. "Now," she said smiling. "About all that nastiness downstairs."

CHAPTER FIFTEEN

All the Details

"They're more vivid every time," Thomas murmured to Elise.

She nodded and waved a tired hand southward along the river as if to say 'Then go tell them yourself'.

They'd been over it already. Of course he had told his wife about the white room and the bright lights, told her about the return of the kind-spoken woman and of the threatening man's disappearance. He'd left out the details concerning the girl's wardrobe, certainly. Besides, it didn't seem a significant detail in light of the current situation.

Following Edward's example, the group now spread themselves out over a quarter mile, the king in the lead and Thomas at the rear. The younger man's previous night of preparations left only thinly stretched willpower to drive him forward. Had they been on foot, he would have had no other choice than to request a halt hours earlier. Instead, he had nodded in the saddle periodically for half a day. With the Greyarc Bridge already in sight, and Edward drawing ever nearer the guard station there, Thomas had decided he could either speak now, or risk being lost in the din as Askon lobbied for Dalkaldur and Edward for a return to King's City.

A wispy bank of clouds had cobwebbed the sky, half committed to easing the heat of the previous day. Had the sun been as blistering, the early morning outburst between Askon and Edward might have been all the worse. As it was, Askon had fallen back to ride alongside John. Some of the sullenness had left him, though he still stared southward any time the two weren't in direct conversation. Thomas assumed the pairing simply reflected John's willingness to follow Askon to Dalkaldur despite the sudden Norill appearances. Once John had decided a thing, little hope remained to change his mind.

After slowly gaining on the two old friends, the young couple approached them from either side, as one might a dangerous animal. Though hours had passed since tempers flared near the campsite, they all knew well how long Askon's anger could retain its heat.

"Well, out with it already," Askon grumbled without looking back. "You've been drawing closer for the better part of half an hour. It's not as if we didn't hear you coming."

"We thought—" Thomas began, raising a hand to Elise. If anyone had a temper to rival their leader, it was his wife. And as of late, she'd been less often the whisper and more often the wit with biting edge. He tried again. "We didn't want to interrupt you. Today hasn't been easy for any of us, especially after what we encountered on the ridge. With the two of you angry, the rest of us are left…"

"Adrift," Elise finished for him. She pawed at the curtain of black hair, looping one side behind an ear. "You and our young king need to sort out this nonsense before the whole endeavor comes apart. For now, we're with you, despite it all, but don't think for a single breath that I—and my piece of your precious puzzle—won't take Thomas and turn back. Now, listen to what he has to say. It might help you convince Edward."

John shrugged a shoulder. "She's got a point. If you keep this up, it'll be a two-man march into the mountains and no map to read from." He lifted a finger. "And yes, I know there's no *actual* map. I was speakin' in proverbials."

A smile rippled over Askon's face. He tilted his head toward Thomas and gave a quick nod. "Alright then. I'm listening."

For the next hour Thomas recounted his visions, starting with the city and Alora's home with her father, the books, and the young man who seemed to be her friend. Then came the dingy relocation, her father's fretting, and her desire to get back to the place with the books. Finally, Thomas made his way to the white room and the kind-spoken woman, all the while being careful to include every detail he could recall.

"So ya said she weren't wearing a stitch," John interrupted, his eyes drifting and distant. "How'd ya know for sure? Could ya see —"

Thomas cut him off. "It doesn't work like that."

Elise glowered. "And even if it did, what might he be able to tell you? I'm fairly certain you can imagine it well enough for yourself without a detailed account. It's as the woman in Thomas's visions says, the anatomy is the same. If you've seen one, you've as good as seen us all."

"Ha!" John scoffed. "I may not have a mind for complicated clockwork springs and little gears, but I've an eye for detail in this department. An' let me tell ya, there's a great deal more to be observed than 'They've all got arms and they've all got legs and they've all got...'" His gaze drifted again, this time not so distantly.

"Breasts?" Elise offered with an arch of the back and light touch to her hair which evaporated instantly as she leveled a glare at John, a crease forming on her brow.

"No." John responded undaunted. "I was thinkin' of sayin', *eyes*. Shows what your mind's up to. Some of us around here have a sense o' decency 'bout such things as that. But so long as you're bringing it up, I'd be a liar if I said they were all the same."

Elise sighed, exasperated. "Dalstone, King's City, Tolarenz even, *you're* the ones who are all the same. Anybody shows a little skin to the sky and you lose the better part of any intellect you had to begin with."

As ever, unaware of when he'd fallen into a trap, John forged ahead. "It was hot enough yesterday. I didn't see you stripping layers and barin' yer bare self to the sun and everybody."

"No, you didn't. But not for some shamefaced shyness as your women seem to. I'll wear what I want and not wear what I don't want on my own terms and time, thank you. And it won't matter one feather who can see, if they're so rude as to stare. In Vitæsta we needn't worry about eyes that pry. A patch of skin out in the open isn't an invitation. If you're invited, you'll know."

Askon shifted uncomfortably in the saddle. "I think, regardless, Thomas has withheld this story long enough, and you seem to be missing the point, John." He leaned over and gripped his friend's shoulder, giving him a rough shake. "Why don't you let him finish?"

John pulled the shoulder away nearly costing Askon his balance. "Alright. Though I'm still not certain if I agree."

"What makes you think I care about your agreement?" Elise raised her eyebrows and leaned again toward him. "There are facts, and then there are opinions to which one may agree or disagree. Vitæsta's customs are my truths to share with you—gods know why I would choose to. They're not up for debate."

When John didn't respond, Thomas finished recounting his vision. The kind-spoken woman had returned, and after getting Alora settled in the white room, seemed ready to make some kind of offer concerning her treatment. Whatever it was, the price would be rooted in the fragments.

"But none of it makes any sense," Thomas said when he had given the last details he could recall. "When it started, we all saw the same thing: a young woman running from someone, hiding the fragments. We wanted to help her. It was simple. Now I'm seeing her trapped, captured, tortured. I'm seeing her memories or imaginings, or possibly other times from her life. And I have no idea where she is. It's a city, that's certain, but which?"

He shook his head heavily and sighed. Elise put her hand out, and he grasped it for a moment before letting it fall. "I'm just tired, is all. Maybe it will clear up after I've rested. Unfortunately when I rest, I only see more of what's happening to her. And it's usually unpleasant, one way or another."

Askon's gaze had drifted again to the south. There, even as they talked, the Southern Mountains peaked above the horizon. If he had his way, those peaks would soon rise, encircling them until finally they found the mountaintop valley of Dalkaldur.

"What about the book?" he said without turning to face the others. "*The Book of the Tear* seems important to her, and it's another item that ties her to us."

Thomas shrugged. "There isn't much for me to see there, except that she's interested in it. I know that Caled makes an appearance and that she remembers him enough to draw sketches of him when her mind wanders."

"Remind you of anyone?" John asked. The others didn't laugh.

With his eyes still on the southern sky, Askon rubbed a hand over his face and chin. "Have you tried sleeping without the Sight fragment? Maybe a little distance between you and it will help you rest."

Elise nodded.

"It's worth an effort, though I think at this point the distance would need to be fairly great. I've kept it in another room back home, and that does little good. The images are less clear, but that's often more unsettling. And I'm afraid none of us wants any part of the Tear very far out of sight right now, what with Norill appearing across the kingdom searching for the pieces."

Ahead of them, now by the better part of a mile, Askon could see Marten circling above Líana. After a few passes, the falcon landed lightly on her shoulder.

With little recognition that he was even doing it, Askon's breathing slowed, and the Time fragment's power grew. He saw her posture change, saw his sister had learned something from the bird, much the same way he could read the falcon's movements like a conversation. Then he felt himself sway in the saddle, a ring of black clouding his sight, and nearly fell from his seat. With a shake of his head, he released the fragment's energy, and the world came quickly back into focus.

"You all right, there?" John wondered. Askon had hoped he had covered the near blackout well enough that the others would assume it simply an adjustment in riding stance.

"We thought you might fall for a moment," Elise whispered, her voice laced with concern, its irritation and edge softened, muted.

"No," Askon lied. "I mean, yes." He rolled a shoulder as if to stretch it. "I'm all right. It's been a long while since I've ridden so far. Parts of me are falling asleep that I forgot could fall asleep."

"Well, I'll agree to that," John said with a chuckle. "Maybe we should have a bit of a rest before we get to the Greyarc. You know once Edward gets his news from the sentries there, he'll start that 'A king has responsibilities!' and 'What about my people?' nonsense." The big man waved his arms as if to encompass the entirety of Vladvir. Askon wondered if there would be more. When there wasn't, he sighed.

"I haven't seen Edward like this in a very long time. Perhaps ever..." Now the others were left to wonder what more Askon might say. Eyes narrowing, he pointed into the distance.

"Do any of you see that?" He drove a finger forward again for emphasis.

"I see Líana," said Thomas. "It looks like she's trying to catch up to Edward. But what does that have to do with anything. She's ridden alone for the better part of the day. Can you blame her for wanting to talk with him before we reach the bridge?"

"No," Askon barked. He poked the air a third time. "*There.*"

It was Marten, of course. And though the bird was small to Askon's eyes, he assumed the others would recognize him at this distance. The falcon flew directly toward them, his winged shape growing.

"You're pointing at Marten," Thomas said after a moment. "Why?"

Askon inclined his head. "He's headed this way for a reason. And Líana's headed in the opposite direction. Something's wrong."

CHAPTER SIXTEEN
Bonds and Bridges

The leather guard received the brunt of the punishment when Marten landed full force on Askon's shoulder. Assuming extended time in the snow and ice of the Southern Mountains, they had all packed additional gear. It could be days, possibly weeks, depending on how well Dalkaldur remained hidden from Thomas and the Sight fragment. Askon had packed the guard for a different sort of practicality, or so he told himself. In his sparring sessions, he felt lopsided without it. Add that to his light physical activity in recent months and frequent second helpings and he simply needed something, anything familiar. So, when Marten's talons wrapped themselves tightly against his former master's shoulder, Askon felt a bit more like himself again.

Marten dipped his head, clear eyes darting as he folded his blue-gray wings. Askon leaned in close, observing the bird's movements, the tiny breathing sounds, the tension in his feet. Together they assembled a picture akin to a game of charades, a version at which Askon was particularly adept. Wondering how his friends interpreted their little dance, he turned to John.

Before Askon could speak, his friend had already begun, "Bird says there's a fight waitin' for us at the bridge, doesn't he?"

Askon cocked his head slightly, for a moment birdlike in his own way. He paused, trying to imagine John—with all of his bullish stubbornness and willful lack of subtlety—understanding Marten's vague, understated communications. "How did you know?"

A grin spread slowly through the curls of beard, and John stretched his arms high above his head. He brought them down and, after a conspicuous flex of his right bicep, pointed toward the bridge. "Ya been so intent on that bird, that ya seem to have missed some o' the more obvious clues." He let the hand drop to his side. "See there. The makings of a bit o' smoke by the bridge. Thin, but clear enough to my eye. Then there's our disgruntulated—"

Thomas cleared his throat, "I think you mean disgruntl—"

"I know damned well what I mean, Thomas!" John barked. "Mind yer betters while I'm instructin' our leader on how to spot an ambush."

Thomas bristled a bit, but Elise calmed him with a look. John adjusted a sleeve and continued. "As I was sayin', our new king up there, who's been *upset* this mornin', is full turned around and ridin' back this way." John nodded toward Edward and Líana, who had indeed begun to make their way back toward the rest of the group. "Now, ya see, that's where it gets interesting by my account.

We've got smoke rollin' up, bands o' crazed Norill, and a king swallowin' his pride. But they aren't at a gallop, nor even more than a trot, so I'd say your bird's seen a bit more'n I have, 'cause I'd turn us southward or wait till nightfall with a list like that."

Askon smiled. "Well that was—thorough," he said, "and not terribly far from the mark, even with Marten's help. You're right, though. I hadn't noticed the smoke or that Líana and Edward are on their way back. A year's time is more than enough to become a bit out of practice in such matters."

"I hope you mean the bird," John snorted, "because I might second guess followin' you into gods know where if you've gotten rusty at seein' things that are right in front o' yer face. 'Course, that would be assumin' you were ever any good at it to begin with."

With a shake of his head and a sniff of a laugh, Askon shrugged, careful not to disturb Marten. It felt good, right some-how, to have the falcon resting there once again. But Marten took flight nonetheless and soon circled high above them.

"Let's hope the rust works itself out sooner rather than later," he said.

Another several minutes closed the gap and reunited the group. Edward's face, usually stern and impassive, grew sullen the closer he and Líana drew to the others. They rode in silence until they were within two long bowshots of the bridge. Askon recalled the ambush there, the fragment's overpowering influence, and their near ruin if not for John's opportune arrival and skillful planning.

Now, at least, the sky was clear and blue, and though a wreath of mist snaked through the stone pillars, it merely sparkled in the sun instead of shrouding the crossing in fog.

With a deepening frown, Edward nodded to Líana, granting permission she would have taken on her own regardless.

"It's unclear whether or not the bridge is safe," she began with unrestrained confidence. "I can see it. Marten has seen it, and by now, I'm sure Askon has as well. The guard stations are empty, signal fires lit at both riverbanks, crows circling the dead. And yet…" She turned to face the bridge.

Askon interrupted. "And yet, we have little choice but to cross. There are no reliable bridges south of the Greyarc until it joins with the Grafdrek at the borders of the South Kingdom." He sighed. "We could attempt—"

Líana's eyes narrowed. "That's not what I was going to say." She glared at him, holding him there a moment, reminding him more than a little of Marten staring icily at John. He felt the urge to pull away.

"I was going to say," Líana began again, "Edward needs to head east, and the Greyarc is the only place to do so. If these Norill are able to take a bridge such as this one, they are unlikely to meet any greater resistance until they reach King's City itself."

Askon turned to Edward. "You can't mean to—"

"I do," said the king. "Even if the Norill are already on their way to King's City, I have to follow. I may be too late. I may place myself in greater danger. Of these things I am aware, but without me, it isn't much of a *King's* City at all. My people, our people, deserve better than a man running about chasing faerie stories."

"But you've seen the fragments, seen what happens there with your own eyes!" Askon fired back.

"Not that I count for much in this debate," John said, "but it seems to me—and I've certainly told the story enough times to know—that you've lived a faerie story already, Edward. Watchin' Askon move faster than ought be possible, seein' places that aren't really there, people we've never met, movin' yourself and the rest of us round with your mind, and—" he hesitated at the last, "watchin' Iramov raise the dead to fight again."

Edward shook his head. "Say what you will, but I have a responsibility to my kingdom's people. It's simple. One of you will carry my fragment to Dalkaldur if you still feel you must go. I make for King's City. Perhaps if I avoid the direct road, I can come upon a garrison or patrol and begin planning how we will enter the walls if the Norill have already arrived."

A few minutes later they had gained the bridge, Edward in the lead at center, Askon and Líana just behind on either side. The others followed, watchful and wary. On their left, the guard station where Askon, Thomas, and Edward had hidden before John appeared at their previous encounter on the Greyarc, stood empty, its door swinging loosely on creaking hinges. The rush of the Estelle muffled the sound, but the grinding metal on metal pierced even the great river's constant drone. Around the deserted station, bodies lay crumpled and lifeless, flies flitting here and there. The crows at least had winged away upon the party's approach. The flies were bolder, fixated, greedy.

"None left," John grunted, his face pinched in disgust. "Bastard Norill killed 'em all, or run 'em off at the least."

Thomas had dismounted, leaving his horse to follow Elise. "Perhaps there's a sign that some of the guard retreated, headed east toward the city?"

Askon and Líana were already busy searching the area, the former scouring the paving stones for tracks or signs that would show where Vladvir's fighting men had gone if they hadn't stayed to the last, and the latter moving slowly from body to body, checking, Askon assumed, for any survivor she might revive. Along with Thomas, they combed the western bank for several minutes while the others talked in hushed voices, gesturing here and there over the river or to the south.

After completing a third circle of the evidence, Askon shook his head. Some tracks led away from the battle, but only a very few in comparison to the corpses left behind, many of whom looked young, inexperienced, and under provisioned. Their armor showed much mending, some of it poorly done. Vladvir had seen little strife over the past year, or so Askon had gleaned from his letters with Líana and the others. A skirmish here or there where remnants of Iramov's supporters lurked, or where the hatred of half-elf or Norill lingered. There had even been word of opposition to Edward's rule after whispers of Codard's treachery spread. But all of these were small and had taken only the barest few lives. It was a lucky outcome by most measures, as the forces of Vladvir's army had seldom been weaker since the Great Darkness.

And so the young, untrained guards had come to be stationed at the Greyarc bridge, where they fought the mindless Norill Askon and his friends had met at the top of the Æsten Ridge. He knelt again, squinting in the afternoon light, hoping for some clearer sign.

"Líana!"

It was Edward. His horse reared at the shout, whinnying and dancing nervously against the Greyarc's stones. Askon looked up as Edward spurred the horse onto the bridge, but he could see nothing through the animal's bulk.

Edward drove the animal forward, lashing the reins again and again until he had crossed nearly half the bridge's span, then leapt from the saddle and struck the ground with an awkward clatter. He knelt for a moment, and then, in a blink, he was gone.

The horse reared, a second scream echoing over the roaring Estelle. Its legs buckled, and the great beast fell against the cold stones. Askon stood now, sword drawn, scanning the bridge for his friend and his sister, but something told him not to advance. And so he retreated a step, then two. John hurried to his side while Thomas and Elise led the other horses behind the guard station, out of the line of enemy arrows. But the same sense telling Askon that now was no time for a charge coursed through his mind. Something was not right. The fallen horse kicked and twitched on the bridge, and there was no sign of Edward or Líana.

They appeared behind him, Líana shaking and quivering like the horse on the bridge. Her eyes had rolled back so far that only the whites showed. The lids, one closing further than the other, fluttered rapidly. In a heartbeat Askon was at her side. The shaking slowed until it became a pulsing jitter. When these subsided, her body merely jerked from moment to moment, a taught bowstring thrumming against the empty air, her face tightening with pain then relaxing and tightening again.

Slowly the convulsions faded until they were no more than a ripple. Sweat beaded her brow, and her skin grew pale, the color leaching from her lips and cheeks. Now, with no color and no energy left to move, she lay still beneath her husband's worried face. He pulled her close, and recognition dawned. He lowered an ear to her mouth, breathed deeply, and nodded to Askon with a sigh.

"Water!" he hissed at Thomas.

Askon turned from them to face the bridge. The horse had begun to struggle again. It rose and, bolting toward them, ran wild-eyed for the western bank. Behind it, a row of Norill advanced. From the center of their ranks, a man emerged. With outstretched arm he signaled them forward over the bridge. Their mouths moved together. No sound carried over the river to Askon's ears, but he knew what the ragged voices chanted.

CHAPTER SEVENTEEN
Confirmation

"Form up the horses!" Askon shouted. Across the bridge, the No-rill and their leader advanced. "We can break through their line and head south."

"South?" Edward barked back. "Are you mad?! Look at your sister. Look at her! She needs a healer. We're not going to find help if we go south. You're obsessed! We have to get her to King's City. I don't know what they did to her, but it's the same as they did to my horse." He struggled to lift Líana's half-conscious form off the paving stones. "Help me!" he commanded.

Together they managed to seat her in front of Edward while Thomas collected the horses and drew alongside the others.

"Whatever we do," John rumbled, "we need to ride like hell. Put some distance between them and us. You two can have it out once and for all when we get clear of 'em."

Askon aligned the horses five abreast: Líana's empty between Thomas and Elise in the center, himself on the left, and John on the right. Edward and Líana rode shielded behind them, the latter still in and out of consciousness.

"They'll have to ride level with us, Askon," John said, as the horses stamped and twisted nervously. "If one of us goes down and they're behind, it'll take 'em down too."

"We have to protect them," Askon retorted. "Edward can't fight while he's holding her in the saddle. And she certainly can't defend herself."

"He's right," Edward said. "It won't work to leave us back here, especially if her horse has no rider."

All the while, the enemy made its slow advance onto the bridge. They had no shields, for which Askon was grateful, but they were too many for the six of them to defeat, especially with Líana in her current condition. At the center of the first rank strode the man whose strange weapon had injured Líana. Askon watched as he reached into a pouch on his belt, then fumbled with something in his hands.

"Alright," Askon growled. "Quickly then! I'll break their line at center. Put Líana's horse next to me on one side and Edward on the other. John, cover Edward's right. Thomas, Elise on the opposite side."

Askon eyed the man across the bridge. He had stopped fumbling, and now held something short and black at his side. A hammer, a club? The object was obscured by the man's hand and body as he led the Norill forward.

"Hurry," Askon said. "We don't have time for this."

A moment later the horses were in position. Ahead of them the enemy showed no sign of retreat, but neither did they seem inclined to attack. Long knives glinted in gray Norill fingers, but they hung limp at the creatures' sides. Had they not faced Iramov's army of the dead, Askon and the others might have been cowed or shaken. But they *had* fought Iramov, and defeated him.

"Charge them," Askon ordered. He drew his sword, spurred his horse, and the others followed.

Hoofbeats clattered across the stones as their wedge surged ahead. A quarter of the distance and Askon felt Edward swerve unsteadily next to him. Half the distance and the riderless horse veered, almost faltering before deciding the best and only course was forward. Three quarters the distance and Askon could see the enemy leader clearly. The man smiled a smug smile and raised his arm, the black object extending from his hand toward them.

It was then Askon recognized it, smooth and dark at the end of an outstretched arm. Aware of the risk should he lose his concentration, Askon glanced at Edward. The king recognized the weapon too. Disbelief lay as plainly on his friend's face as Askon had ever seen it. He turned back to the man who marched undaunted toward them.

"Brace! Brace yourselves!" Askon called.

The man grinned, steadied his hand, and fired at Askon.

It came on slow, the object that issued from the black weapon, a capsule or cartridge of some kind. Two slim metal prongs protruded from the end nearest him. The casing attached to the prongs was equally black. The whole apparatus reminded Askon of the crossbows and ballistae he had seen in use across Vladvir's fighting forces, only this was much more compact, had no cross-bar, and clearly loosed the strange projectiles instead of a bolt or arrow.

As he took in the details of the object, Askon considered stopping it midair as he had the arrow at the battle of Dalstone, considered capturing the device so they could study it if they were able to escape. Perhaps Thomas would be able to understand its mysteries, given enough time.

But then he felt the slow darkening around the edges of his vision, the mounting sensation that consciousness might slip quietly from his grasp. His concentration wavered, and the fragment's power began to fade. As it did, the pronged object picked up speed. In equal measure Askon's vision cleared, the darkened ring receding slightly. Then the flow of time slipped entirely from his grasp. The object hurtled ahead, and with an effort, Askon angled his sword and sent the strange object pinging off the blade back toward the enemy line.

Their horses smashed into the Norill ranks. Askon saw one of the creatures fall convulsively to the stone, twitching and jerking as Líana had done—as the girl in the vision had done. But he caught no more than a glimpse as he turned his attention to groping hands and slicing knives.

"*Sors!*" they chanted. "*Vladvir sors!*"

Askon parried and cut the clawing attackers, batting away their weapons, severing hand from arm, felling two Norill outright, all the while cautious to keep his sword tightly in hand.

CHAPTER 17 | CONFIRMATION

And then he was through.

Edward galloped along beside him, clutching Líana tightly. Askon stole a look back; the others had broken free as well. Thomas and Elise were only a few paces behind. John a few again further. The hoofbeats changed from clatter to thunder as they left the bridge stone and pounded over the grass.

Back on the Greyarc, the Norill clambered after them to the edge of the stone, then stopped stock still in perfect ranks. The man emerged, again rearming his weapon. He raised it, squinted, reconsidered, and turned back to the motionless forms of the Norill force.

Askon and the others rode hard, until the enemy was no longer visible, until neither river, nor its trees, nor the great stone bridge touched his far-reaching sight.

And then they rode further.

Miles away and hours later, along a thin clear stream, they finally stopped to rest. The horses flagging, the riders' energy equally sapped, Askon tumbled from the saddle in a heap next to the cool water. Night had begun to fall, the last of the day's sunlight faltering like a spent ember amongst the ashes. His eyes were bleary, his muscles exhausted. They had ridden long and hard, but he felt as though he'd fought a days-long battle. Unable to stand, he drank noisily from the stream.

John helped Líana off Edward's horse. She too sunk immediately to the ground, though her eyes glimmered once again with the light of awareness, and color had returned to her cheeks. Edward dismounted beside her, knelt, and upon seeing her well, crossed to the stream.

He fell to his knees next to his friend, took a breath. "I—"

"You saw it too," Askon said.

A long quiet moment stretched out over the trickling water and panting horses.

"You saw it too," Askon repeated. "I know you did. Just before I knocked it away, you recognized what was in his hand."

Edward's face stared beyond Askon, beyond the plain, as if he might somehow see inside King's City itself. "I did," he said.

"It's the weapon they used on the girl in Dalkaldur. They used it on her, and now he's used it on Líana." Edward shook his head. "Wherever the Norill are coming from, it's the same place we've seen with the fragments."

Thomas looked down upon his kneeling friends. "The man on the bridge wore a circlet, like the one she wears, like the ones the soldiers were wearing in the vision. They're from the same place."

Askon tried to rise, found he could not, and instead sat heavily next to the stream. He searched his memory for a glimpse of the man's forehead, trying to recall if he too had seen a circlet there.

"I don't remember seeing one," he said finally. "I was too concerned with the weapon."

"Well, that's obvious enough, don't ya figure?" John said lumbering alongside them. His head and beard, fully soaked, dripped water onto his clothes. "If *you* didn't see the pretty princess tiara that slack jaw of a commander was wearing, I did. Plain as plain. Same color and kind as the soldiers in yer little jewelry show."

"Did you see what it said?" Thomas asked.

"O' course I did, Thomas!" John cooed, as a mother might to her child when he discovers an obvious truth. "Why, I saw it, stopped and asked him its maker and material, and invited him to luncheon with—"

"That's enough." Elise cut him off. "You waste our time with your endless sarcasm and constant insincerities. If the man leading these Norill truly wears a similar circlet to the woman in the visions, I think it's clear what must be done next." She looked back over the distance they had traveled, her pale face bronzed by the lingering sunset, and Askon knew she wasn't looking for a possible pursuit or even contemplating the enemy at the Greyarc. She was thinking of the baby, now far away in Tolarenz, realizing she would be forced even further from him before their errand had finished.

"There's more," Askon said tiredly. "And I think I'm not the only one to feel it. I've used the fragment many times since Morrowmen first gave it to me. Initially the power came by accident and, as we all saw, did not always work in my favor."

"Sounds like understatement doesn't work in yer favor either," John said under his breath.

"Perhaps not," Askon replied lifelessly. He took a slow breath and rubbed his eyes with his fingers. "But I've used the fragment reliably for a year, sometimes more often, sometimes less, but something is different now."

"It saps your strength," Líana interjected. They were the first words she had spoken since the attack on the bridge. She too looked drained and fragile. "Back in South City, I was able to heal myself and others with the Life fragment. Afterward I felt tired. For a small hurt, it was akin to running a flight of stairs. For something more grievous, John's wounds for instance, which I never did fully mend—"

"Now don't you go worryin' about all that," John said softly. "I'm right as right, and a scar's as good a story starter as any."

She smiled at him, and he seemed to stand a handsbreadth taller. "Even those wounds simply exhausted me, like a day spent climbing in the mountains. But using the fragment last night on the ridge, and today when I was clear enough of mind to attempt using it on myself, felt like being suffocated." She looked down at her hands and said no more.

"Yes," Askon agreed after a moment. "I've felt it now a number of times. It's more than simple tiredness. It's taking something from me that I can't easily take back."

Elise laughed. Warm and full, the sound seemed to surprise her as much as it had them. "I know it also, but in more ways than the two of you." A faint smile graced her face, then faded. "It's how I feel during the stretches when the baby won't sleep. I'm sure Thomas has known it as well, especially the first few nights after our son was born. Neither of us slept properly. Well, none of the three, I suppose. It goes beyond exhaustion, far beyond tiredness of hand or back. Beyond the bones. You feel a shift, something primal. The need, above all else, to rest."

Thomas placed a hand on her shoulder, remembering.

"You know that's how they get," John said, shattering the moment like a muddy boot in a clear stream. "Once they've popped out a baby or two, it always reminds them o' somethin' or other such. Next we'll be hearin' about—"

"And how many fragments of Alora's Tear have you carried?" Elise's voice cut like steel. "None. And how did your efforts at killing Iramov turn out?"

John made an inarticulate sound.

Elise mimicked him, then forged ahead. "I, on the other hand, ended all of that. I, on the other hand, carry the Death fragment, here." She indicated her wrist. "I, on the other hand, used it to bring down Norill after Norill on the ridge."

She paused, slowing her breathing. "And I know firsthand the feeling they describe. I just *happen* to have another experience to which I can compare."

Thomas placed his other hand on her shoulder. She shrugged them both off.

"I grow weary of your second guessing, your 'that's how they get' and other gems of so-called common sense." She shrugged a second attempt from Thomas, more violently this time. "The next time you think you have some scrap of enlightening wisdom concerning women, keep it to yourself. Or you might find yourself learning 'how we get.'"

John shrugged and spread his hands as if to indicate that this sort of thing was exactly what he had been talking about. When the others said nothing, he snuffled an awkward laugh.

"You know," Líana said after a moment, some of the energy returning to her voice, "she's right. How often have I sat across from some noble, trying to entertain his wife, who's already trying to entertain me—and herself—only to hear him prattle on about what we *women* discuss," she laced her hands primly in her lap and took on the elevated posture of those born to wealth, then dropped it with a glare directed at John, "when I can shoot, sharpen, track, and fight better than any of them. In fact, most are so painfully inept, in their crisply pressed clothes and feathered hats, that I'm forced to pretend to be awed and confused by their fine swords with gold-wrought hilts. Instead I feel only disbelief that anyone would trust so soft a metal as gold to protect their hands in battle."

She sighed heavily. "John," she said after a moment, "don't be one of them."

The bearded smile had faded by the time she finished. And at the last, he let his head fall. Elise had settled into Thomas's arms while Líana spoke, and now it was her turn to smile.

"What about me?" Thomas asked through a deep yawn.

Elise looked up at him, the smile turning from vindicated to playful. "Oh, you think you need correcting on this issue as well?"

Uncertain of the appropriate answer, Thomas mumbled an unintelligible string of semi-words while the women looked on, the end of which said, "No, not that," and after another wide-mouthed yawn, "about the Sight fragment."

"What about it?" Edward coaxed.

Thomas eyed Líana and Elise. When he seemed certain enough that neither would attack, he said, "I've used the Sight fragment. With all of you back in Tolarenz, and unintentionally since then. It's how we know anything about Alora and Dalkaldur, the place where they hurt her, the white room, and all the rest."

"White room?" Edward asked. "I don't recall seeing anything like that."

"You haven't," Elise replied. "He sees things in his sleep, dreams them."

Thomas smiled. "Only they aren't dreams."

"Maybe that's the difference," Edward offered. "You aren't intentionally using the fragment—unlike the rest of us. Instead, the fragment almost seems to be making use of you."

"Another thing to consider," said Elise in the timid whisper she seemed to employ less and less often, "is that we're using them when under serious threat. Perhaps, Thomas, you don't feel what we do simply because you aren't trying so hard to draw upon its power."

"It doesn't matter," Edward said with finality. He had begun setting a makeshift camp. "We need rest either way—just look at Thomas—and we know now where we have to go next."

Askon forced himself to his feet. "Edward, I understand that you—"

"We're going to Dalkaldur." He didn't look up. "I could ride for King's City. I could travel some of the distance using the Space fragment. But what would happen when I reached them? What if more Norill come? I'll be trapped there, powerless."

Líana laughed quietly to herself. A smirk lingered on her lips.

"I know. You understand the feeling," Edward said to her. "After what we saw on the Greyarc, it's clear that the threat to the girl in Thomas's visions and the threat bringing these Norill into Vladvir are one and the same."

He patted the bedroll over the quickly cooling grass. "Thomas, since you aren't feeling the fragment's effects, why don't you take the first watch?"

"Let him rest," John grunted, still staring at the ground. "He's been up since the gods' first breakfast, and is more than half-likely to fall headfirst into the dirt before you've situated yer bedroll. I'll take the watch. I'm not feelin' all that restive just now."

Thomas's sharp intake of breath, the precursor to a correction, came to an abrupt halt as Elise's elbow jabbed into his stomach. She took his hand and, while he tried to recover his breath, led him to their horses to unpack their own bedrolls.

Soon, with John awake and staring quietly at the glimmering stream, they fell into fitful sleep.

CHAPTER EIGHTEEN
The Careful Lie

Bang, bang, bang!

By the second knock, her father had leapt out of bed, scooped up a hammer from the work table, and crept close to the door.

Bang, bang!

He raised a finger to his lips. His usually well-kept hair stood on end to one side where he had slept on it. Wide and owlish, his eyes, meant to be serious and alert, instead made her laugh, a sound she suppressed, but only just.

Bang, bang, bang!

Quietly, quickly, she slid from her bed near the wall, the powder blue cotton nightclothes she wore making no sound at all. She tugged the shirt down where it had curled above her midriff while she slept, doing the same with the long sleeves, and straightening the loose fitting pants.

As though the door might come crashing in on them at any moment, he followed her movements with his owl-eyed expression. But she knew it was all a show, the simple theatre he so often indulged in. *They* were after him again; he'd be sure of it.

She also knew he couldn't see much more than indistinct shapes and bleary lights without his glasses. In a few steps, she lifted them from the worktable and walked them over. Sidling away from the door, he took the metal frames and slipped them over his nose. Then he jerked his head, chin first, toward the other side of the room. By the time she'd backed away, arms folded, eyes looking up from inclined brows, she'd begun to wonder if the person assaulting their door had given up out of sheer boredom.

Bang—

Her father wrenched the door open with such force that she felt the air stir on her side of the room. Like a madman, he leapt into the frame, ready to strike. Though he might have thought different, he didn't cut a particularly imposing figure.

But neither did the door's attacker. He stood, hunched and timidly furtive, rubbing the fist he'd pounded against the cold metal. Whatever his message or meaning, showing up in the dead of night, it certainly wasn't a threat. Not from him anyway.

The two stood there for a moment in the doorway, one wild-haired and gray with upraised hammer, the other cowering and slight, skin so dark he seemed only eyes and a shadow. After the moment grew spectacularly awkward, the shadow made the first move. Her father cocked back the hammer.

Raising his hands palms outward, the figure outside glanced briefly down at a long leather satchel which wobbled against his side. It was then she recognized him in the dimness, and it was all she could do not to burst into laughter. The two of them were like some parody of the clandestine operations she'd loved so much in *The Black Eagle* and *Thurmond's Plot*. They weren't her favorites, of course, but a little spycraft, good spycraft that is, was always welcome.

This, the clumsy exchange at her doorstep, was not good spycraft. Her father and her friend eyed each other and gestured like exaggerated cartoons. After the third "there's something in the bag" head nod and the fourth "I *will* hit you with this hammer" chin wag, she had had enough.

"Oh, stop it!" she chided. "Daeron, my father is not going to bludgeon you to death."

Arms still folded, she strode across the room, pushed her father back, and yanked on the shoulder strap of Daeron's satchel. "Get in here!" she barked in a whisper, then closed the door.

Her father relaxed a bit, upon seeing that Alora recognized their visitor. But the hammer still hung in midair, almost as if he had forgotten about it. She reached up and slowly pulled the weapon down while her other hand extracted it from his grip, placing it again on the work table.

"Father, this is Daeron. I've told you about him, remember?" She pulled up a stool for her friend and sat on another.

Her father looked the young man up and down. She'd caught Daeron doing the same thing to her as they crossed the room, though the square-cut cotton nightclothes were about as suggestive as a floor-length burlap sack. Her father's look, obviously threat assessment and not lingering gaze, nevertheless proved equally awkward. After a long moment she drummed the table with her fingers.

"This. Is. Daeron…" she said again, intentionally drawing out the first syllable of his name as she had heard women do when talking to a stranger's baby. Then she gestured meaningfully in the dark-skinned young man's direction.

"Right," her father spluttered as if she'd only just awoken him. His hand shot across the table in greeting and hung there for a moment in the sickly lamplight.

Slowly, Daeron reached out and shook it. "Nice to finally meet you, sir," he said, so low that his voice was little more than a whisper.

"No, no, no…" her father said, shaking his head. "Not *sir*. Call me Corwin." He laughed to himself. In the silence that followed, no explanation was forthcoming. She gave him a meaningful look, tilting her head in his direction and raising her brows.

"Oh yes, call me Corwin." He laughed again. "Just don't call the authorities."

"Now, can you tell me about your father?" the kind-spoken woman said, brushing back a lock of shapeless wavy hair. It was blond, after a fashion, and trimmed a bit below the jawline. She was older than Alora, significantly, but not old. Fine wrinkles touched the corners of her pale blue-green eyes, and her lips were red and glossy.

The question floated in the whiteness around her. White walls, white sheets, the woman's white lab coat, her own white clothes.

In all of it she felt decidedly dingy, even the lovely copper of her circlet seemed offensively *other* within the white room.

After a moment, the woman drummed her fingers on the table next to the bed. She sighed. "My dear, this will go much more quickly if you simply answer in a timely and forthright manner. All that we require is your cooperation. As I said, that nonsense in the basement is indeed nonsense, but he's a willful one, the keeper down there. I can't be sure he won't petition to have you transferred back."

Not that.

It must have shown on her face, though she hadn't willed it to. The kind-spoken woman smiled a broad, comforting smile, but Alora felt no comfort. They'd been at this an hour already. She'd explained what they were after, why it was urgent (a version of it) and that though Alora's time in the darkness had ended for now, without her continuing cooperation it had not ended entirely.

They'd talked about seemingly trivial things: the room, the fit of the clothes, her face and eyes, her circlet, even a couple of uncomfortable questions about her figure and body—the entirety of which the woman had already seen as Alora lay sprawled upon the floor after first awaking in the white room. She assumed the last had been to unsettle her, to make her remember how terribly exposed she had been, to occupy her mind when the real questions came. This was the first, and it was a test.

"My father is about as ordinary as you could imagine," Alora said, flexing her foot within the bandage.

A semi-smile flattened the woman's red lips. "Well now that will get us nowhere quickly. If I wanted to imagine Corwin for myself, I likely wouldn't have any use for you. Let's elaborate a bit, shall we?" She drummed her fingers again, the red nails producing brittle clicks like rats in the dark.

"Salt and pepper hair. Glasses that always slide down his nose. The worst jokes." The list wasn't what the woman wanted, Alora knew, but if they were going to test her, she would at least test them back—find the boundaries, the limits of the woman's patience. At the very least, it would buy more time.

The woman wrinkled her nose and scribbled something on the page before her. "Glasses? I see…" she said without looking up. "And how about a story? Why don't you tell me something about your time with him, a moment that really defines him as a person, the way you see him, anyway."

"Daeron, why are you here?" she asked, after neither man seemed likely to speak. The silence between the three of them had stretched far beyond her patience. "It's the middle of the night. Don't you think that's a little odd?"

The young man rubbed the back of his head again, ruffling the dark hair. "Yeah. I mean—of course. So, well…" He reached into the bag and pulled out a heavy volume, old beyond reckoning, and set it on the table—*The Book of the Tear.* He slid it toward Alora. "Here," he said with eyes that hoped he had done the right thing and a face that said he wasn't entirely certain he had.

Her fingers were already on the cover, tracing the ridges of its embossed letters. "I thought you couldn't take this from the library," she said, opening the book and turning to the page where she'd last left off. "The Knight of Vladvir," she murmured. "I was looking forward to this, and I wasn't sure I'd get to read it. Father tells me I shouldn't be going back."

Across the table, a sharp intake of breath animated the bespectacled man. He shot her a look that spoke of plots and prying eyes and the still unanswered question of why a librarian had shown up in the dead of night to bang on their door as if to stave it in.

She shrugged it off. "Why would you bring me this?"

His eyes hadn't left her. More green than blue, and piercing against the darkness of his skin, they held for a heartbeat, turned a glance toward the door, then met hers again. He drew a breath.

"I knew it!" her father blurted. Daeron's eyes grew wide, flicking from Alora to her father and back again.

Knowing she'd regret it, she reached across and placed her hand on Daeron's as he rose from the stool, his whole body tensed and ready to bolt. He looked at the overlapping hands, sat back down, looked at her, then back at the hands, those aquamarine eyes equal parts fearful and stunned. "Let me deal with him," she said, retracting the gesture.

Already on the other side of the small room, rifling through the papers on his work table, the older man hardly noticed them. "They'll have followed him," he mumbled. "Probably sent him." He rounded on Daeron. "Are you working for them?!"

Alora placed her hand on her father's shoulder. It flexed briefly, and he was breathing hard. The muscles in his jaw were tight, the lower teeth projecting forward in frustration. "Stop," she whispered gently. "He's a friend. And you're scaring him half to death."

Her father's eyes softened, but his arm still twitched with tension. She waited a moment while his jaw relaxed. With a deep shuddering sigh, he pushed his glasses back up to the bridge of his nose. "Alright then, scared friend, explain yourself."

The young man scooted his stool closer to the table, then fell elbows first onto its surface with his face in his hands. He lay there a moment, the brass circlet on his brow pushed high on his forehead into his hair. "Daeron," it read. And Alora thought that in that moment, it couldn't have been more accurate.

With deliberate determination he turned his face up to meet her father's unfaltering gaze. The circlet perched on his curls, making him look more fairytale princess than furtive nighttime librarian. Alora laughed at that, imagining Daeron in full regalia, then herself cloaked and armed for swashbuckling. She scrambled the costumes, mentally editing and rearranging until they both became covert royalty run away from home to battle brigands encamped in the wilderness. Just as she had begun assembling their backstory (the families of their peasant friends had recently been robbed or otherwise harmed by said brigands) her father cleared his throat.

"Well?" he asked.

Daeron was staring at her while she stared into the nothing and everything that was her imagination. Cultivated equally by mother and father as a child, these days a chastisement would be more likely than encouragement, accompanied by "a woman of your age." In its absence the noble storybook pair evaporated, leaving the three of them seated, awkward, and silent around the table.

When the pause threatened to grow uncomfortable, Daeron turned back to her father whose shoulder still tensed and relaxed rhythmically while he waited. The young man pushed the circlet back into place and let his hands fall, one over the other, onto the table.

"I was cataloging the day's returns," he began, his eyes fixed on his own crossed hands. "Nothing unusual, just the end of an ordinary day." A half-smile arched the corner of his mouth. "Your book was there, out on the desk."

Alora's eyes narrowed. "Doesn't it make more sense to shelve it again?" she asked. "You generally seem to find them very quickly."

She caught herself before saying any more. His nervousness had lulled her, lowered her defenses against argumentative Daeron. She waited for the inevitable retort concerning some arcane sorting system or stack pattern. None came.

"He leaves them out so he'll be the one to bring them to you," her father said with a smirk and a skeptical eyebrow. "If he shelved it, you might just go to that location and get it yourself. Or, in the event you show up during another person's shift, they won't be able to find it for you. Clever, in a way, I suppose." He angled his head at Daeron. "Have I got it right?"

Face reddening in the way it always did around her, Daeron shifted uncomfortably on the stool. "Not always," he said.

She thought of the times when she'd finished reading something and was ready to move on. It would have been impossible for him to know which title she'd pick next. And she read so much and so often that there were dozens of times when she was searching for something new. And there it was.

On days when she needed a new book, there was always, *always* a reason for Daeron to come along. Sometimes he claimed it would be difficult to find, or that he'd need to get a ladder, or he was returning some volumes to that shelf anyway, and on and on. And yet, never had he been anything besides a helpful companion through the aisles until he'd be off while she carried her volume to the garden or one of the spacious interior seating areas.

She watched him now, as he struggled with whether he would say aloud all that she had just been thinking. She stopped him before he had the chance.

"The end of an ordinary day," she coaxed.

"Right," he said, tugging at the tip of an ear, his thumb running back and forth over the point. "I'd left *The Book of the Tear* out in case you'd be back for it. Of course you'd be back for it. That's when the patrol arrived."

"I knew it!" Her father erupted again. "That's how it starts, you know. They—"

She shushed him, tipping her head toward Daeron.

"Well, he's not wrong," the young man said. "It was only two officers, in uniform obviously, but no helmets, so I didn't think anything of it. They approached the desk and asked if there had been any unusual requests lately. I laughed and asked them what that would even mean. There are thousands of titles on all manner of subjects and categories, some meant to entertain, some to educate, some to catalog, and many more besides."

Her father chuckled. "I'm sure that went well."

"No it did not," Daeron said earnestly. "They became agitated, listed some of the characteristics, though they didn't seem to want to say—or didn't know—which title outright."

Alora ran her fingers over the gold lettering on *The Book of the Tear*. "Let me guess: large, little used, historical, mythological?"

Daeron nodded. "And that's not all," he confessed. "I had been reading the book, trying to see what you found so interesting about it. I'd already been through the waterfall cave where the monks or priests or whatever had protected the Tear. They gave themselves those tattoos." He placed his hand above the title's final word. "When I said nothing out of the ordinary had been checked out— which was true, I might add—they could tell something wasn't right. One of them grabbed the edge of the desk, gripping it and asking again, only this time sort of growling it. They were trying to intimidate me, and it was working."

"Did you tell them?" her father asked. "Alora, if he told them, we have to go. Now."

"I didn't," Daeron interrupted. "Not after what I saw."

Her father was already back at the worktable, shuffling his papers into a travel bag. "What did you see?" he said.

"When the officer grabbed the desk, his hands were bare. Between the thumb and first finger, there was a teardrop-shaped mark."

"Hmm." The kind-spoken woman scratched beneath the rim of her circlet. It was deep metallic purple, pearly and shifting, a lacquer over a baser element as was fashionable in certain circles, expensive. She scribbled another note.

Alora had spent the last quarter of an hour in a kind of trance, focused on telling the most convincing lies she could think of about her father. Each detail had to be precise, but not too specific, both true and untrue, meaningful enough that the woman would stop threatening her and meaningless enough that she was really giving them nothing.

She'd been trying to retell the story of Daeron and the book, though she'd changed everything about her father's distress and paranoia to fatherly bluster about young men calling on young women in the middle of the night. But the sound of pen against paper had drawn her attention. She watched the woman's hand travel back and forth over the page, a teardrop mark standing in contrast against the room's unending white.

CHAPTER NINETEEN

One Song

Líana pulled her feet from the stream, listening intently to the constant cluck and chuckle of its water. Every now and again a deeper, resonant gulp arose and she smiled. The river had a rhythm, a consistency she admired. She wondered how long she'd have to sit, to listen, before she could predict the notes, before she could know its song. *Forever*, she thought. And this was just one bend of one nameless stream. How many streams were there, and how many songs? Or maybe it was all one song.

With the eastern sun beginning to warm the surrounding plain, she smelled morning, cool and clear like the stream, dewy and sweet. By afternoon the sweet would turn to salt, to dust and horse, leather and sweat. And though she preferred the former, she appreciated the latter. Both were marked improvements over the smells of the city.

King's City. It too lay to the east. When Edward awoke, and it would be soon, she would see the indecision on his face. It was a rare sight. He was always so confident, so guided by duty, by responsibility—even when the responsibility wasn't his. He shouldered the blame for his father's betrayal. That she knew. Many times he'd sat and listened as a parade of his citizens requested audiences in which they aired a grievance with Codard's alliance to Iramov. Word had traveled, but Edward's defense made the pairing sound more rumor or manipulation than outright collusion, and that was nearer the mark anyway.

She ran her hands up and down her leggings, reconsidering for a moment the decision to bathe her feet in the stream at so early an hour. The motion warmed her a bit. Then she stopped, her right hand resting on two small punctures in the leather. They might've been mistaken for a snakebite. She knew better, of course. Beneath the leggings her skin was unharmed; she'd seen to that before ordering her brother and John to rest. Askon had tried to resist, as John had resisted earlier, but she refused to hear his protest. She'd seen how tired he was, wished he would let her carry some of the weight.

When she'd used the Life fragment to heal the wound left by the strange weapon, her vision had clouded and her balance betrayed her. Even so, after a moment, she felt as rested as before, though the sensation of using its power had become somewhat unsettling as a result. She hoped today there would be no need.

The stream's song played on while she watched Marten take flight above the water. He knew the music too. Each wingbeat thrummed with it. Out here, Marten was free. Out here, Líana was free.

With a last vigorous movement of her hands over her thighs and calves, she stretched, dried the remaining droplets from her feet and slipped on her boots. The others would be awake soon.

✢ ✢ ✢

Elise gasped awake, her hands clenched so tight at her chest that the nails left marks in the palms. The boy wasn't there, and no amount of waking this way would bring him to her. And yet, when she sat up, when the instant panic subsided, she felt refreshed and to some degree unburdened, though she knew Thomas would feel more the worry and less the relief. Then came the guilt. Why had she left him?

She felt Thomas stir next to her, his arm wrapping gently around her hips. He sat up and, with a stretch, rubbed his eyes.

"Same dream?" he asked through a yawn that stopped short, seeming to think better of it. "The one—"

"Where I forget him?" She breathed deep. "Yes."

Thomas smiled, or so she assumed. She hadn't looked at him, but for sheer probability she knew he was smiling at her.

"You know, it's not so unusual," he said gently. "There are places where parents and children cross paths only once in the evening or morning. Many of the nobles—"

"Are feather-stuffed, idiots and simps!" she snapped, shifting a glare his way. "I don't want our child to be 'seen and not heard', or 'neither seen nor heard.' He's our son. He should be with us."

Thomas moved his hand to her back, then up over her shoulder. "Soldiers, merchants, shepherds, so many fathers spend a great deal of time away from their sons and daughters."

"And look how that turns out," she said dryly.

"You could say the same for those who refuse to part with their children," he countered. "The time you spend—the quality of it—that's what matters most in the end."

She pulled her knees up, crossed her arms, and leaned into him. One of them, she decided again, had to go back. How, she was still uncertain, but she hoped it would be soon. They were still days from reaching the Southern Mountains. Beyond that, even if Thomas could find Dalkaldur using the Sight fragment, the journey to their destination could be longer than she dared imagine.

+ + +

The visions were coming faster now, more reliably, more clearly. Every night, no, every time he closed his eyes to relax, he saw the girl and the kind-spoken woman, and wherever it was they resided. He'd tried to use the fragment, tried and tried, with limited results, but since the visions had increased, he couldn't summon the power at all. It was as if the ability retreated when it was done with him, receding into the background until it needed to call upon him again. He had rarely felt so useless, even when he'd first joined Askon, before the fragments, or Elise, or their son.

He thought of the boy often, of course, but the mornings were the worst. At home in Dalstone, his cries or his laughter awoke them. Those sounds began the day as surely as the sun.

CHAPTER 19 | ONE SONG

Without them, he knew that as much as he might be thinking of the child, his wife thought all the more.

Given the choice, Thomas would stay with the boy at every opportunity. Other men spoke of fatherhood as part accomplishment and part burden. From the first day, he had seen only equal helpings of joy and blessing with a small sample of challenging puzzle for dessert. For Thomas, parenthood was a complex combination in which each individual element was to be appreciated, relished even. For Elise, it seemed innate, a duty to defend, to protect. There was care, of course—and love as well—but he knew that she would give anything to defend them. He hoped such a call never came, for he was all too certain of how she would answer.

But they had further to go. Much further. Thomas looked out across the whispering grasses while Elise pulled on her boots and quickly nicked the laces into place. Determined as she was, he knew that inside she fought the pull: the pull of him, the pull of the boy, the pull of Askon's unwavering plunge into whatever dangers came next. The pull would eventually break her, if Thomas let it. But he had no intention of doing so. He knew about duty, responsibility, and he knew what it was like to be struck like a bell by what you are meant to do. Askon was a forge fire. Elise was the hammer at the anvil. And there was work to be done.

+ + +

Askon watched Marten circling above them. The falcon ranged wide but never out of sight, always keeping them in the center of his loops. He was watching them and watching out for them. And though the bird would not return to his shoulder, Askon knew what this pattern meant. Somewhere, distant as they might be, the Norill and the man with the strange weapon had taken up the trail. Their pursuit must have been slow, otherwise Marten would have warned Líana, but his incessant circling spoke to his concern: the enemy was far behind, but they hadn't given up.

So they rode, not so fast or so hard as their flight from the bridge, but hard enough that horses and riders were tired and blasted by heat and wind when the sun touched the edges of the western horizon.

"How long are we stayin' off the road?" John grunted. It seemed hours since the last time anyone had spoken.

"As long as we can," Askon muttered.

"And why would that be?" Líana asked. She rode on her own now, fully recovered from the effects of the attack the previous day. Beneath the deep purple hood, her eyes glittered.

Askon didn't respond.

"The way I see it," she continued, "we should stay clear of the road until nightfall. Then we follow it until we give in to sleep." She looked off to the right, in the direction of the road. They'd been traveling alongside the wide strip of packed earth for some time now, nearer when it suited them and farther when necessary. After a moment she turned to Edward and asked, "Where does this road lead?"

His eyes narrowed as he imagined the patterns scrawled on a map somewhere in King's City. "If I remember correctly, we're following one of the most frequented tracks into the foothills of the Southern Mountains, which isn't saying much. It likely skirts them along all of Vladvir's southern border, though it's not so much a formal border as a practical one. Technically the Southern Mountains are a part of Vladvir, but you'd never know it from the councils in King's City. A bit of Vladvir in name only, I suppose, as very few know or care enough to keep record of what happens there or even how many subjects make their home in such a place."

"Finnestre," John grunted again, a sound that was more sneeze or throat clearing than word.

Thomas perked up in the saddle. "What was that, John?" A small smile rippled over his face.

John frowned. "I said, *Finnestre*. What are ya, deaf or somethin'? The road leads to Finnestre."

The smile returned, this time accompanied by a gently quizzical eyebrow. "That's pretty far south for a man of Dalstone to be familiar," Thomas said, setting what to Askon seemed like the world's most obvious trap.

"Not so unusuary for a soldier to travel to all parts," John said, a little too quickly.

Askon expected a correction from Thomas, but the mistake went unacknowledged, a further sign that the young father was baiting his older, grizzled friend.

"I don't recall many patrols or operations this far south," Edward said.

"Nor do I," Askon added.

Thomas leaned to one side with a conspicuous casualness. "Yes. Quite far south," he said, the grin on his face growing wider. "Quite far indeed."

John's shoulders tightened, and he rounded on Thomas. Had they not been on horseback, Askon imagined this particular altercation would have been more physical. As it was, John had only his words for weapons.

"Oh, ya know damn well why I'm familial with this place!" he barked. "Are ya gonna tell 'em or are ya gonna weasel your way along until I do?" He jerked the reigns and drew closer to Thomas. The scowl deepened. "Well, weasel? What'll it be?"

Thomas and his horse shied away from John's imposing presence. The young man's posture shifted as he reconsidered. Askon was thinking of Caled, of something he had said when Askon was still only a boy. They'd been hunting in the woods near Tolarenz, a training session, a chance for Askon to sharpen his tracking skills. Young and eager to impress his mentor—the leader of Tolarenz— he'd picked up a bear's trail and suggested they attempt to capture it, even going so far as to explain the snare he'd use.

Caled, eyes sparkling in the shafts of forest light, had only smiled at this and said, "*Remember Askon, if you track and trap a bear, you deal with a bear in the end. It is one thing to set a snare, and entirely another to return to a beast at bay.*"

Now, Thomas played the part of Askon's younger self. And though all those years ago Askon had taken Caled's advice and left the bear alone, Thomas's trap was already set, and the bear already inside. All Askon could do was watch as the hunter confronted his unwanted quarry.

"Yes!" John went on shouting, "I know the damn place. Been there but once. Though once'd be enough if I never stepped foot there agai—"

"Set foot," Thomas said reflexively. "The saying is 'never *set* foot there.'"

John checked his horse and pulled it hard into the retreating Thomas. The impact jostled the younger man's mount, and himself in the saddle as well. By the time he regained his balance, John's great paw was about his collar. "Set, stepped, tell 'em if ya will..."

And then Thomas was on the ground, scrabbling through the grass as his horse cantered out ahead of the group. He looked all too similar to the Thomas Askon had met on the plains as they made their way to Austgæta.

"Ha!" John bellowed, his laughter rolling on as the younger man collected himself. "Better watch who yer pokin' at there, boy. Takes more than a wife an' kid to make a man." The laugh subsided to a chuckle, and John rode out ahead to Thomas's horse.

He turned back, scratching briefly at his beard. "Still thinkin' o' turnin' over that rock just to see what comes out from under it?"

Thomas shook his head and dusted off his trousers. John snatched the reigns on the younger man's horse and let him catch up. "Alright then," he said before handing them back. "I figure that's one lesson learned. Only half a hundred dozen more to go."

He smiled, but it wasn't the broad, toothy expression Askon knew and that they all loved. John's lips were tight, his jaw and shoulders still set. He did not return to them until the group took to the road in the fading daylight.

CHAPTER TWENTY

Just One Story to Himself

A moonless sky peppered with stars scattered out before them, bright and brittle as shattered glass. The earth, dull and lifeless, offered them up to the vastness above. Streaks of purple shot through the points of light, cloudy and complex and beautifully purposeless at the same time. Dawn was a long way off, but they could go no further.

Edward turned from the road first, silently commanding the others. John didn't argue. The king knew their limits as well as anyone, and they had all reached them. They picked along a thin trail, the road growing dim and distant, then farther until, John guessed, Askon's far-seeing eyes felt the same. Fire wasn't an option. The night was cool, but not cold, and none of them had the stomach for food at this hour.

"I'll take it again," John said. He'd hardly spoken since Thomas had put his nose where he shouldn't. No one spoke at all now. For once, John liked it that way. They hobbled the horses and bedded down for the heavy, fitful sleep of the road.

All of them, that is, except Askon.

For a while the half-elf pretended to be asleep, lying still, breathing slow, knowing that in the dark, John wouldn't be able to see him. And that was just about right. He could see Askon's blurry form. Not much more than a shadow in the dark. He'd get up when he was ready. John saw it coming a mile off, moon or no moon. So he stared at the endless starry sky and waited.

Askon sat up.

"Figured you wouldn't let it rest," John said before his friend even made a move to stand. "Can't a man have one story to himself?"

"He can," said Askon quietly as he rose and stood by John. His feet didn't even make a sound. Always so quiet, careful, right up to the moment he needed to be, then louder than a boar in the brush and with half the strategy. Less than half, most times.

An hour is a long while on a night's watch. Some nights, a minute's an hour and an hour's a day. Whatever the case, the minutes that passed between them were long. And John took no issue. Askon was like a dog with a bone, he'd worry it until there was nothing left. Why not have the upper hand? Make him beg. It didn't take long.

They'd made their way out from the camp so as not to spook the horses or wake the others. At the top of a rise, just high enough to see a short way into the night and, more importantly, if they were quiet, to hear for what seemed a hundred miles, John inhaled deep as if to speak. Then didn't.

"Alright," said Askon, right on cue. "There's—"

John raised a hand. "What happened to lettin' a man have just the one story?"

His friend paused a moment, but John knew it wouldn't be a long one. He listened close, and just as Askon took a breath...

"It was quite some time back. 'fore I met you, a sight more. The whole thing, that is." John sensed Askon's weight shift, but he went on staring out into the night.

"What happened to keeping 'just one story to a man's self'?"

"Hrmm..." John mumbled. His half-elf friend would expect a wisecrack, a smart-ass jab of some kind. He wouldn't get it. This wasn't that kind of story. "Ya think ya can let a man tell it his own way?"

Again a shift of the weight. "Well, I suppose—"

"You're gods damn right you suppose. Now stop supposin' and just listen."

One last time, John waited to see if Askon would butt in again. Maybe he was hoping for it, trying for a bit of distraction, even an argument to avoid the telling. When no interruption seemed likely, he bulled ahead.

"Like I said, it was before you and I ever met. I might've been the same number o' years as you are now. Maybe a notch less, but thereabouts. It was a summer day. Sun wasn't out, though. Clouded over thick as smoke in a smelter. Just as hot, too. The whole command was out that day. I wasn't very high up at the time, even just countin' the recruits. I held my own well enough, o' course, but we were all of us equal parts young and stupid anyway.

"So we're sweatin' and raisin' hell down the streets of King's City, maybe a dozen of us or so. Callin' and whistlin' at girls, makin' passes and gettin' nowhere like any other crowd of soldiers on leave starved for certain attentions and with a license to blow off a bit o' steam.

"After a good many attempts, and not a small share o' slaps to the face, we had the sense to give up the effort, for a time that is. Someone—a bunch o' Jacks and Sams, they were—"

Askon stopped him there. "Jacks and Sams?" he asked.

"Oh, men ya train or serve with for a stint and then don't re-member all too well. Happens most often when there's nothin' so serious as a war or people bein' brought back from the dead to fight it. At any rate, those sorts are all named Jack or Sam or Cal or some such. It all blends together."

"I see," said Askon. He brushed off a wide flat rock that faced the steep hillside and took a seat. "I suppose I've had more than a few of those in my time."

"We all have," John added, brushing off a seat of his own and lowering himself onto it with a stretch. "Now, I can't have ya in-terruptin' me all the time or we'll never get to the end. The point, I mean."

"Alright," said Askon. "I'll try to keep my questions to a min-imum."

John breathed for a moment, stared up at the shattered-glass stars and picked up where he'd left off.

"So me an' the Jacks figured a drink would go well against the heat and, as all young men do, figured it would smooth our chances with King's City's loveliest. Nearest tavern was the Goat's Beard. Ya know it?"

"Of course I know it," Askon said. "Edward and I had a drink there when I arrived in King's City to speak with Codard…" His voice dropped, a hesitation, and then, "About Iramov and what he'd done to Tolarenz."

A touchy moment, that one. John avoided the subject. It had not been his finest hour. He'd been angry at Askon for leaving them, angry at the Norill for winning the battle, for killing his friends, for *being* Norill. He hadn't known about Iramov. Either way, he'd never doubted Askon's story, and certainly hadn't wanted his friend locked up—or cut down. But that was neither here nor there. What was done was done. And they were a long way from that day in Codard's throne room.

"John?" Askon prodded.

"Now what'd I say about buttin' your way into the story?" John countered. "It's like I was tellin' ya. We piled into the Goat's Beard, one right after the other, loud as cats fightin' in an alley. The owner takes one look and waves his hands, both hands, at us. 'No, no, no!' he says, wavin' 'em around a bit more, tryin' to show us that they're full up. 'You'll have to go somewhere else. I can take five. No more.'

"Now we weren't necessarily married to this particular barkeep or his bar, but we were lazy and hot as a sun-dried carcass. The five in front bellied up to the bar, gave us a grin, and started in on the barkeep. The rest of us spilled back into the street. Some went one way, some another. How many stayed along with us, I don't remember, and it didn't matter for long.

"Our next attempt was at the Ham Hock. If ya been there, ya know it's a damn sight worse than the Beard, which is already a sight worse than any place good. Thing was, it wasn't crowded, and the keeper didn't seem to mind us when we came barreling in loud as if we were still a dozen.

"'Evenin' says the keep. And we looked around at each other.

"'Don't ya mean, *mornin'* or *afternoon*?' I said.

"He looks back at me, gleam in his eye and all that. 'This's a bar, ain't it? It's always evenin' around here. Folks drink more that way.'

"We laughed and the rest o' the boys took up a table. I stayed at the bar. Talked to the keep a bit, 'til he made his way to other customers. And that's where the real story begins."

"Begins?" Askon scoffed. It was just the reaction John had been waiting for.

"Every good story needs a run up. Gotta set the stage, fill in the background, so the listener's there with ya. Now normally, I'd do a bit less, but in this case there's no cuttin' it short."

Askon snuffled a laugh. "It's too bad we're not actually in the Ham Hock. At least then I could call for a drink while you work on your 'run up.'"

"Ooh," John crooned. "It's that way then? I figured you'd want to stay sharp or some such, but if that's the case…" He produced a leather flask of brandy and handed it to his half-elven friend. "Will this do for a substitute?"

Askon popped the stopper and sniffed. "This is strong enough for two substitutes, but with a run up like yours, I might need it."

"Drink up then," said John. When Askon had, he took the flask back, had a sip himself, and stoppered it again. "Now where was I? Ah, that's right, the important part.

"I'm at the bar, and the barkeep has moved on. That is, the first barkeep. I'm a drink and a half in by now, and up out of the pantry comes a woman—"

"Of course it's about a woman," Askon interjected, but John was already living the story.

"Six feet if she were an inch, and likely a bit more besides. Taller than you by a notch or two, though shy o' me by a bit, thick hair, sandy brown, arms with some strong muscle for hammerin' barrels and carryin' kegs or whatever you please, and legs thick and powerful, like to break a man if he found himself in such a situation."

"So she was a big woman?"

"Gods no!" John laughed at that, a hearty laugh. "And I suppose yes. But she wasn't some doughy daughter of Count Stuffshirt Gilden Stockings. She was just a good strong woman of pleasing proportions."

"Did you speak to her? Did she have a personality, or a name? Do you remember anything besides a list of her body parts?"

John huffed. "You sound like her. A good description goes a long way, and once you've settled it, your audience knows what to imagine. I'll make it quick. Aside from lookin' powerful, tall, and still with enough o' curvature just about everywhere a man could want, she had a face…a face like…warm bread."

"What?" Askon shuffled on the rock where he was seated. "I don't know if that's the sort of description—"

"Some women have faces like flower petals or snow that nobody's put a boot in yet. Some are like a ripe fruit, sweet and fragile. Hers was like warm bread—"

Askon shifted again. "Are you saying her face was brown?"

"Oh, you could say that. She'd seen her share o' the sun, but that's not really what I mean. When I say her face was like warm bread, I mean it was a face you count on, a face to come home to, one you'd not just want to see but that ya needed to see. I mean, a man can look at a flower, if he has a mind to. They're not much for nourishment, though. Now warm bread? Take all the rest away and he could live on that by itself."

And so John had, for a great deal longer than any other face he cared to remember. She'd come up out of the pantry that day and struck him dumb, not just the look of her, but what she said and how she said it, what she cared for and what she didn't. When she'd gone, he'd been struck even dumber. For now, though, he was busy basking in the beginning of it all.

"Took me a couple attempts 'fore she finally came over. Felt like hours, my mouth shut tight for fear I'd say some fool somethin' before she got a chance to make my full acquaintance."

Even in the dark John saw the smile break over Askon's face. "Well it wouldn't be the first time."

"Wouldn't for bein' a fool, sure," John replied flatly. "Might'a been the first time for keepin' my mouth shut that long, though." No use denying the blatant truth. He'd been cautious from the start. "You keep on smilin' over there, because my carefulness paid off. Eventually she came over, asked if I needed another tankard. I did. I would have said so anyway just to keep her standin' there. She could tell, so she started in talkin' about her work at the tavern."

Askon raised a sarcastic eyebrow. "Bartending? Seems riveting."

"From her it was. She'd taken the work not as a simple serving girl or kitchen hand but as an apprentice to the tavern owner. Lookin' to be an owner herself at some point, but more importantly apprenticed to him at his brewery. Ya see, while the Hock wasn't much to look at, or to smell, the drinks there were so powerful damn delicious that you'd go there anyway. Now the owner, Salman his name was I believe, cared not one jot about the tavern other than to sell his drink, and he wouldn't sell it to the other taverns either. He just kept on takin' any profit he could and funnelin' it back, as it were, to the brewery side o' the operation."

"And now I see," said Askon, taking the flask again and raising it. "She's a beauty and a brewess. What more could a man want?"

John sighed. Askon meant it in humor, he knew, but it hit the tree and missed the forest. "Her name was Isilda."

"Was?"

"She's not dead," John corrected. "It isn't that kind o' story. But hell if we didn't hit it off right then and there in the Ham

Hock. Pretty soon she's tellin' me her life story, cozyin' up to the bar, followin' me out when her duties were finished for the day. We were from then on unseparateable, as they say, and in more ways than one." John beamed and let a sigh roll out long and slow. That sort of detail was always good to make Askon uncomfortable. The sigh would get him to squirm.

"But it's not that kind o' story either, though there's material to spare: her quarters at the Ham Hock, my quarters at the barracks (tricky, that one), a couple o' barns…" He chuckled and the smile turned peaceful. "That time down by the lake. We even caught a pair o' fish that day, length of your forearm, made for a hell of a supper after. Then there were the real interesting opportunities. For instance—"

Askon held up a hand. "I think I understand. There was no lack of intimate relations between you. I thought you said it wasn't that kind of story."

"Ha!" John barked. Then with a lower voice and a glance back toward the camp, "Well just because for once it ain't the most important doesn't mean it ain't important at all. Let's just say she was downright hungry in that department, and persistent, and *con*sistent.

"So just based on my ramblings about our more romantic affairs, you'd know that we weren't some kind o' leave day meet and greet and get out o' town. I kept comin' back to the Ham Hock and to Isilda for the better part of a year. Two years? Anyway, it was a long time. We talked about her work, and sure enough, I knew at some point she'd be through with her apprenticery, which would mean a change in our ways. What I didn't know was how soon and how gods damn different it would really be." John found his fist grinding into the dirt next to him, a shard of gravel jabbing between the knuckles hard enough to have drawn blood on weaker hands.

"Gimme' a swig o' that," he said gruffly, snatching the flask out of Askon's hand. The liquid sloshed inside and spilled a drop or two with the jostle.

He knocked back two long swallows and stoppered the bottle. "She left," he said, suppressing a belch, blowing the air through his lips.

"And that's it?" Askon said. "There has to be more than that."

"Oh, there is. Some that I'll tell." He paused. "And some that I won't." John stood, staggered a step, caught his newfound balance, and drew his half-elven friend up from the ground. "I tried to pin her down—in the figuratory sense. Bought a simple marriage ring, just some iron with a pattern beaten and inscribed on it. Barley tops and stems, woven round how they do on carvings and what-not, on account of her makin' ale and the like. Thought she'd appreciate that." An unwanted smile pushed its way onto one side of his face. He pushed it back down.

"And gods damn hell if she didn't. Cried, even. And she wasn't one for cryin' over any little thing. In fact I seen it only twice before. Whacked a finger with a hammer one day. Nail turned black and fell off after, but even then it was only a couple tears. And once on the occasion of talkin' about her family—all dead of the fever. She cared for 'em right to the last breath: mother, father, and two brothers. That time had a good deal more tears, and for good reason. But she cried at that ring." A tear of his own was working its way up. Then it spilled onto his cheek. He brushed it away, knuckling his eye as though there might've been something in it.

"Didn't agree to it, though. Said it wasn't the right time. Said she had to go home, back where she came from. Said it was where she'd intended to build the inn of her own all along. The whole time, Salman, the Ham Hock's owner, had been sending fractions of her pay and a runner to look after the place she had in mind. Said it wasn't much, but that it'd be somethin' when she could do the work on it herself.

"I said I'd go with her. Even offered to leave the king's service, but she wouldn't have it. There was no changin' her mind. When I asked her why she'd never mentioned it before she said, and I'll never forget it, 'Some things just have to stay buried. If we dig 'em up, no good comes of it, and we miss out on the times we would've had before it all came to the surface.'

"She was right o' course. I just didn't want it to end that way. She said she didn't either, but that a calling's a calling, whether it be hers or mine, and she swore up and down that my work with the men in the army, with swords and shields and—more importantly, she said—at firesides after the fight, was my calling as much as brewing a good mead was hers. Then she went home."

Askon put his hand on John's shoulder.

"To *Finnestre*," they both said.

The shattered-glass stars, shot through with beautiful cloudy purple, sparkled in the night. Askon turned away from him and took a step or two back toward the camp. Then he stopped.

"She's right, you know," he said. "About your calling. It's why I put you in command after the battle at Austgæta. Men follow you, listen to you, admire you. And it's not because you're a fearsome warrior—though you are. And it's not because you're crass or just because you're funny—though you are. It's because you make them feel like part of something, that they're not just one man with a sword against a foe who wants them dead and forgotten. You make them feel that they're in it together, that they're not just Jacks and Sams, but Thomases and Edwards…and Askons."

John smiled, though he didn't turn to face his friend. Another tear or two might've run down his face, but as a wise person had once told him—some things just need to stay buried. He heard Askon take a slow step toward the camp, and another, then called out, "She took the ring."

Askon's steps stopped again.

"Do ya think she still has it?"

"You already know she does, John. You already know she does."

CHAPTER TWENTY-ONE

Finnestre

The day had greeted them with a handful of traveling parties headed north. At each meeting, Edward warned of the road's dangers, though he refrained from specifying more than was necessary. When they had encountered the first group of travelers, Askon feared Edward wouldn't be able to keep his identity secret, that he'd announce himself as king, not to exert power, of course, but to help protect the people who were unwittingly headed into danger. Even so, Edward had remained discreet. The roads were always dangerous, and after saying as much, the first group had agreed to keep a wary eye. The rest had done the same.

And so evening had descended with dark clouds and a chill wind tugging at their cloaks—a summer storm. In Tolarenz such storms happened like clockwork. For days the town would suffer oppressive heat, then suddenly a change, a deep-breath sensation that stilled the world. First the skin, tingling and crisp, then straight through to the bones with the thunder. You could smell it on the wind.

Askon had been admiring the ever nearing peaks of the mountains to the south, grim spires cloaked in snow and wreathed in dark clouds. The storm swept in from the southeast where the mountain range eventually collided with Ellmed forest further off than even Askon's sight could reach. Wind whipped the grass in fits and starts, and though miles of blue sky lay behind, ahead lay only black.

"Storm'll be givin' it to us proper soon," said John, who hadn't said much of anything since he and Askon had spoken the previous night. Finnestre, like the peaks of the Southern Mountains and the oncoming storm, had spent the day drawing ever nearer. In the hour before the distant rain obscured it, Askon had glimpsed the settlement's outline. He'd said nothing of it to the others.

Thomas adjusted his cloak, wrapping it tighter around his shoulders. "Do you think we should try to find shelter and wait it out?" he asked.

Líana shook her head. "I don't." A strong gust sent her cloak billowing out behind her. Quickly, she wrestled it back into place. "Do you see any shelter? I haven't for miles, and even that would have been little help to us."

"It seems to me," said Elise, speaking for the first time in nearly as long as John, "that stopping would only allow us time to become miserable while we wait for the storm to pass, especially here." She gestured to the surrounding plains, now as much blue-green sage as golden grass. "I say we go on, be miserable in the saddle, and hope the road leads us somewhere sooner rather than later."

"I agree," said Líana. She shrugged the deep purple cloak into place, reached behind her, and tucked her long braid inside. "Earlier, I think I saw some buildings, but they must be hours away. Depending on our pace we'll be lucky to reach them by nightfall."

"I saw them as well," Askon added. "Nightfall would indeed be optimistic, even on a clear day. With this weather, it'll be a stretch, and we'll be slowed further when the sun goes down."

John trotted up beside them, scratched vigorously at his beard and spat. "Well I for one would rather be half drowned by this storm than go into that town. But it seems like there's nothin' for it. Finnestre's the last known civilized place before we head into the hills. Just rock and snow and freeze-yer-ass-off cold up there. Might as well find someplace warm and dry where we can get supplies and the proper gear first."

Edward nodded, his eyes far away again, this time in the direction of the mountains, and crouching somewhere in their snowy labyrinths—Dalkaldur. Rain began to patter in the dust.

An hour later and they were soaked through to the skin. The storm started out cool and refreshing, dappling their cloaks then dampening them. Askon had even bared his arms and head to the rain, but soon the summer shower became a downpour. When the sun set, and even the distant blue to the north went silver and black, what had been a pleasant reprieve from the heat of the road, turned to unforgiving cold, pounding down in sheets so heavy they could scarcely hear their own voices.

Thunder boomed in their ears, and the horses spooked beneath them, threatening to bolt. Where to, Askon was uncertain, as the storm wrapped itself from horizon to horizon. Beside him, Líana clung low against her horse, speaking steadily to it, her purple form nearly one with the beast in the blur of windblown water. Marten remained, sullen and sodden, at her shoulder. Askon knew he would need hours of sun before flying properly again.

A few times the rain lifted for a moment, and the wind took its place, slicing through the protection of their clothes and covering Askon's arms with gooseflesh. He began to shiver. As the wind roared, he shouted to John. Either his friend couldn't hear him or he refused to. The large man rode upright and stoic, "Takin' his knocks for bein' so fool-headed as to ride to Finnestre," he'd later say. For now he merely rode on, face and beard streaming with water, buffeted by gusts of wind.

The road too had taken a beating, the packed earth churned to mud, the low places filling with puddles wide and deep, the wagon ruts running brimful like frothing little rivers. After an hour or so, Askon had watched as Thomas's horse missed its footing. He feared a fall for horse, rider or both, but beast and man recovered. The whole group slowed their pace.

Askon wiped his face with his sleeve, a motion he'd repeated half a hundred times. The droplets beaded again on his nose and cheeks almost before he'd lowered his arm. Long since having gone from refreshing to bitterly cold, they now grew itchy and frustrating. He shivered again and shook his head in another attempt to clear them.

Lights appeared, glowing blearily through the shroud of rain. The deluge unceasing, Askon rode on. His horse surged ahead, apparently as eager to reach the shelter of Finnestre as he was. In truth, they'd been among homes at Finnestre's edge for a mile or so, but the houses were small, as were the fields surrounding them. Agriculture it seemed, though a part of every village or city in Vladvir, was not Finnestre's main source of prosperity. Under the constant battery of wind and rain, Askon found very little to be prosperous about this place at all.

With bowed heads and the sound of hooves splashing in a sop of mud, they rode into town. All shivering, all clinging to their horses, all wishing for an end to the storm, all of them except for John. Still riding upright, he followed Askon and Edward's lead, but even John's determination had worn down against the relentless rain. His burly shoulders hunched and his hood was pulled low.

At the only building large enough to be an inn or a tavern, they tied the horses and approached the entrance. Twisting the end of their cloaks, they wrung what water they could from their drenched clothing. It made little difference. John pointed a thick finger at the sign hanging above the door: "Bones n' Stones Inn" it read, the words encircling a pair of skewed dice with the appropriate markings.

John looked pointedly at Askon. "This'll be the place," he shouted over the thundering storm.

Askon snapped his hood over his ears, indicated that Líana do the same, and drew close to John. "We have to go in," he said loud enough for John to hear him, but not the others.

The big bearded man stared back at him with a sigh and turned again to gaze at the placard. With an effort, he smoothed the anxious look from his brow and extended his arm, signaling that Askon should enter first. "Brains before beauty," he said.

Askon smiled and gestured to the rain-soaked forms of Líana and Elise. "Then where would they be?"

"Just open the damned door," John growled.

When all six had made their way inside, Askon closed the door behind them. Instantly the roaring storm fell away, muted on the other side of the heavy wood panel and sealed tightly with the sort of craftsmanship he would've expected in the keep at King's City or the Tolarenz town hall.

In the breath after closing the door, everything seemed so quiet. Then they exhaled, and the din of a busy tavern rose up all around them—and music: pipes, a lute, soft drumming, and at least one singer, not to mention a crowd of patrons all braying along with the familiar tune. Muffled thunder boomed outside.

Cold and dripping, the six of them found a table near the fire, somewhat away from the musicians and their audience. Despite the hour, neither showed any sign of tiring nor preparation to leave.

"Oi!" a slight man at the bar called. "Be with ya in 'bout half a moment." He bustled about busily at his work, pulling cups of ale and horns of mead, sliding them across the long, polished wooden surface, collecting coin here, marking a tab there. Askon wouldn't have called him frantic, his smile was too genial, his wink too easy, but his hand flew from tap to cup to bottle and back like a dancer. And then, if it hadn't been obvious enough from the start, Askon realized it *was* a dance. The audience at the other end of the long room clapped with the musicians' rhythm, the words to the song lost behind their collective percussion. And somehow, pleasantly between the beats, a cup would contact the bar, a drink would pour, and with an unexpected catch like a sudden gasp, the bartender would wrap his hand around the cup and send it hissing down to its owner, connecting two beats, sometimes three. After several of these Askon could no longer tell if the clapping rhythm was intended for the music or the barkeep, and the dance went on.

Soon, all the rounds had been filled, and the song ended. Energetic applause filled the room then slowly faded away. One especially well-watered patron went on clapping, slow and grateful, a taut smile pressed across his reddened face.

"Dansil's the name," said the barkeep, appearing as if by magic. Stirred from his observations, Askon startled a bit, then turned to the man who had extended a hand. Askon shook it, careful to keep his head low.

Edward lowered his hood and reached across the table, offering his own hand. "Pleased to meet you, Dansil," he said. "We're here to—"

"No," the barkeep interrupted with a grin. He lifted a finger, tapped the end of his nose, and eyed the six of them again. "I'm gonna guess…" He pivoted the finger to Líana. "Half-elf." Now to Askon. "Half-elf." Over to Elise. "Hmm, that one's tricky." Now on to Edward. "Nobility." Thomas. A pause. Back to Elise. "Something with these two." And then finally John, who had lost what seemed half of his height, two thirds of his breadth, and all of his bluster in an effort to remain unseen. "Half—mercenary? No. *Not* nobility." He brightened at this for a brief moment, the smile broadening. "Soldier." He glanced around the table again, dark eyes glittering. "Have I got it right?"

Edward leveled his hand as if to say enough was enough. And the barkeep's pleased expression turned apologetic. He ran slender fingers through his sandy shock of hair.

"I'm sorry!" he said breathlessly. "'round here we often forget the importance of stayin' in the shade, as it were. I'll let ya in on a secret, though. Half-elves? Long as everyone minds their own business, you won't meet with much trouble. Nobilities on the run? We see it from time to time. Everybody gets that wanderin' tingle or the need to put tracks between the family's way and their own." He glanced at Edward. "We understand that, too. What I mean to say is that here in Finnestre, we're so far out in the hills that we're pleased enough to see new folk at all. Long as you're friendly—and don't go brandishing all that," he indicated their weapons, "everything should be just fine. You can let down your hoods. It's alright. In fact, there's pegs to spare up on the hearth. Dry 'em out, enjoy some music, and for the gods' sake, order a round o' drinks!"

Elise had already removed her cloak, and Thomas's, before the barkeep finished his speech. Dansil extended his hand again, a little wave of his fingers saying she should hand them over. Another song had begun at the other side of the room, and he moved gracefully with it over to the hearth to hang the cloaks.

"He's a charming one," Elise said, elbowing Líana gently.

Thomas took a breath. Hesitated. "Yes…" Then almost to himself. "He is."

During the brief exchange, Dansil had returned. "Now don't be shy," he coaxed. "No worries for half-elves or old soldiers here."

Reluctantly, Askon lowered his hood and handed over his cloak. Líana did the same. His friends were right. Dansil did have a boyish charm, a lively energy about him. And in addition, Askon read Elise's assessment to mean that he was also quite attractive, with mysterious dark eyes and blond hair cropped close at the back and upright at the front. Askon found it difficult to guess his age, and curiously more difficult to look away when he was talking.

John sat silent and still, hunching further into his seat when the barkeep returned. "Suit yerself," Dansil chirped. "What'll we all be havin'?"

"Your finest," said Edward.

With a chuckle, Dansil leaned toward the others. "Told ya he was nobility. Didn't I say that? Alright, good sir. Just one problem…"

"And what's that?" Edward asked.

"Everything's the finest here. The proprietor simply won't tolerate anythin' less." He smiled broadly down at them.

Edward grinned back, cocking one eyebrow. "Well then, I'll have your highest recommendation. I leave myself at your perceptive mercy." He gave a small bow.

Askon shook his head, a partial smile lifting the corner of his mouth. It was Edward's usual way to assume the customs of whatever people he encountered when he traveled. If the stay was long, he'd even adopt their style of dress and speaking habits. Askon wondered if it was a conscious decision or if his friend even knew he was doing it.

"I'll have the same," Askon said.

Dansil nodded.

"And us as well," Líana chimed in, pointing to herself and Elise, whose look had settled somewhere between curious and dangerous as she studied the contours of Dansil's handsome face.

"And how about you?" Dansil asked Thomas.

"Well…I—"

"Say no more! It's wine. Yer friends're all havin' the recommendation of the house, which right now is an ale to positively write home about. But you—*you*—no. It's wine for you. Maybe even a white. I think—yes. There's a vintage that'll just about hit the mark."

Thomas said no more. Dansil rounded on John, whose elbows had slid over the table until the entirety of his upper arms rested flat, his whole form coiled into a taut ball. He looked more like a pile of knotted cloaks than a man.

"Hrmphtha," mumbled the pile.

Dansil leaned in, one hand splayed over the table's smooth surface. "What was that again?" he said softly, gently almost.

"*Water!*" the pile barked.

Dansil jumped back a bit, for the first time taking on an expression other than the purest, most gracious geniality. The reaction evaporated a heartbeat later, replaced by a knowing grin. "Indeed," he said smoothly. "Alright. I'll be back shortly, or someone else will. And I'll send some hot soup and bread as well. Seems ya been on the road one too many thunderstorms worth for anything else, at least to begin with."

He turned, bobbing his way along to the now rollicking music, and slapped both hands on the bar. "Barmaid!" he shouted, drumming with the beat as he waited. After a moment a woman emerged from the pantry. She had a motherly face and wore a thick brown braid. Her shape too was motherly, not heavy, but sturdy, with strong arms and solid determined steps. She strode over to Dansil and gave him a playful slap across the cheek. He took the blow as if it would spin his head around, one hand leaping to his face where she had made contact. Then he laughed. The patrons along the bar would have heard him if they too hadn't been laughing—and cheering—already. *The proprietor*, Askon thought to himself. He looked at John, then back to the bar as Dansil spoke a few words with her and she disappeared into the pantry again.

CHAPTER TWENTY-TWO
Dansil and the Damsel

A song or two passed before the motherly woman reappeared. She carried a wide wooden tray laden with steaming bowls and a round loaf of bread. "Good evening," Askon said.

She frowned. "Hello." Her round face furrowed a bit at him then relaxed. She passed the bowls around and set the bread in the center of the table. "'Round here we learn to keep our elbows off a table," she said in John's direction.

He didn't look up until she'd disappeared behind the bar again.

The soup was good, thick with potato, carrot, and onion, with plenty of chicken. They ate hungrily, even John, who kept his face low to the bowl and never once moved his elbows. Warm, but clearly baked much earlier that morning, the bread too set their spirits higher. The crust was solid, and held the pieces together when Askon dipped it in the soup, while the center was light and airy, sweet even. They had fully engaged in the meal when the woman returned once more, this time with their drinks.

"Dansil sends his regards," she said flatly. Her eyes were heavy, with dark circles beneath them. She was exhausted. Askon knew the feeling. She went to John first with frown. "I *said*," and here she thumped down a heavy glass mug full to the brim with a drink darker than any Askon had seen before, "Dansil sends his regards."

John lifted his eyes to hers, long enough for them to make contact, then they shifted to the bar where Dansil beamed. He gave John a wink and went about his business with bottles and glasses.

"What is it?" John said to the table.

The woman's frown flattened. "The darkest, richest brew this side o' Grafdrek swamp water. We usually only pour it for special occasions. In a word, our finest."

"Your *finest?*" Edward said, indignant.

Her flattened frown became a smile, after a fashion. "Dansil said you'd say that." She stepped over and patted Edward on the shoulder. "He also said to tell you that though the Finnestre black is indeed a special one, it's better aligned with spirits such as your hunkerin' friend and that the Cold Mountain pale will be more to the rest of your liking." She handed him his mug.

Edward raised it in the direction of the bar. Dansil gave a gesture that spoke to his utter confidence in choosing correctly for them before continuing his bustling dance of mugs and horns and cups.

She passed around the rest of their drinks, lastly making her way to Thomas. With her left hand, she lifted a remarkably delicate glass, the like of which Askon had only ever seen at Apopsé's most lavish tables in South City. As she set it down, Askon caught the glint of metal on her finger.

Without thinking, he drew upon the Time fragment in an effort to get a more thorough look. Around him the music wavered, slowed, stopped. Her finger, perched on the edge of the finely made glass, showed a ring of plain craftsmanship. He focused on the metal's surface. And the edges of his vision grew dark. Then quickly, *very* quickly, the blackness drew in. He released the fragment's power for fear of falling into the void.

When his sight returned, his head had lolled to one side. The tired woman looked at him curiously. "Maybe a bit more soup 'fore you get too far into that cup," she said, tucking the tray under her arm. "If you need anything else, either I or Dansil will be back around in a bit."

They thanked her, all except John, who remained silent.

Thomas sipped the wine, and with a broadening smile, swirled it gently, breathed a luxurious breath, and sipped again. "Oh, this is *magnificent*," he exclaimed. Holding the glass by its fine stem, he lifted it toward the bar and settled comfortably into his seat.

Askon pushed the thought of the darkness from his mind, how swiftly and easily it had come, as another song began at the back of the room, fluid and graceful, a ballad like those that sung of Alora and Heraphus. Askon listened as his friends talked of the weather, the food, the small things.

A woman, the lyrics went, a woman no longer young but not yet old, had been bathing in a stream. Askon rolled his eyes. He knew how such songs went, and yet in all his travels not once had he accidentally stumbled upon a fair maiden naked and alone in the forest.

The tune played on. Before her bath had finished, just that sort of stumble had come to pass. A man had found her, huge and heaving, surprised her, had his way. It was a series of events as common in Vladvir as the lone maiden naked in the woods was in stories. It occurred in all manner of places with all manner of women falling victim, regardless of their state of undress. Askon took a long pull from his mug.

She'd lived, of course, because if she hadn't—another genuine occurrence common enough to turn Askon's stomach—it would have meant the end of the song. She'd survived, determined, tempered like a warrior's blade. She told the townsfolk; they mocked her. She should have more sense, they'd said, that only fools in songs went naked bathing in forest pools. And what was more, they'd said, no one had ever seen the offender, not after nor before. It was like he had simply vanished.

Here the music became quiet, subtle, furtive, as she made her plans.

Next day, a snare she set—and made herself the bait. Naked again she waded in the waterway, though this time both were only to the waist. It wasn't long she lingered till her quarry rutted through, and as before so did he now intend to do.

He approached, and she, with gleeful wickedness slipped her steel into his thigh—once, twice, on either side—stabbed him with knives she'd kept in the trousers worn on her clothen half, cut where the blood drains the fastest. There was a joke in the song then, about what else she might've cut, but Askon didn't find it particularly funny.

Now the song turned sorrowful, instruments from dark to dour, as the woman returned, her grisly proof to present. They called her murderer, said she'd done it for sick pleasure, said she'd meant it all to happen from the very start. They ran her out of town.

And so, outcast and with broken spirit she set more traps, each increasingly complex. The fools that men were around that place, they kept appearing, kept thinking they'd outwit or overpower her, but no one ever did. There were loops and falling logs, pits with sharpened stakes, poisonous snakes, vicious dogs, and many men —all dead. Askon found the tactics to be somewhat suspect, even for the gullible rubes that populate such stories, but the ale was good, and so was the music, and for the first time in weeks Dalka-ldur faded into his most distant thoughts.

Then came the grand finish. One day, when the woman had grown well experienced in her art, and years had passed since first she was attacked, a hero appeared. Askon knew the type. He'd taken pity on her—but had really been fixated much the same as all the others. He would save her from her fate. Turn her from evil, show her the ways of love. For his, you see, was different and pure, honest and good, not like those who'd preceded him.

Across the table from Askon, Elise—well into her third cup— had laughed at this verse. "Let him try!" she called. Her face had grown red, her speech thick. She pointed to the stage. "Well, would you look at tha'—t!" she cried. "He sings, too." She smiled to herself. Thomas looked worried.

Askon turned to face the stage. Up until now, he had been too intent on his friends and too swept away by the song to look behind him and see the musicians. Amid the lutist, piper, and original singer, who now played a stringed instrument which Askon did not recognize, stood Dansil. His voice pure and clear, singing the song as if he'd sung every word he'd ever spoken, his eyes smiled at them.

"This really is the finest," John grumbled into his drink. His only eye contact had been with their second server, and that only for a flicker.

Dansil sang on about the hero. He'd professed his love, admitted to having watched her at her work, lavished her with compliments about the shape of this and the curve of that, how each pretty piece set his heart alight. He'd blindfolded himself, stripped naked, and left himself to her mercy. This last intrigued her, stopped her stock still. She'd called off her dogs, killed the snake she held, thrown her knives into the pool's deepest reaches. The last thing she'd cast away were the trousers she wore beneath the water.

Hearing this, he'd rushed to her, blindfold and all, smiling and sighing. "Faster," she'd called. "Hurry." It had been so long.

The music beat with a rapid, pattering quickness.

And then he'd pressed himself to her. She'd wrapped herself around him. She breathed into his ear.

"I prefer women," she whispered—and drowned him with her bare hands.

"Woo!" Elise cheered, tears in her laughing eyes. "Oh, that's bloody *fantastic!*" Her applause cued the rest of the room, a second thunder to match the storm outside.

Later, much later, and on several occasions, Askon had tried to retell the story. No matter how he told it, no matter how *John* later told it, they never received the response that Dansil had that night in the Bones n' Stones. The patrons laughed and laughed, slapping their thighs, giggling until their faces went red and they coughed and spluttered, took long drinks, and laughed some more. It was something in his voice, his charm, his perfect timing. And after a shocked moment, Askon was laughing too.

John, on the other hand, was not. He huddled morosely over his mug, hardly moving at all through the song's entirety.

Askon slapped him on the back. "Oh, come on!" he cajoled, a bit bleary at the drink himself, "That one should be perfect for you, John. It has all of your favorites." He smiled, but his friend didn't look up.

"Seems 'bout right," he mumbled. "Lure a man in, set him up so as he's thinkin' he's found the right girl, then drown him in a river."

"It was a lake," said Líana playfully. "And besides, it seems to me he may have misinterpreted some of the signs."

"Gods' damn hell!" John shouted, loud enough that both Edward and Askon shifted forward unconsciously to defend her.

She glared at the two of them. "Stop that. Both of you." She reached across the table and placed her lithe hand over John's huge one where it rested on his mug. He drew back a bit, then relaxed. "What's gotten into you?" she asked.

"Hrm'srly," John muttered.

"What was that?" Elise asked dryly.

"I'm sorry," John said. He didn't move his hand or show any sign that he wanted Líana to either.

The crowd had demanded an encore, and Dansil had complied. His second song was unremarkable aside from his natural presence in front of an audience and smooth, clear voice. A bit more raucous than the Lady in the Lake, this one was clearly meant to encourage patrons to buy another round, or two, and to further enjoy the drinks they already had.

Things began to settle down after that. There were rooms enough for all of them, which they paid for when the woman Askon knew only as "barmaid" returned after their final cups were empty. Her demeanor hadn't changed. She still frowned most of the time, and smiled only when it seemed she was playing some joke at their expense.

Askon elbowed John as she collected the coin from Edward, who had insisted on paying.

"What?" John bristled. "Why do ya keep doin' that?"

Askon eyed their server and tilted his head her way in an attempt to keep John's secret.

"No!" he snapped. "Just let it lie, would ya?"

People had begun to filter out of the inn, though perhaps ten or so remained, finishing their drinks, talking of the day to come, putting off thinking of the same.

"Ya see?" John continued. "I tell ya one thing, and I even ask for just one story to myself, but no. Ya can't even—"

"*Sors!*"

The room flickered purple. Askon's head jerked up and away from John at the sound.

"*Sors!*"

He saw Líana and Edward, their eyes wide. Elise stood, knocking her chair over, her hand on her sword hilt. Thomas had yet to process it.

"*Sors!*"

They were surrounded, and the flashes continued. What began as five or six, quickly became ten, twelve, fifteen. By the time their leader appeared, Askon and his friends had drawn their weapons. The motherly woman remained, frozen between them and the bar. The chanting stopped, and the Norill's limbs went slack, their cruel knives glinting.

"What do you *want?*" Askon said. He felt his blade waver a bit as his ale-addled balance tilted and swayed the world, or him, or both.

The commander, now wearing a helmet like they'd seen in the vision of Dalkaldur, his eyes covered by the strange glass plate, said nothing. A slow smile crept over his mouth. He raised an arm.

John tensed, glanced back at the bar, and sprang for the servingwoman just before the commander fired.

Askon breathed deep, reached for the fragment's power, and blacked out.

CHAPTER TWENTY-THREE

The Unexpected

She was safe and, John hoped, sound under the weight of him. That was good. He hadn't considered what damage he might do when he dove for her. At the least it had to be better than whatever that weapon did to its targets. Seeing it hit Líana had been more than enough. Difference was, Askon's sister had signed up for this, taken on the danger of her own free will. The folk at the Bones n' Stones had not.

He heard the other drinkers rise up, hollering about folk coming to their town and trying to cause harm. Some of them, he'd seen throughout the night, were already armed. Nothing so serious as a sword, but there were knives here and there on more than a few belts. How many were left, John couldn't say. The rest, it seemed, were content to grab whatever was handy—chairs mostly.

John rolled off her. "Get behind the bar!" he hissed.

"I'll get wherever I please," she said, "and whenever I feel like it."

John waited a breath, expecting Askon to put a stop to the Norill, or at very least to initiate a counter attack. And then his half-elven friend's body landed with a heavy thump next to his chair. So much for that.

John collected himself and rose, drawing his sword in the process. He'd nearly reached his full height when something whistled past his ear, so close he felt the wind of it. He whipped around to see Dansil with a crossbow leveled at the enemy commander. Another inch to the left and he'd have put a quarrel in the back of John's head.

The commander cried out. John turned again, watching as the wounded man clutched at the bolt. Dansil had hit him in chest, near the heart, a good shot.

"Kill them, you useless—aargh!" the commander wailed as another quarrel struck him, less accurate this time, winging him in the opposite shoulder. With a cry, he peeled the helmet from his head. It skittered to the floor.

But his Norill servants heard him, and then the fight began in earnest. Askon was still on the floor, unconscious it seemed, though dead might be just as likely, considering how unpredictable that stone of his was.

Elise had a blade through a Norill neck before John could even choose a target. She drew back and clashed with another, face tight, jaw clenched. In her eyes, a spark turned to flame.

John parried a wild slash from a Norill knife, the metal on metal peals pinging through the taproom. He sent the attacker reeling with a kick and brought his sword down hard, as he'd done so many times before. Few of the Norill were big enough to take a solid stroke, and he gave this one two, then a third, and the pommel, just to be thorough.

And while he was at it, he brought the pommel around with both hands to smash the back of a Norill skull that seemed to be getting the better of Thomas. When the creature fell, it landed bonelessly on top of the younger man, who pushed it off and rose from his pinned position in his seat.

John grinned at him, saw the look on his face, and felt the bite of steel across his left arm. He winced, whirled around with a roar, and shoved the enemy back. It stumbled a step and regained its footing. John heard a meaty cluck. The Norill spasmed, clawing wildly, and fell with a bolt lodged in its spine. He looked to the bar. Dansil was in the process of reloading his crossbow, but *she* stood with hers leveled. And still she didn't smile.

There was no time for it. The other patrons, stunned momentarily by the beginning of the fight, charged the remaining Norill, cutting and battering at the enemy. An older man, wiry and quick, managed to stick two with a broad hunting blade before a third rose up behind him and plunged its knife into his neck. A heavyset man bludgeoned one with a chair leg, finally spearing it with the broken end. But in his victory his boot hit a patch of blood, and he lost his footing. Two Norill were atop him then, slashing, biting, clawing while the man screamed.

Líana had reached him after that, but too late. What remained of the large body John mentally placed in that vault where warriors keep the stories they won't tell. Then with a precision he'd never seen in all his soldiering days, the half-elf woman jabbed, cut, parried, strangely beautiful in dealing death to the two atop the heavy man and another two who approached her from either side at the same time. She was so quick. Quicker than Edward, much quicker than John himself, even her brother, save when he had the fragment on his side.

John marveled for another moment only to realize that when the two who'd taken on Líana were dead, the fight was over.

In all, two patrons died, John received a wicked gash on his bicep, Thomas had a knock on his forehead, while Elise and Edward would have the classic patchwork of bruises that came after a good battle. Líana and the two behind the bar were unscathed, and Askon still lay sprawled under the table. It was a miracle, John thought, that they hadn't preyed on him as soon as he fell. Líana ran to him.

A purple flash rippled through the tavern's shadows. John turned on the enemy commander. He'd counted on having one alive—well, partly alive—who'd be able to say more than that one word. Problem was, the commander was nowhere to be found. It had taken only a few steps to find where the man had fallen. There, blood marked the floorboards, streaked them toward the corner. Following it, John saw nothing but an end to the blood. That left only two options. Either the commander had stopped the bleeding and managed to run away in the commotion, or he'd flat disappeared. Both seemed farfetched. However, they'd appeared in a flash of light; it only made sense that they might disappear back.

With heavy steps, John stalked over to the man's strange helmet. He kicked it and sent it spinning.

"Don't touch that!" he heard Thomas shout. And, "Líana, don't!"

Thomas scampered over to her, grabbed her wrist—the side where she wore the ring—and pulled it from Askon's body. "Don't use it," he said panting. "You can't use it."

She jerked her arm free, those eyes, one blue and one green, catlike and feral as if she'd as soon chew his hand off as look at him. "I need to help him," she said icily.

"No," said Thomas, lowering his own hand. "You don't. He's just unconscious. See? He's breathing."

He was, but John didn't see how that made a bit of difference. Breathing or not, Askon was out like a snuffed candle flame, and smoke doesn't give off any light.

Thomas rubbed the lump on his head, lacing his fingers into his hair with not one bit the casual appeal of Dansil doing the same earlier in the night. He scratched the scalp.

"Say what you're thinkin' and get it over with," John ordered.

"This more or less proves it," Thomas said, his hand still in his hair. "I didn't say anything at the time, but I saw Askon trying to use the Time fragment earlier tonight. It was when the barmaid came the first time. Don't ask how I know, I just do. Maybe it's this." He gestured to the bracelet on his wrist which held the Sight fragment. "Or maybe it's just me watching people, noticing things. I like details. Regardless, I *know* he used it, or tried to at least."

"And what does that have to do with anything?" John wondered.

"Do you ever listen?" Thomas smiled and shook his head. John didn't like that one bit, but he held his tongue. "It's like we guessed back in Tolarenz. They're following the fragments. More specifically, and I'm sure of it now, they're following Askon's fragment. The only exception I can think of is the Æsten Ridge. Everywhere else they've appeared, Askon has used the Time fragment. Maybe not right at the moment they arrived, but at some point. I think they're tracking him with it somehow."

Edward had been talking with the remaining patrons as Dansil and the woman behind the bar gently urged them out, back to their homes, emptily reassuring them that the danger had passed. He left them to it and joined the group.

Líana looked back to Askon, then up again at Thomas. The fight fled from her eyes. "So you think if I use the fragment to heal him, they might find us again?"

Thomas stood. "I don't know. Up until now, it's only been where Askon has used the Time fragment. If he's not injured, aren't we better off *not* using any of the other fragments, in case it brings more of them here?"

Her gaze rested on her brother for a long while, until Edward knelt beside her. "Let's see how he fares on his own first. If he isn't awake by morning, then try the Life fragment." He helped her up.

John didn't like how the plan was shaping up. "Seems to me, we need to beat like hell outta this town before they show up again. Wherever their commander went, he's likely flickered off for reinforcements, don't you think?" He pointed to the commander's helmet. "And what about this?"

"Don't touch that!" Thomas cried.

John scowled at him. "Ya told me that once already. Now tell me why."

With a giddy smile, Thomas knelt beside the helmet. "Because *I* want to," he said, like a child with a new toy. He examined the strange glass visor, running his finger across its edge from one side to the other and back again. "This material is denser than bottle or window glass, stronger somehow," he mused, moving his hand to the inner surface. "Oh! I was right."

"What?" John asked.

"The circlet fits into place here." Thomas pointed at the inside rim of the helmet. "I'm not sure why, but it seems they wear these all the time, even under their armor."

"Who?" John asked. "Who is this *they* ya keep talkin' about?"

"The people from the visions—" said Edward, "wherever they're from—are always wearing them, and they usually have an inscription. So far our best guess is that it says their name."

Thomas reached further inside, then drew his hand back with a start. "It's *cold*. Very cold." Slowly this time, he pinched the metal only to draw back his hand again. "I think it might freeze my fingers if I kept them there. How strange."

He grabbed a fork from a nearby table and jammed it into the helmet, prying against the circlet inside. It resisted. Thomas pulled harder. It popped free with a dull *ping*.

The others gathered in close, trying to read the lettering on the gleaming ring of steel.

"Gaelin," said Thomas.

There was nothing more to say. Nothing more to discover. That's what the circlet said. They couldn't touch it for fear of damaging their hands, and when they tried, it only snapped back into place within the helmet as if by magic. Thomas had said something about metallic attractions, or some such nonsense, but John figured whatever the cause, magic was a good enough description for him.

"Let's clear this place out and try to get some rest," said John heavily. "We've got a long road, and we don't even know the way." He gave the slightest nod to Dansil.

The barkeep ambled over, eyeing the broken bits of what had once been a pleasant evening. "I don't understand what happened here, and I'm double afraid that all of Finnestre will be scared to their bones tomorrow. But I'll help." He smiled weakly. "What can I do?"

CHAPTER TWENTY-FOUR

Glass or Polished Stone

"You can't wait me out," the kind-spoken woman said. "You understand that, don't you? We will have what we want. One way or another."

Alora examined the woman's face again, tried to read the pale blue-green eyes, the painted red lips, followed the curve of her short blond hair, saw the points of her ears peeping above the curls. She seemed so ordinary

What was her name? The shifting pearly surface of her circlet made the inscription impossible to read. Alora had tried. Thus far she had simply thought of her captor as the kind-spoken woman. She was, up until the last hour or so, just that, her voice always calm and level. Of course, the words it carried were threats. This was, after all, an interrogation. The woman had said as much. However, each question, each prodding for more information, even the threats themselves were delivered with honey-sweet words and the warmest of faces. It turned Alora's stomach.

The room, with its featureless walls had, a time or two, tricked her eyes. Stare long enough and they suggested an endless white void, as if she could walk across it, and keep walking into infinity. Once, between questionings, she'd even got herself out of bed and limped over to test the lies her eyes were telling her. And lies they were indeed. The wall was solid stone. Maybe glass of some kind?

It made perfect sense that the walls would lie. Everything here was a lie. The woman was not kind. The room, clean and white and brightly lit, was not safe. There was no conflict between her two captors, not truly. However they might bicker, they were on the same side in the end. The questions they asked, those too were lies. They already knew everything about her father. Probably knew everything about Daeron as well. What they really wanted was to know about the fragments, about *The Book of the Tear*, about its author. *His* was the information they really wanted, Thomas of Dalstone, or barring that, someone who knew what he knew.

"How did you escape, that night? How did you know we would be there?" The woman's voice turned brittle, her red lips pressed into a firm line.

Alora considered another lie. She'd told enough of them already, and they fit perfectly with everything else in this horrible place. But no. That only played into their hands. She considered the truth. They'd escaped because they'd known, somehow, what would happen—before it happened. But that wouldn't work either.

At best it would confuse her captor. At worst, it told too much. She tried another tack, summoning her own kind-spoken voice.

"I… We… Could I just, perhaps know your name? I think it would help. I've been here a long time, if I recall properly. If I knew who I was talking to, I might feel better. The answers might come easier. I'm sorry." She ducked her head and feigned a wince, reaching for her wounded foot.

The woman's voice shifted, her expression easing around the mouth, to which she lifted a hand, pen still between her fingers, and touched her red lips with concern. False concern, just as false as Alora's wince. She saw it in the eyes: greedy, hungry, sparkling at the thought of Alora's compliance, giddy in the hopes that they'd finally worn her down.

"I do think it would help," Alora said, keeping up the pretense: eyes on the floor, favoring her injury.

"Do you…" The words, gentle as a cooing dove, rang hollow. Alora looked up to find the woman so close to her face that not even a handsbreadth remained between them. The eyes turned cold, the face twisted, the red lips curdled into a sneer.

"You stupid lowborn *bitch*," she hissed. "I'll give you something to whimper over." As if she'd planned it (of course she'd planned it) the woman reached to the side table, grabbed an empty vase—white of course—and smashed it into the side of Alora's head. She felt it shatter, heard it crunch with the impact. She fell to the floor.

Dizzied and bleary, Alora blinked. Tears filled her eyes. She touched her temple, winced genuinely this time, and plucked a shard of shattered ceramic from her skin. Now the tears fell dripping from her cheeks and nose. She lowered her hand to the floor, polished white like the walls, watched as the clear teardrops dissolved into a smear of blood, brilliant red against the hateful whiteness, and wondered if the walls and the floor really were glass. Was someone outside watching, laughing, relishing in her torment?

Above her, the once kind-spoken woman loomed like a warrior queen from The Perilous Isles, bitter and vindictive or… Alora laughed, a short uncontrollable laugh. Even bleeding and broken, imprisoned, interrogated, she still told herself stories, like she was living out one of her books.

"You dare laugh at me?" the woman growled. She looked down at Alora, who now struggled to collect herself, to stand.

The woman stomped hard on her injured foot, and Alora screamed, writhing, flailing against the cold stone, trying to pull herself free.

"Like I said: *filthy, lowborn*, hardly worth *feeding* to the dogs." The sickening smile on her face rippled. "My name, since you ask so politely, is Sehlín. Though it won't do you much good." She twisted her heel. Alora wailed again, struggling to pull her foot away. "Perhaps there's some Norill blood in there making you so endlessly, utterly stupid. Tell me what I want to know. *Now!*"

Somewhere thunder boomed, crackling off into the distance.

How were they doing that? When the room was empty, when Sehlín's twisted face wasn't screeching down at her, she'd heard nothing but absolute silence and her own breathing. It had been as if the room were sealed to the outside world, buried somewhere deep underground, and yet somehow high above the place she'd been held before, in the darkness, where she'd certainly be going again. She tugged at her throbbing foot.

Mindlessly, as if she had just crushed an escaping beetle, Sehlín lifted her foot and turned toward the door. She'd heard it too, the thunder. Her eyes flicked back to Alora's whimpering form, then again to the door.

Wind whistled now, and raindrops pattered. Thunder crashed again. Were they piping it in somehow? It sounded so close. On the other side of the door, she heard the storm grow louder. Sehlín rushed over, flung it open, and slammed it behind her.

Alora writhed, sat up, tried to wipe the blood from the floor only to smear it further. Two beads dropped heavily. She drew back her good foot and kicked the shattered remains of the vase. It skittered away. She screamed again, pain and rage. Again, for fear of the darkened room and scratching rats. Again, as if to tear her voice from her throat. And then, futile whimpering sobs into the unending whiteness of her prison.

The thunder rolled on.

CHAPTER TWENTY-FIVE
The Hospitality of Strangers

Askon awoke, but his eyes did not open. Beyond the eyelids there was light. He could sense it. Then sleep pulled him back down. A moment, an hour, a day later he surfaced again, this time hearing the muffled, distant voices of his friends. He commanded himself to rise, but something heavy and vast pushed him back down into the bed, and he slept again.

"He's been fitful the last three times I checked," his sister's voice called over the roar of water.

That couldn't be right. He looked for her, behind him on the open plain, off to his right where the river ran inexorably to the cliff's edge. Her words flitted between the ripples. He turned, looked again. Hide and seek. Hide and seek, his feet silent in the soft grass.

"Wake him," said Edward. "What if the Norill, these people, find us again?"

Askon wanted to reassure Edward that they wouldn't be found. Not out here. He laughed to himself. Who would follow them here? He gazed through the mist and thought he could see all the way to King's City.

"If you really intend to search for Dalkaldur," said a new voice, smooth and bright yet tinged too with sorrow, "you'll need all the daylight you can gather. The chill settles less than half a day from here by horseback. By tomorrow morning you'll have frost on your boots when you wake."

Sleep pulled again, and Askon went with it. It was beautiful, the wide empty country where the world fell away at his feet. He thought of his family, wondered where they'd gone.

"Alright. That's enough o' that," John growled. But the river thundered on.

Askon settled back in. Then a blast of brilliant morning sunlight struck him. He clenched his eyelids tight. The warm blanket in which he'd been wrapped vanished. He was left cold, his upper body exposed and shivering. "What? Where—"

"Don't try to sit up," Líana said. He felt her hand on his shoulder. "John, you didn't need to open the curtain and the window."

"Need? I know what I need well enough," John laughed. "But I know what he needs better than you. You're lucky I'm feelin' graceful this mornin'—"

"Gracious," said Thomas, from somewhere far away.

Askon attempted a smile, settled for a grimace, and blinked. The light was fierce. He squinted against it. "And what would have been next: the water bucket or the frying pan?" He tried to sit up. Líana's hand went from gentle to firm, holding him down.

"I thought I might get inventitive an' go with a basket o' live crickets this time. Figure we could roast them after."

Now Líana's hand wasn't enough. Askon wrenched himself upright, the muscles in his back complaining at the effort. "No," he said. "First of all, they had better be alive." Crickets were a half-elven luck charm. No one in Tolarenz ever intentionally killed a cricket, and if it happened by chance, there was an elaborate set of counter charms to be applied. His father had known them all. "And second, invent what you will, but leave the crickets out of it. We've had enough bad luck as it is."

"Told you I'd get him awake and about again. Just needed to let an expert do his work." John grinned proudly around the room. No one seemed to be impressed.

Líana and Edward, John, Thomas's voice, and that other voice. The barkeep? Were they still at the inn? Askon thought for a moment. "The Norill appeared with their commander. What happened? Where's Elise?"

"They're all sound. Don't you worry about them," said the other voice. Askon reached for the name, found it, felt it slip through his grasp. "I'm Dansil. We met last night. I helped your friends bring you here after the fight."

The fight. Had there been a fight? "I don't remember," Askon said numbly.

"Well no, ya wouldn't," John chuckled. "You went out like a bent candlestick 'fore anything even got started." He puffed up, and in his best barroom storyteller's voice explained the battle, down to the last detail. There were special flourishes for Líana's sword work and the marksmanship from behind the bar, Dansil and the barmaid—the *proprietor*—Askon remembered.

"Where is the barmaid?" Askon wondered.

Dansil smiled. "She's in the kitchen. This is her house. Flarah might look like she'd as soon kill and eat ya as take you to a seat, but she's welcoming enough behind all that. A good heart, that one."

"Flarah," Askon said the name again. He looked to John, whose face seemed unperturbed. "Her name is Flarah?"

"That's right," Dansil said. "You know, I'll go tell her you're awake. She'll be glad to hear it, I'm sure. Maybe we can all get something to eat before you head into the hills. We'll need to be quick…" His voice faded away as he went chattering off toward the kitchen.

Askon looked at John.

"What?" the big man asked. He drew his knife and set its point to a fingernail.

"I'm sorry," Askon said.

"For what?" Edward asked.

"First of all, I'm sorry for what happened in the fight. You probably had to take extra precautions to protect me after I blacked out. I think it must be the fragment. When I reach for it now, all I encounter is darkness. And second," he turned to John, "I'm sorry she's not here."

John dug in again with the knife. His expression wasn't sad, it was intent, on the nail, on the blade. "What?" he said again, distracted. He looked up and recognition dawned behind the bristling beard. "Oh! Don't worry about all that," he said. "It's nothin' to be concerned over." He turned his attention back to the knifepoint.

The others looked confused, and Askon remembered that John hadn't shared the story of Isilda with everyone. Thomas seemed to know, but he and Elise were somewhere else in the house, nearby Askon guessed. When nothing was forthcoming, Edward turned and headed out into the hallway.

Líana patted Askon's shoulder again. "We'll let you get dressed. I'm glad you're doing better now," she said, following Edward to the kitchen. Only John remained.

"I tell ya one story," John said without looking up. "And you go blabbin' it to the gods and everybody."

Askon flushed at this. "Well, yes. I did forget that detail. I suppose when you're out cold for several hours, your mind needs time to—" He paused a moment. "I'm not the only one who knows. Thomas brought it up in the first place."

John still didn't look up. "Oh, Thomas thinks he knows, just like he thinks he knows everything. He knows there was a woman, and that Finnestre has something to do with it. You're the only one I told the rest."

"Well, I'm sorry."

"Why?"

"If Flarah is the proprietor..." Askon waited, "...that means Isilda..."

"Ha!" John barked. "That I made the name up?" He flipped the knife over and slipped it back into its sheath. "Flarah's not the proprietor." He laughed again. "An what the hell d'you take me for? Ya known me longer than that. Flarah's ten years older than me if she's a day. And that look on her face all the time." He gave a performative shudder.

Laughing all the while, John pounded the door frame with his fist: once, twice, and again for good measure. Then he turned back to the bed. "Get dressed. And stop worryin' over it so much."

He closed the door behind him.

Askon's clothes lay neatly folded by the bed, and he pulled them on, slowly. Despite not having fought in the battle, he ached all over. At first he felt it in the muscles, but it went further than that, down to his joints, into his bones. If the Norill appeared again, he'd have no choice but to ignore the Time fragment. Calling upon it took too much from him.

He laced up his boots, the leather straps popping rhythmically as he set them to the hooks. His sister and Elise were feeling it too: their escape from the Æsten Ridge, the near miss at the Greyarc. None of them could depend on the fragments for help if things came to a fight. At least, not without some careful experimentation and practice in the meantime.

Though Edward hadn't seemed to be drained by his use of the Space fragment, he also hadn't used it as frequently. Askon was unsure what degree of effort tasks undertaken with it required. Perhaps it was easy to move a person from place to place with one fragment and extremely difficult to stop an arrow in flight with another. And then there was Thomas who could use the Sight fragment with no negative side effects whatsoever. They'd guessed several days ago that it was because he couldn't properly control it. That might have been right, or it could be that the easiest thing in the world is opening one's eyes to see.

As he cinched the laces tight, Askon resolved that the problem stemmed from *control*. Exerting mastery over the fragments had begun to take a toll on them, a rapidly increasing toll if the previous night's failure on Askon's part was any indication. His instincts told him he was exerting the most control and Thomas the least.

They'd been busy while he was asleep. Not only were his clothes laid out for him, his whole pack was prepared. He hardly recognized it. First of all, it had grown much larger. There were furs and a pickaxe, metal spikes, and a length of rope, thick gloves, and quilted trousers. Much of the clothing would be far too hot in Finnestre but not once they reached the Southern Mountain snows, where their search for Dalkaldur would truly begin. He left the new supplies for the moment and followed the sound of the others.

"They'd better not come here," Flarah's voice said, as if a second Norill invasion would spoil her seating arrangement for breakfast. "What assurance can you give me that I'm not just waitin' to be overrun?"

Askon rounded the corner to find Edward standing next to her at the kitchen counter, mincing vegetables which she scooped up and scattered into a skillet of eggs and sausages. Apart from the two in the kitchen, the others sat at a long table, each with a cup of tea. The pot sat at the table's center, its lid slightly askew.

"Honestly," Edward said, pausing his work, "there's much we don't know about these Norill and their leader."

"Well, that seems obvious," Flarah huffed. She cupped a handful of whatever red vegetable Edward had been mincing.

He grabbed a different one, green this time, and cut into it. "Yes. We're fairly certain they won't appear in Finnestre again, though there have been cases where they have shown up more than once in the same place."

"It's quite rare," Thomas chirped from his seat at the table.

"So it is," Edward said with a nod.

Flarah batted Edward absently with short towel. "Alright, that'll be enough." She shooed him out and scraped the bits of green into the pan, where they sizzled loudly in a puff of steam and an earthy smell. Askon's mouth watered.

"How are you feeling? Back to your old self, I hope," Líana asked. Edward sat down beside her on a bench meant for two but that by necessity held Elise as well. The table and its chairs weren't quite enough for Dansil, Flarah, Askon, and all the others, even with the bench, so John sat apart in an armchair, carefully sipping his tea. Across from him, Dansil had claimed a wooden rocker, the last piece of furniture upon which anyone could sit without being horribly impolite to their host.

"You can have my place, Askon," Dansil said, rising with a flourish, his beardless face gentle and concerned.

John clacked the cup against the small table next to his chair. "And why would ya do that?" he thundered. "Seat ought to go to a person who did some work. Our boy Askon here decided to take his beauty sleep through the whole thing!"

Dansil's dark eyes made their way over to John. He placed a thin-fingered hand on his broad shoulder and patted it twice. "And that only tells the quality of the rest of us. Wouldn't want to lose it now, when there isn't even any danger to face."

John sunk into the chair slightly. He reached for his cup again, and Dansil's hand fell away as he moved into the kitchen to offer a helping hand to Flarah. His other hand snapped up a sausage, but the barmaid was too quick. She slapped the offending fingers, which dropped their prize. Then as with Edward, she pushed Dansil out of the kitchen. He grinned, and she graced him with a rare smile. He returned to the others and leaned against the wall, as comfortably, as easily, as if it had been the wall's design all along.

CHAPTER TWENTY-SIX

Barley Tops and Stems

An hour later they stood at the top of a rise outside Finnestre. The town was small compared to King's City or South City of course, even smaller than Dalstone, but it reminded Askon how tiny his own village really was. Before Iramov came with the Death fragment, Tolarenz was little more than a speck in a vast world. He wondered how many of Vladvir's people carried hate in their hearts for the half-elves, even after Iramov's defeat. One neighborhood in King's City would be enough to outnumber everyone in Tolarenz. He turned away. They had hosts to thank. And the time had come to say goodbye.

The hill where they'd stopped spread out toward the mountains in a wide plateau. Nothing like the vastness surrounding Austgæta or the great Vladvir plain, but a large flat area loosely wooded with gnarled, hard-scrabble trees. He figured crossing the little forest would take no more than a few hours, once they set themselves to the task. But even now, only a handful of miles from Finnestre, he could feel the cold creeping in.

Beyond the plateau, the trees failed and the mountains began in earnest, jagged and stony. The wind whipped down from their snow-tipped peaks, rattling the stout branches and rippling Askon's cloak. Morning light glistened on the mountaintops, over the trees, and onto the sparse grass. At the edge of the forest, their horses snorted and stamped, shaking their manes in the wind.

"You'll have to keep a steady pace if you want to make Kalmuth Pass by nightfall," Dansil was saying.

Askon followed Dansil's gesture, which pointed toward the peaks, where gray stone turned to white snow. "We will keep that in mind."

"Truly," said Edward, "we can't thank you enough."

A wry smile appeared on Flarah's motherly face. "Oh, I think kings have plenty of ways to thank their subjects when it comes down to it."

Edward laughed and stood straighter. "How long have you known?"

She approached him, pointed to the ring on his finger, the stitching on his clothing, gestured widely to his posture, and his horse. "Our Dansil here isn't the only one who can read a person for who they really are, especially when the book's written in as clear a hand as yours."

Dansil elbowed her with a smooth smile of his own. "Ya know, just because we're the end of the civilized road doesn't mean we aren't civilized." He nodded toward Líana. "We've heard that the king's bride is a beauty of a Half-elf—"

"And a queen because of it," Líana interrupted. "So one might tread carefully."

Dansil, apparently unperturbed, went on. "That might very well be, but you didn't seem the type to look for praise according to that station."

"You'd be right about that," she replied.

But Dansil wasn't finished. "And finally, you've got John of Dalstone with you as well."

John, who had been listening perfectly intently, glanced around as if the charming innkeeper's words had woken him from a deep sleep. "Wasn't aware I was so famous around these parts."

Flarah took a step toward him. "You lock that clatterbox of a mouth back up. Do you think for one minute we'd have let a bunch o' strangers into my house without knowin' who you were, John?"

John, large as he was, much larger than Flarah and a great deal more threatening in any other situation, took a step back. He put up his hands, wide meaty palms outward.

"We know exactly why you came this way. Tellin' us that you're lookin' for Dalkaldur. Well, good luck! You'll freeze, most like, but that wouldn't stop a fool like yerself. No, not for a jackrabbit's heartbeat. You could o' gone any place along the foothills, but you came here."

John retreated another step. "Isild—"

"Don't you say that name to me!" Flarah snapped.

For the first time, Askon watched Dansil's warm persona waver and crack. His brows pinched, his smile faltered.

The motherly barmaid advanced again on John, jabbing at his chest with her finger. "She's gone, ya stupid brute. No longer with us, as they say. And you have the nerve to come—"

"That's enough!" Dansil cried, his voice pained and keen. He stepped between them, put his hands on Flarah's shoulders. "Why don't you let me talk to him?"

She slapped one hand away, turned, and stormed off toward the horses. "Tell him whatever you want. It won't be anything you haven't already told him before," she grumbled. "And it's not like to change anything."

"Can you give us a moment?" Dansil asked, regaining some of his composure.

"Of course," Edward said with a bow. "I'd like to thank our host, but she seems…"

"I'll let her know," Dansil said, with most of his comforting charm intact. "It's still too close a thing for her."

"I haven't told them," John said. "They don't know about Isilda and me. Well, all save Askon there." He looked away, losing most of his bluster. "I had to tell somebody before we got here. I didn't intend—I mean—it wasn't our intent to—"

"Why don't you come with me?" Dansil said. "I won't be so harsh as Flarah."

Askon and the others made their way toward the shelter of the trees. They watched as Dansil led John to the edge of the hill on the Finnestre side. They called their thanks to Flarah as she passed. She said they were welcome, and shot a glare at Dansil and John before riding off back to town.

John and Dansil talked animatedly for a few moments, one pacing, the other gesturing widely. It looked like a lecture as much as it did a conversation. Both men raised their voices at times, though over the constant wind, Askon heard little more than the shape of it. At no point could any of them understand what the two said.

"Hmph," Elise laughed after the two had been back and forth for nearly a quarter hour. A smirk found its way onto her face.

"What?" Thomas asked.

She brushed her black hair away, hooking it over an ear. Then, crossing her arms, she pointed over to John and Dansil. The smirk lingering.

John stood with shoulders hunched, hands on his hips, his head down. Dansil, at arm's length, smiled, turning his palms outward. His head was also inclined, though it seemed he simply meant to make eye contact with John.

After a moment John looked up, weary and raw. He extended a hand. Dansil resumed his graceful dancer's posture, cocking his head slightly, considering John's offer. He reached out, pushed the hand slowly away, and wrapped John in a wild embrace, kissing him full on the mouth.

Thomas gasped audibly. Elise's smirk broadened. Askon's eyes went wide. There, on Dansil's hand, glimmering in the morning sunlight was the ring he had worn the night before, and though it would have been much too far for the others, Askon's half-elven eyes saw the truth: barley tops and stems etched into the metal.

Before Askon turned away, he saw John pull Dansil close in the windblown grass with Finnestre spread out below as if no fragments, no visions, and no world could stop him.

It was a long time until anyone said anything.

They'd ridden well into the scrub pine forest, weaving between squat trees which hugged the ground as though the unrelenting weather had convinced them to never again stand straight. Askon remembered the trees in his family's garden and wondered what his father would have thought about these determined old pines struggling up through the rocks and into the bitter wind.

Finnestre had long since faded from view, descending below the horizon as they climbed the ever-steepening slope. Dansil too had disappeared, though he'd remained at the hilltop until long after human eyes would have been able to tell. He was even small and indistinct to Askon by the time he finally turned back.

An hour had passed since then.

"Tell 'em the rest, he says," John mumbled to no one in particular and everyone in general. "What's private is private, he says, but when they know you're keepin' a secret, it's the knowing that turns to poison."

Silence stretched out over the windswept trees, a long deep breath in the storm's sunlit wake. With a rush, the world exhaled.

"Isilda was his given name," John said softly. "He took it up again, and the clothes, and the long hair when he came to King's City."

Cautiously, Askon eyed the others. They did the same, none daring to interrupt.

"At first, I didn't know. Nobody did, and that was the point, o' course. King's City, especially under Codard's command and Iramov's influence, didn't take kindly to those who were different. And Dansil's different. Askon, I'm sure, bein' a half-elf, ya knew this as well as anybody, still do probably, even with Iramov dead. The world can't change in a day."

John sighed. "Anyway, when I met Dansil, he was goin' by the name of Isilda because it was the easier of the two choices at the time. He needed to work with Salman at the Ham Hock, needed to learn the trade, wanted to learn from the best. And he did. He just had to do it as Isilda. But that's done now."

He looked back toward Finnestre where his gaze lingered for a moment. The others held their questions and listened.

"I was over and back for Isilda, before he told me. It was that day at the lake, Askon. What really happened was him telling me. Said that Isilda was temporary, told me about his plan to go back to Finnestre, where they knew him for who he really was." At this, John sniffed. Askon couldn't tell whether it was sarcastic or sorrowful.

"Said it didn't change anything between us, said nothin' had to change. Well, I was young and a sight more bullheaded than I am now, if you can believe it. I didn't take so well to it at first, just said all the wrong things, and thought even worse. I left." He stared at the ground, the rhythm of his horse jostling his shoulders up and down.

"You just left her there?!" asked Thomas. The others, still too tentative to speak, said nothing.

"Him," John said. "I left *him* there." He smiled for the first time since they had left Finnestre. "For once, I'm the one correctin' you."

Thomas lifted a hand to his flushed face. "I'm sorry. I didn't–"

"Don't be," John laughed. "It took me long enough to figure it out."

"To figure what out?" said Thomas.

John shook his head. "The *him* instead of *her* bit. Should've been the easiest thing in the world, changing those little words, but it took me the damned longest time to get it right. If I saw him or talked about him more often, I'd probably still make a mistake of it here or there. So don't let it get to ya. Just so long as you're makin' the attempt and gettin' it right most of the time, you're doin' better'n most."

"So what happened?" Líana coaxed.

"Well," John said, sitting a little straighter, "I came back after a while and took my knocks, as it were." He smiled and his eye gleamed, though he fell short of a wink. "He was still sitting there by the lake when I'd made my fool way back, drunk o' course. Me —not him—though by the end of it we both were, I suppose.

"I told him I was wrong and stupid. He said I was right about that at least, and his words just made me all the more sure."

"Sure of what?" asked Líana.

"Sure I'd rather be without Isilda and with Dansil than without both. It's easy enough to change what you call a person, I figured, and half the reason I'd gone over so hard for Isilda was she seemed more than half one o' the boys most times anyway."

Thomas looked from John to Elise, back toward Finnestre, and then to John again. "I don't understand," he said. "So Dansil, he's…"

John chuckled smugly. "I'll spell it out for ya if I must. Dansil's decided to live as a man, which he's always been, but the rest o' the gods and everybody's seen a woman. They only ever took who he really was to heart in Finnestre. He ain't—" he paused a moment, "—assembled the way we are, but instead," he tilted his head toward Líana and Elise, "like they are."

Thomas processed this for a moment, as did Askon if he was being honest with himself. He'd known of such people in Tolarenz when he was younger, though they had been, as John had so curiously put it, *assembled* as men and living as women. In fact, most people, even in Tolarenz, hadn't known their whole stories. Caled, of course, had known them all, and Askon by proxy as he trained with the town's leader. He wondered if any such folk lived in Tolarenz now.

But Thomas, it seemed, couldn't help himself. "Dansil 'lives as a man'?"

"He *is* a man," John corrected.

Thomas nodded, his face expressing something between apology and fear. "Then why did he kiss you?"

There was a moment of silence. John's eyes narrowed. Then he burst into a booming laugh that echoed on the wind. "Same reason I kissed him, I figure. Same reason you kiss that wife o' yours. Same reason anybody kisses anybody." He shook his head. "If you're askin' if Dansil, bein' a man as he is, would kiss a woman that way. Or, as I figure, if you're askin' if he'd go to bed with one, I'd say the reasoning is the same."

Poor Thomas, intelligent as he was, didn't seem to Askon as if the world had equipped him to understand such a statement.

"Thomas," said John, "you've gone to bed with a woman. I've gone to bed with a woman. Edward and Askon—"

"Alright," said Elise. "We understand the premise. Get on with it."

John shrugged. "Dansil would, probably has too, and for the same reasons."

"But," Thomas stammered.

"But nothin'," said John. "I told ya already that part o' what I liked in the first place was how Isilda acted like a man sometimes. That included a mutual appreciation for the maiden form, as it were."

Thomas shifted in the saddle, looked for a long time at Elise, and then stared off into the trees.

The smirk crept back onto Elise's pale face. She waited a moment as a strong gust rushed through the trees, then said, "In Vitæsta, as the Norill live, this is not uncommon. You saw them. Their bodies are more similar than ours between the male and the female. I would guess that many whom you thought were men were women, and the opposite as well. One finds comfort where one finds comfort." She looked at Thomas. "One finds love where one finds love."

"Don't say it," John rumbled.

"And the world is how it is."

CHAPTER TWENTY-SEVEN

The Bitter Wind

Askon rode beside John for the next several hours. The forest, if it could even be called that, spread deceptively further up the mountainside than he had expected. Now well past noon, he wondered how deep into the mountains they could travel in a day. Besides a few words from Flarah and Dansil that morning about where Dalkaldur wasn't, Askon still had no idea how they would reach their destination. Regardless, he could see the end of the forest, and knew it would be the last easy shelter they would enjoy for quite some time.

It took significant resolve not to question John further concerning Dansil, not so much the details that so tangled poor Thomas's thinking on the matter, but the details of the future. Would John return to Finnestre? Would the two even have a future? The prospect seemed terribly unlikely. There was Dalstone to consider, though John had left that behind before. And though John seemed comfortable enough with the idea of kissing a charming, graceful man in the fields on the edge of nowhere, the image of the gruff commander and Darts of Grafmark leader would be shaken if anyone other than his closest friends had borne witness. Perhaps Dansil (as John told it) had been right. Maybe the two needed to be separate to become the truest form of themselves. Each would achieve success, but would do so miles apart, never knowing the other's happiness, yet always keenly aware that there could be no other way.

The thought weighed heavily on Askon's heart when John finally spoke again.

"Know why I hate that Norill sayin' so much?" John said as though they hadn't ridden for hours through the forest in complete silence. He didn't take his eyes off the jagged mountain peaks in the distance.

Askon nearly gave several reasons why that might be: an innate hatred of the Norill that couldn't easily be scrubbed away regardless of his fondness for Brâghda and her warriors; a powerful distrust of Elise with her constantly shifting temperament and shallow tolerance for John's less refined qualities; a need for ideas to be simple and easily reduced to right and wrong. The list went on, and all unsaid, as John answered his own question.

"It's that it says everything and nothin' at the same time. World's full o' contradictions, sure. We want to be free to do what we like, but we've got laws and rules to spare, and with good reason. We drink a pint and it's a good time, too many pints and we're sick and miserable, a sight worse than at the start. Food's the same way. The kind that sticks with a person best, helps 'em march a good day uphill, and the most delicious too, is the kind that puts ya in an overfed noble's chair, getting bigger all the while until walkin' from the sleeping chamber to the table seems like a hard day's work."

"It sounds to me as if those examples prove the Norill right," Askon said gently.

John looked back, pulling his horse around broadside. "Hell if it does!" he growled. "It says to ya that they got everything figured out, but it misses the most important part."

Now that they had stopped, the others were drawing closer. Askon lowered his voice. "And what is that?"

John pointed out past the edge of the forest to the crooked, rocky horizon. "It only tells how the world *is*. Well, I got news for the Norill, and anybody else who keeps sayin' those words. There's no accountin' for tomorrow. Might be that things are how they are, for now, but we don't live the same way as folk did in the Great Darkness or during the Scouring. Things can be different, Askon, I believe that down to my guts, and I know you do too." He nudged the horse along, moving out of Askon's way.

"There's no accounting for tomorrow," repeated Askon.

"That's right," John said, though Askon hadn't been expecting a response. "I know where I stand right now, and where I plan to go, but that don't mean I'll ever get there."

"And it doesn't mean you won't get there, either."

John smiled, his eyes sparkling a bit in the hot sun. "No," he said with a deep breath. "It doesn't."

Askon listened to the dry scrape of hooves on rocky soil, listened as it slowly shifted until hardly any soil remained amongst the rock. After that, each step grated like cracked glass. When the forest had failed, the wind picked up, cold and unforgiving. He watched green and gold fade to gray as they followed the narrow track toward Kalmuth Pass. Beyond that, the maps Askon had collected in Tolarenz grew contradictory and confusing. A few, however, attempted to depict Dalkaldur itself, but the lines were only indistinct suggestions by the cartographer. They certainly couldn't be trusted.

The best map had come from Dansil. Naturally, the regional efforts were much clearer and more recently drawn than those Askon had been able to find back home. Thanks to their host, he knew the track would grow narrower and sometimes disappear entirely into a sea of broken stones. He also knew the pass would be covered in snow. From there the trail plunged into deep valleys and crawled along icy cliffs, but even Dansil's map went only a few days beyond Kalmuth, and it didn't indicate Dalkaldur at all.

Askon flipped the hood of his cloak tighter around his face. The wind gusted, pulling the fabric from his fingers and baring his head to the deepening chill. The sun, westering now after a long, quiet day, provided heat enough between the bouts of rushing wind, but each period of warmth accomplished less and less before the wind came again.

"Do you think we should change our gear?" asked Thomas. He and Elise had ridden quietly, a fair distance behind Askon and John for the better part of the day, talking softly to one another and to Líana and Edward as well. "Maybe unpack the furs and have something to eat?"

"We could," Askon replied, "But I'd rather we didn't. So far we've yet to enter the Southern Mountains proper. Kalmuth Pass is most likely within our reach today. If Dansil's maps are right, we'll spend the better part of tomorrow making our way through it. I'm hoping to be sheltered from some of this wind by then, but we can't count on it." He replaced the hood again.

"I agree," John said, his eyes still fixed on the line where rocky gray turned to brilliant white. "We're going to need those furs and such. Cold's like to cut straight through to yer bones soon enough. I'd say we save puttin' 'em on until the last minute."

Thomas squinted into the wind toward the line of white. "There's some advantage to waiting, I suppose. It seems to me, though, that we need to be dressed warmly before we reach the freezing point. If we aren't, our bodies will lose what heat we have left thanks to this wind and, if my guess is correct, failing daylight by then. My suggestion is to suffer being too warm now, and then have plenty of heat as we cross into the snow."

No longer able to allow herself to be left out of the decision making, Líana rode up beside them. "Either way," she said as though she'd been there all along, "we're going to be uncomfortable—and fast—then miserable. The whole question is about when and how we become so. Whether that has any effect on our survival once the cold overtakes us, we'll have to find out."

"Dalstone and Vitæsta spend more of the year suffering the winter than Tolarenz and King's city put together," Elise added dryly. "Wouldn't you say, John?"

He nodded.

"If the other side of this mountain looks like that," she indicated the snows up ahead, "then we're in for more than we can likely handle." She gestured back down the slope toward the forest, and the plain below. "If it looks like that, we can at least have some hope."

She was right. Heading into the mountains wouldn't guarantee anything. They could freeze while traveling through the pass or succeed in navigating it only to run out of firewood or food. If they did find temperate areas, below the snow line, there might be no clean water. But they had known the risks when they left, and after their encounters at the Ridge and on the Greyarc and in Finnestre, Askon was certain they had made the right decision.

They had to find Dalkaldur.

"We'll wait," Askon began. "I want to be as far up this slope as possible before nightfall. If we reach the snow, we put on the extra gear and continue until there's light enough only to start a fire. We'll keep it small tonight—assuming there will be more nights spent in the cold—and set out again at daybreak."

Unsurprisingly, the furs were as warm as they were pungent. They had clearly seen use and must have been difficult to clean. Askon tried to ignore the smell as the snow deepened around his boots. Thomas had been right in his reckoning. The heat that had made the furs itchy and difficult to bear in the late afternoon, when they had passed from rock shard track to crystalline frost, carried along nicely into the evening.

Their boots too, had been augmented for the journey. Each had a small latticework buckled with leather straps at the toe and heel which widened the area around their feet to keep the boot upon the crusty top layer instead of punching through. The apparatus, however awkward at first, would be essential anywhere the snow grew deeper than a foot.

Askon shrugged and rubbed his shoulder where he usually wore the leather guard. He looked out over the plain and wondered when Marten would make it back to Tolarenz. As they had drawn nearer the summit, and the cold had crept in, Líana had been adamant that Askon teach her the proper signals to send the falcon away.

"He'll freeze out here," she had said. "And I can't use the Life fragment to protect him without drawing the enemy to us. Tell me how to send him back to Tolarenz."

For a moment, Askon had seen the fiery young girl he'd left in his village, before her transformation and all the growing she'd done since then. It rarely showed itself anymore, that childish streak. Of course, the child-*like* playfulness they often saw was as much a part of her as anything, but this brief flash of demanding petulance somehow warmed Askon's heart even more, a light not entirely extinguished, even after the damage Iramov's darkness had wrought.

"Alright," he had said with a smile. "I want him safe as much as you do. Though I can't promise he'll go along with it."

She laughed. "I'll convince him."

Now, in a long silent line, they led the horses further up the slope. With the snow deepening, and drifting in the wind, Askon was uncertain whether their mounts too would be better off turning back while they could find their own way back down. But he knew the truth. They needed the horses, needed them to carry their equipment, needed them to ride if the path cleared, and last of all—in case things went very wrong—they needed them for reasons he preferred not to consider.

No one had spoken for a long time. Anything that needed saying had already been said. Now their goal was what mattered, and all their focus was bent on it. Despite their determination, they climbed slowly and rested frequently, conserving their strength for the days to come.

In a low valley they would have been forced to make camp. Up on the mountainside as they were, and before entering the fork between two towering peaks, the sunlight lingered. Askon figured it had bought them another hour, perhaps two. Even so, the edge of the sun finally dipped below the horizon, over the plain far away beyond the river Estelle. They needed to make camp before the light went out.

Askon called a halt and, after directing the others, built a small fire against a collection of white-capped boulders. Here, the wind did not reach them, though when it was strongest, a fine spray of icy dust drifted down. It was as ideal a shelter as they could have hoped for without building something themselves. They ate, spoke of small things, of the road ahead. John volunteered for the first watch, a shift that would have more concern for losing the fire than a surprise attack by the enemy. And, uncertain what would happen when they crossed the pass, when they left Vladvir behind to face endless uncharted wilderness, they tried sleep.

They did not discuss how best to find Dalkaldur. After all, they had already debated it more times than anyone cared to recall. Under the shelter of the great stones, with the little fire burning merrily, there was nothing left but to see it for themselves, to trust that between the six of them, and the unpredictable power of Alora's Tear, they'd find their way.

CHAPTER TWENTY-EIGHT
Tears and Blood

With a wet sniff, she wiped the tears from her eyes, a streak of blood trailing across the length of her forearm. Heavy sobs wracked her frame. She was never getting out. Another wave hit her, despair and childish fury. All around her, the room's gleaming whiteness shone on, undisturbed by the marks she'd made, the stain they'd easily erase. She obliterated the smear of blood and tears on the floor before her, her hands flailing in the mess, her throat raw against the muted animal cry escaping her clenched teeth.

A piece of the shattered vase skittered away toward the door. And there it was, wedged firmly in the frame, another fragment. She brushed the tears away and looked again. The door was open, a crack, but it was open. Despite slamming it with enough force to make Alora jump, Sehlín had not accounted for the broken vase. It had stopped the door before latch or lock.

Slipping on the broken pieces, she clambered to her feet. She couldn't take anymore. She'd tried to be strong, tried to wait them out, tried to keep her secrets, but there was no use. No one would come to rescue her. She was alone, and so would have to free herself. Battered as she was, and bleeding again, even a quick capture and whatever consequences they might devise seemed worth the risk.

Leaning experimentally, she tried her injured foot. It sang with pain, but bore her weight nonetheless. She fought the urge to cry out, swallowed it and, shifting to her good foot, scooped up the largest piece of the shattered vase. The jagged triangle would probably do as much damage to her own hand as it would to an attacker, but she felt better with it in her grip. If nothing else, she'd do her best to hurt them before they had the chance to hurt her again.

Thunder boomed beyond the door. Her bare feet tapped softly as she limped forward. With shaking fingers she reached out, grasping the cold metal, widening the crack ever so slightly until she could see through it. On the other side lay an empty hallway, featureless as the room where they'd been keeping her. Not white, only drab gray.

"Come with me," said Sehlín's voice, irritated and impatient.

Alora ducked at the sound, shrinking reflexively away from the door. Then came a muted response. It sounded painful.

"I think not," Sehlín said. "Wait here while I fetch someone. They'll see to your wounds."

Alora listened hard. A rustling sound. Another low painful moan. Footsteps moving away.

"Don't die while I'm gone."

A long silence followed. She waited. One breath, two, five… Another sharp crack of thunder, and she slipped through the door. At one end of the corridor she saw the person Sehlín had spoken to. He sat with his back against the wall, one leg outstretched and limp. It was all she could see of him. She watched his boot move weakly, fall, then move again with the next wave of pain.

Alora struggled against her own wave; it pulsed all along her face and through her foot. She turned to find nothing more than open hallway in the opposite direction. Clumsily, she stumbled step after step, steadying herself against the wall. Then, with a curse at her own foolishness, she tried in vain to clear the handprint she'd left behind.

The storm, louder now that she was free of her white prison, roared again. She ignored the wall mark and made her way to the end of the hall—whatever window she might have to escape closing with every step. Rounding the corner, she pressed herself, back to the wall, in a mirror of the injured man Sehlín had left behind. A shuddering breath shook her body, then another. On the third, the air came more smoothly, the control more easily. On the fifth, she was ready to move again.

Stairs. She needed to find the stairwell. If she could get there, an exit couldn't be far. The building was large enough. The question remained, however, up or down. She'd been trapped so long that her sense of depth or height had failed her.

Keep calm, she thought with another deep breath. Setting her jaw, she exhaled forcefully, stood, and continued down the hall.

Seventeen, eighteen…twenty-seven…forty-seven. She'd been counting the lighted columns as she passed, carefully checking each corner before proceeding. The building's design expressed no personality, no style or decor, simple gray repetition over and over. At twelve, she'd passed two large windows spanning almost the entire length of the hall. Inside, workers pored over long tables strewn with papers and glassware filled with colored chemicals bubbling brightly against the lifeless surroundings. Lowering herself as best she could, she'd crawled beneath the window to the next turn. At thirty-two, she'd been forced to double back to a fork, at the time hoping it would be the stairwell. It wasn't.

Fifty-seven, Alora mouthed, rounding the next corner. There, two men in white uniforms stood, speaking quietly. Surprised, she drew back with a gasp. When it seemed they hadn't heard or seen her, she peeked again around the steel pillar.

"Just keep focus on sector seven," the taller of the two men said. He had wild hair streaked with silver, and unusually long ears: a highborn. "They'll need the element of surprise if this operation is ever going to succeed."

The other man clutched a writing board similar to the one Sehlín had used in her interrogations. He drew it closer to his chest. "I wish they'd just call the places by their names instead of these codes."

"Too dangerous," said the wild-haired highborn. "Too tempting for people who don't have it so well here. Less risk if you don't know where each one goes."

A wash of pain flooded Alora's senses. *Quiet!* she thought, squeezing her eyelids tight and biting down hard. Another rush welled up, and a muffled whimper slipped past her defenses. The voices went silent. Panic gripped her.

"Did you hear…" asked the highborn, tilting his head in her direction.

"These halls," said the other man, seemingly unruffled. "A person gets to the point where they'd imagine someone walking them rather than remember the truth. 'Stay at your station. Finish your projects. Speak only of official business.'" He said the last formally, as if reading from a card or manual.

"Maybe you should take your own advice," the highborn said.

Alora waited, listened, heard the door click softly shut. When she checked again, the two men had disappeared inside the workroom. It was another with wide windows all along one side. As carefully as she could, she peered through.

One end of the room was not unlike the others she'd passed. The wild-haired man stood at a metal work table, while the other ferried supplies from a cabinet on the far wall back to the workspace. They made several notes, filled a glass container with bluish liquid, then measured the contents. After a second round of this process the wild-haired man dipped one hand into the substance and lowered the other, fingers splayed, against the table and pressed down.

Alora gasped as the black circlet on his brow, virtually invisible to her up until now, began to glow. At first, the light was faint, then red, then orange, and finally white. The brilliance pulsed a half dozen times, each time fading bit by bit until it was black again. As astonishing as the process was, the two men didn't react. Neither showed even the slightest interest in what they were doing. They simply made more notes, then carried the bluish liquid to the other side of the room where the real wonder awaited.

On the opposite wall, a glass cylinder stood, nearly the height of a man and an arm's length across, filled with the same bluish liquid. Beyond it, a dais rose a step above the room's floor. There, beyond the cylinder was an open window. *No, not a window,* Alora thought. She looked closer.

Upon the dais the room simply became something else, somewhere else. No place in the city looked like what was on the other side. Snow covered the ground. Furious wind blew swirls of crystalline dust across a landscape where a pale moon rose over looming mountain peaks. And beyond, a breathless array of stars as if the sparkling spray had scattered itself through the black. It was beautiful and fierce, and foreign. Through the twisting clouds of snow, a weak orange flame flickered.

The highborn poured the liquid he and the other man had been working with into the cylinder. On the dais, the frosty scene wavered, then dissolved, rippling like a reflection on a pool. Nothing remained but an empty wall.

Furious, the highborn stormed across the room. With a menacing grimace, he smashed the container to the floor and grabbed the other man by the collar, drawing him dangerously close. The highborn screamed into his face, spittle flying, his wild hair terrifying above his popping eyes. He shouted again, then shoved the man away and dropped his gaze to the work table. The other man reached out and placed a tentative hand on the highborn's shoulder. He thrust the gesture away and stared at his hands as if someone had severed them at the wrists.

Then he looked up.

This time she'd been caught. There would be no shrinking away, no last second gasp and near miss. Their eyes met, held for a fleeting moment, a moment of recognition. Briefly she wondered if he would believe what he was seeing. Then the livid green eyes narrowed and he lunged for the door, calling out to his assistant. He didn't get far.

Sliding on the broken glass at his feet, he lost his balance and fell, catching himself only at the last second, knuckles white as they gripped the table. His assistant knelt to help him, and Alora saw her chance. She bolted down the corridor, past the door, and on to the end of the hall where the path forked again.

This time there'd be no second chance, no doubling back. Whatever time the highborn's fall had bought her was sure to run out, and quickly. She thought of her father. *"What does it matter? Left or right, up or down, heads or tails, they're all equal probability. Neither is inherently better,"* he'd often said.

Not helpful she thought. Behind her, the door latch rattled.

Another nauseating wave of pain assaulted the memory, threatening to suffocate it. Her father's voice came again. *"But you know, sometimes right is just right, right?"*

She hurled herself down the fork to the right, the door still rattling behind her. Had they locked it? Had it jammed somehow?

Realizing she'd clenched her eyes shut against the pain, she opened them. On either side of the new hallway were rows of wide windows. Through the glass a half dozen workers stared agape at her momentarily, then sprang into pursuit.

Mistake! she thought, catching her momentum, reeling against her injured foot. She grew lightheaded, dizzy. Little flecks of light sparked at the edge of her vision, and she remembered endless stars fanning out behind a pale mountain moon.

But she did not fall. Gritting her teeth so hard she thought they might crack, she sprinted as best she could, lame and hobbled as they'd made her, frantically clambering for the left-hand fork. A man was shouting. The highborn? His assistant? She didn't know. She didn't even look up.

Colliding with them both hard enough to knock them and herself off balance, she ran on, the wall saving her from a crash against the cold floor. Somewhere far away, the storm thundered again weakly and died.

She struggled for the door, their footsteps drawing nearer. The latch clacked heavily as she struck the metal slab. Her heart did the thundering now. What if it wouldn't open? She pushed with all the energy she could muster, and the door gave way.

On the other side, she tried to catch herself, tried to slow her momentum, but she sailed through, rudderless and out of control.

For an instant her mind felt nothing but joy. *The stairwell!* And then nothing but fear as she misjudged the landing. Her throbbing foot was too slow, too swollen and clumsy. It fell, skewed and heavy on the corner of the first step, lost its traction, and thumped down.

Pain lanced through her leg, all the way up to her face. She cried out, unable to suppress it any longer, and fell in a tangle of arms and legs down the first flight of stairs. Dazed, though still conscious, she writhed against the screaming of her battered body. Prying herself to her knees, she crawled to the handrail, dragging herself upright again.

Stunned and utterly submerged in relentless pain, she stumbled down the next flight, and the next, flailing wildly at a step here, a platform there as her balance betrayed her and her consciousness failed. The stars sparkled again at the edges of her vision, creeping in and out as if uncertain whether they'd like to stay. Footsteps echoed on the stairs above.

Forcing back the stars, breathing raggedly, she descended again and again until she came to a door unlike the others. This one, wooden and ornate not featureless metal, was sure to be the way out. The footsteps drew closer.

Without a glance, she put all her weight against the wooden panel. It slid open silently, and so effortlessly that she spun into the room on the other side, falling again as her foot gave way. Choking back tears, she gaped at the room around her.

Three floors high, with balconies at each level, the space was nothing short of cavernous. Along one wall, shelves neatly lined with ledgers stretched further than she could count. Hundreds? A thousand? She couldn't tell. On the opposite wall, a similar set of shelves sat mostly empty, though the ledgers had already begun to fill one end. Across the length of the room, the balconies were interrupted by huge stone pillars ringed with lights. But the true wonder lay across from her, opposite the door where she'd entered.

A vast wall of glass panels, the immensity of which she'd never thought possible, rose from floor to ceiling. Momentarily unaware of her pursuers, she limped toward it. The closer she came, the more astonishing the structure grew. It was so tall, so profoundly heavy, and yet so clear as to be made of nothing at all.

Now she was pressing her hand against it, feeling its weight and surprising chill. Beyond it, thick as it was, she saw the city sprawling out before her and her heart fell. Her body followed. On her knees, tears streaming, she gazed through the glass at the city, hundreds of feet below. They were holding her in the High Spire. Of course they were.

Behind her, footsteps ruptured the silence in the huge room. She wept, unrestrained. There would be no escape. They would put her back in the white room, or worse, the black. She could already hear the rats skittering.

Ticka-ticka-tick.

Lifting her head, her whole body shook, exhausted and beaten.

Ticka-ticka-tick.

But the sound was too close, too real. She wiped the tears from her face. On the far side of the room, the workers she'd disturbed had gathered, the wild-haired highborn at the center. He too was bleeding.

Ticka-ticka-tick.

"I think you've lost your way," he said, eyes glimmering. "Stay right where you are. Rest a bit. Sehlín will put you back where you belong."

Ticka-clack! "Alora!"

Their faces—all of them—snapped at once to the ledger-less side of the room, where a door had opened. A figure stepped through, his face shadowed within the hood of a deep green cloak.

She tried to fight the sparkling stars, but they engulfed her, drew her down, then winked out in peaceful yawning darkness.

CHAPTER TWENTY-NINE
Sight

Thomas was on his feet, scrambling through their tiny half-frozen camp when Askon awoke. He'd scattered the embers and the ashes so thoroughly that only an experienced tracker would be able to tell a fire had been there at all. The others were waking, and Thomas chattered on.

"We have to go," he said, scooping up his bedroll. "Edward is on watch. He hasn't seen them, but they'll be here. I know it."

"How?" Askon wondered, but he had the answer before Thomas could reply.

"I've *seen* it," Thomas said, "in a dream that wasn't a dream." He rose to his feet and stuffed the bundle into a saddlebag. "The fragment showed me…"

"What?" said Askon. "What did the fragment show you?"

Thomas shook his head. "No. Not yet. Can't tell you yet. Just… it showed me that we're being watched, and a lot more than that. We need to go, now!"

The moon rode low in the sky, its round body partially eclipsed by the mountain peaks. Morning would arrive before long, but for now darkness reigned. The others were slowly collecting their things, and Thomas went frantically to each of them. That is, except for Líana. Edward, it seemed, had woken her before. The two of them stood peering out into the whirling snow, looking for a sign, any sign, that the enemy was near.

Askon stuffed his own supplies hastily into his pack and readied his horse. When he'd finished, he followed his sister and the king into the wind.

"Is there anything out there?" he asked.

"Not to my eyes," Edward replied. "But that isn't saying a great deal when the two of you are present."

Líana leaned into the wind. "Half-elven eyes or not," she said, "I don't see them either."

"The wind and snow aren't helping," said Askon. He pulled his cloak tighter, adjusting the furs beneath it. "Has anyone else used one of the fragments? If that is how the enemy is tracking us, someone must have."

"Only Thomas," said Edward. "If they've managed to converge on him, we have a larger problem than these ill-trained Norill forces. They don't fight well. We've seen that. Their greatest advantage is finding us and appearing when least expected."

"What's the larger problem?" said Askon.

Líana turned, her eyes slits in the howling wind. "We need Thomas to use the Sight fragment to find Dalkaldur. Without it, we're lost. Up until now, Thomas has been able to experience his visions without drawing their attention. If they can find him, our already difficult road becomes even more dangerous."

"Then let's hope they can't," Askon said.

In a cloud of icy dust some hundred yards distant, a purple light flickered, glowed, and faded. Askon's eyes gleamed. Thomas was not wrong.

"Now. We have to go now!" Líana shouted. They turned and ran for the camp.

"That's what I've been saying," Thomas rambled as they raced to the horses. "I said they'd be here, and now you've seen it for yourselves."

Elise had already mounted her horse, as had John. The two waited, sheltered from the wind where the fire had once burned warmly. The rest did the same, what little camp there had been, now all but obliterated.

"What?!" shouted John, "Are ya waitin' for one o' your damned messenger birds? Let's get the hell away from here. It's one thing for Askon to pass out in a tavern brawl and another entirely out here where we're as like to see a snowstorm as a sunrise."

They spurred the horses and rode away from the camp up the mountainside toward Kalmuth Pass. Then the clouds rolled in, covering what remained of the moon. John's prediction seemed to be coming true. No sunlight glimmered at the horizon, but the moon dipped below the peaks and shrouded itself in thick dark clouds.

With Askon and Líana in the lead, they strung a length of rope from each rider to the next. They had hoped to use sound to lead each other through the dark, but the wind drowned out any hope of that. Instead, they would follow by feel.

They carried on for nearly an hour. Still no sign of light came in the east. Snow began to fall, and the wind grew more intense. Finally, not even Askon could see the way forward through the dark whirling blizzard. They halted against another rocky outcropping, sheltering as best they could.

"They can't follow us in this," said John, batting the snow from his cloak.

"And we can't stay," said Thomas. "If we stop, if I fall asleep, they'll find us."

Elise glanced at her wrist where the Death fragment glowed red. "None of us can. Not safely any way. Not anymore. Who's to say we don't tap into the fragments while we dream? It could happen to any of us."

Líana nodded. "It's true. We'll have to be careful, but we're not nearly far enough ahead of the light we saw back there. We need to go on."

"I agree," Askon said. "But I'm not sure how until we get some light."

With hunched shoulders and a look of shame, Thomas turned to face them. "I have an idea."

"Do ya now," growled John. "Looks to me like yer guilty as a thief with his fingers on the purse."

Thomas sighed. "I am," he said. "I've been practicing."

"Practicing?" John didn't seem to understand.

Askon wrapped his cloak tighter against the wind. "He's been using the Sight fragment, testing what he can do. He knew he'd have to make use of it at some point, and up until now it hasn't been drawing the Norill to us. Do I have it right, Thomas?"

The younger man nodded. "I hoped that only a little use wouldn't be enough of a signal to them. I think I was right, but then I had the dream. Perhaps the combination of my using the fragment—just a bit—during the day and the vividness of the vision..."

"You did what you had to," said Elise, though her words were directed at the other men, rather than Thomas. A challenge.

Recognition washed over the young man's face. "Maybe that's exactly what we have to do," he said excitedly. "Somehow, either by me or through me, the fragment can see what is happening somewhere else, even in places that are far away."

"Like Dalkaldur," Líana offered.

"Yes, like Dalkaldur," Thomas agreed. "It shouldn't require nearly as much energy to see ahead of us a short distance, as long as I can access it properly—"

"Which is all but guaranteed," John scoffed.

Elise moved to respond, but Thomas waved a hand in her direction. "He's right, though I'd only need a split second. Imagine entering a room with your eyes closed, opening and closing them as fast as you can, then recalling the furniture. You could remember quite a bit."

Askon smiled, his lips tight in the cold. "And you could do it in the dark."

Thomas nodded. "I think so. But that isn't everything. Edward, I'll be our eyes in the distance, but you'll be what gets us through the storm."

"And how is that?"

"You're able to move yourself and other people when the moment calls for it, correct?"

"Yes."

Thomas pointed at the rocks above them. "And what do these do but move the snow. The rock is displacing it. If you can do that around us, perhaps only when the storm is the strongest, we can make our way much faster."

Edward shrugged.

"Let's hope it's not too much of an effort," John grumbled. "I can't carry all of ya off this mountain by myself."

"Either way, we need to make the effort now," Líana called. "They're out there. I can feel it."

Thomas's directions, scattered and unpredictable as they were, revealed the path ahead, and the use of the Space fragment proved particularly ingenious. Edward shielded them when they most needed it, though it exhausted him quickly. The horses had panicked then, as the fragment's power faltered. They bolted through the snow and out of sight, taking the lion's share of the supplies with them as they headed for cover and lower ground.

When the storm finally cleared, they stood on the southern side of Kalmuth pass, the midmorning sun brilliant yellow in a pale blue sky. Its light over the snow nearly blinded them. And below, countless miles of frozen wilderness sprawled, dotted with green and gray in the valleys and canyons. Askon wondered how many passes they would have to climb to find what they were looking for and how far this cold country spread before its icy fingers reached the end of the world. He wondered if Finnestre really was the last speck of civilization on a map vastly larger than he'd imagined. And he wondered if somewhere beyond his sight, people dwelled who had never heard of Vladvir or half-elves or anything he found familiar at all.

"No time to start second-guessin' yerself now," John said while the others took the opportunity to rest. The bright sun, warm and refreshing after hours of blowing snow, had melted the frost in his beard. He brushed the glimmering beads away and grinned.

Askon didn't turn back. "Why? Aren't you?" He fanned both hands out at the far-reaching view. "Look at all this. It goes on forever. What hope do we have of finding one mountaintop amid what must be hundreds?"

"No hope," said John flatly. "Not in the sense you're thinkin' anyway. Don't need hope, though."

"And why not? We don't even have the horses."

"We've got skill, and more importantly we've got our boy Thomas with his shiny stone."

Askon turned his gaze back to the others. "What good is seeing a half hundred yards in front of us now that there's daylight?"

"None," said John. He grabbed Askon's shoulder, spinning him back toward the expanse of the Southern Mountains. "But look how far we can see without any effort at all. Days' worth. Days and days."

"Exactly," said Askon. "That's what I'm saying."

John tapped a finger to his nose. Then, twisting Askon around again, he pointed back to Thomas. "Exactly wrong maybe."

Askon shrugged and shook his head, frustrated with John's game.

"Think about it. If we can see this far without any help, Thomas can see just as much fragment-wise, easy as you please."

This time, Askon spun himself, facing again the numberless peaks and long valleys. "And from that, we could at least rule out where *not* to go."

"Moreover," Thomas said, startling them both. He smiled a tried, apologetic smile. "Voices carry farther than you'd think up here."

John crossed his arms, shaking off his surprise. "Speak your peace then. More than what?"

"If I begin by visualizing Dalkaldur itself, I can trace the path backwards from there to here, assuming it's not hundreds of miles away. But based on Morrowmen's stories concerning the Great Darkness and the coming of the Elves, it can't be that far. They moved the whole of Vladvir's remaining population—or their best attempt at gathering it—to Dalkaldur. Even if no one knows where to find it, it can't be farther than the distance we can see from up here. Behind one of those peaks, Dalkaldur is hiding. Our task is to decide which one."

"And survive long enough to get there," Askon said. He worried that no amount of mapmaking or visions from the Sight fragment could solve this final problem. Even if Thomas was right, and they could locate Dalkaldur, even if he could trace a perfect path from where they stood to the lakeside where they'd seen the girl in the vision, seen her hiding the fragments from the strange soldiers, even if they did so while outrunning the Norill and their commander whose weapons and gear told them that they came from the same place as the vision of the girl—even then they still had to avoid freezing, falling, starving. For now, they were as well supplied as could be expected, though a great deal of their food and firewood had gone with the horses into the darkness and swirling blizzard. With only snow and ice all around them, what they had wouldn't last for long.

"Well," John barked, "get to it, Thomas. It's not like we got time to spare. Those slack-headed Norill and their excuse for a commander could show up at any time."

"And more likely sooner rather than later if you're using the Sight fragment, no matter how lightly," said Askon. "Get some space. Clear your head, and find it for us. We'll keep watch."

Thomas climbed a few feet down to a flat rocky area at the edge of the path. John and Askon sat with the others, keeping their voices low, trying to rest, trying to stay warm, trying not to expect too much.

An hour went by, then two. Askon paced back and forth, as had the others when they grew too cold to sit. At one point, impatient and hovering, he had gone back over the summit to the northern side of the mountain. Nothing but a trough of drifting snow had greeted him, though he succeeded in sapping the warmth of the southern-side sun. When he returned, John had a small fire going. They ate and drank, then extinguished the flames before consuming too much of their limited fuel. All the while, Thomas sat motionless at the edge of the world. Askon watched him twitch from time to time, as if woken from a shallow sleep, watched him shift his position, angling himself further and further west. At his wrist, the Sight fragment glimmered pale blue.

"There," said Thomas rising from his perch. He moved like an old man whose joints call out his age with every aching step. Then he stretched, twisted a bit at the middle, and cuffed his thighs and calves, getting the blood flowing again after sitting for so long in the cold.

Thanks to his grueling work in the night, Edward had fallen asleep almost immediately after Thomas had begun his deliberations. The others slept as well, regaining what they could of the previous night's precious lost hours. Askon too had dozed for a moment or two, though with the others sleeping and the Norill following somewhere behind, he feared leaving Thomas alone with all his focus bent on Dalkaldur and the road, track, or trail that would lead them there.

"What does that mean?" asked Askon, meeting Thomas halfway back to where the others slept.

"It means it's done," Thomas said brightly.

"What's done?"

"The map to Dalkaldur."

Askon made a scoffing sound. "You don't have ink or quill or parchment, and it's too cold up here anyway. Even if you had it, the ink would freeze."

"Here." Thomas tapped his temple. "And here." He tapped the fragment in the bracelet on his wrist. "Think of it however you want. The map is made clear in my mind by the fragment, or the fragment somehow remembers the map I made with my mind. Either way, it's done." He pointed southwest, tracing down the mountain side, through a long valley where running water glinted, then he lowered his hand.

"Did you lose it?" said Askon.

Thomas shook his head. "After the valley, the way wraps around the next ridge, across a river, up onto another ridge, then a level climb to the rim of Dalkaldur. If I'm right in my reckoning, and barring any sort of unforeseen difficulty, it would be a three-day journey."

"Would be?"

"Yes," Thomas said, gesturing to the ice and snow all around them. "If we were in Vladvir or even Grafmark, the distance would take three days on horseback. Out here, on foot, it's hard to estimate. Even with clear weather we travel much slower in the snow. It's impossible to be sure."

"As long as you're certain the path will take us there…"

"It will."

"Alright then," said Askon. "That's better news than we've had in some time." He grabbed Thomas's shoulders with both hands, shaking him a bit. "A little luck goes a long way."

Thomas looked uncertain. He held Askon's gaze for a moment, drew a breath, then shook his head. "You're right," he said without much enthusiasm. "I'll wake the others. We need to cover as much ground as possible before the light fails us. It's too dangerous to try the descent in the dark, even if we use the Sight fragment."

A ripple of wind stirred Askon's cloak. Thomas turned and headed back toward the others. Askon remained, staring out over the Southern Mountains, following the valley to the ridge line where it disappeared. Beyond, lay the answer to it all: the girl, the strange Norill, the place where his people had entered the world all those generations ago: Dalkaldur.

CHAPTER THIRTY

Fracture

It was all too much: the girl, the Norill, a half-blind journey to the place where Askon and Líana's people had first appeared in the world. Thomas shook his head. Not to mention what he had seen in the last vision, what he hadn't told Askon. He'd thought he might say it while explaining the path, but he couldn't bring himself to do it, still couldn't even understand it fully. Who could construct such a building, such a city? How would they even accomplish the feat? An enormous wall made all of glass. Strange energies fused into stranger fluids to accomplish strange tasks. And a figure in an unmistakable deep green cloak.

As he bent to wake Elise, he relaxed. She slept so peacefully up here, her dark hair askew in the gentle wind, her pale eyelids fluttering almost imperceptibly, likely at some dream. A smile rested on her face. It was a good dream, he guessed. Then a red glow crept over her cheeks and chin. For a moment he thought she'd gone flush, but then he saw the source of the light. The Death fragment pulsed brightly at her wrist, faded, pulsed again, and the smile curdled to a grimace, her eyelids and jaw clenching. She woke with a gasp.

But he was there, with his hand on her shoulder as her eyes opened and she sat up. "It's alright," he said.

At first she didn't respond. Instead, she glanced rapidly around the snowy path as if something precious had gone missing. Her eyes landed on him last. In them, he saw raw fear.

"They took him!" she said, her hands flailing in the snow as she tried to stand. "I tried—I tried…"

Thomas felt her shivering. He wrapped his arms tightly around her. "It's alright," he said again. "You were dreaming."

She relaxed a bit as another shudder coursed through her limbs. "I tried to hold on, but they took him, our son!" Tears welled in her eyes. "Your dreams are real enough, aren't they? We shouldn't have left him. Why did we come here?"

Thomas too felt the guilt. They had left the boy—still so young—in good care. Safe, yes, but that didn't ease the pain of not seeing him, didn't ease the worry. Even in their own home, on the best of days, the worry was inescapable. The simplest things became dangerous threats. A staircase, a kitchen knife, a chill wind, all were as good as deadly. Or so the worry told him. He couldn't imagine what Elise felt in the boy's absence.

He pulled her closer. "We came because it was right. We came because we're the only ones who can do anything about it. And, more practically," he said, falling into his usual pattern, "we came because if anything is unsafe, it's strange Norill appearing in people's houses and trying to kill them."

She let her head fall against his chest, the dream's panic subsiding. "And we came to help *him*." She indicated Askon, still staring out over the mountains, cloak billowing in the wind.

"We did," Thomas said. "After all, without him we'd never have met."

Elise sighed. They weren't the words she had wanted to hear. "No, perhaps not."

They sat for a moment, enjoying the quiet before waking the others. In traditional fashion, Thomas gathered up a handful of snow and doused John with it, leaving him a spluttering, frosted mess. They had all managed a tense laugh, even John, but Thomas knew it would only be a matter of time before his turn came.

When all were well and fully alert, they began the descent. Askon asked if Thomas wanted to lead, but he declined, settling instead on directing Askon. As long as they managed to traverse a mile or so west, they would end up in the intended valley. From there, Thomas hoped, the going would be easier for a great deal of their journey. In the fragment he had seen level ground, large sheltering trees, and a clear stream to follow.

For now, they had wind, snow, and a treacherous, icy path with which to contend. *At least there is a path*, Thomas thought to himself. In fact, they'd had to remove the snowshoes that had so greatly aided their climb through the dark. The clever lattice work slipped too easily on the ice and made for awkward footing and strange angles on one's ankles. And so they slowly traveled down the mountain and to the west, aiming for the relief of the green valley.

"Reminds me o' that winter up on the Face 'tween Vestgæta and Tolarenz, Askon," John called from the back of the line. "You remember that one?"

"I do," said Askon.

Edward's foot shot out, slipping on the ice. He grabbed Líana's hand to steady himself and frowned. "I don't."

"O'course ya wouldn't. That was 'fore we knew ya." John thought for a moment. "Might o' been my first assignment with our fearless leader here."

Thomas carefully stepped over the sheet of ice that had tripped Edward then helped Elise across. On their left, a long jagged rock formation sprouted up, dictating the path. A smaller mirror of the formation rose on the right, high enough that they couldn't see over it. Snow had drifted into the tunnel between but only covered one side. With hands splayed and feet slipping here and there, they crossed the ice and continued through the corridor.

"It wasn't the first," Askon said, sidestepping a large sharp stone. "The Face was the first winter, though. I finished my training earlier that year, in the spring."

"The Face?" asked Líana. After it had gathered an impressive array of ice crystals, Askon's sister had hidden away the long braid that usually hung loosely through a slit in her hood. Without it, Thomas felt like he was looking at a different person, or, as if in some grim accident, someone had removed one of her limbs. "You've mentioned the Face twice," she said. "I've never heard of that before."

Thomas watched Askon glance at John, presumably waiting for the latter to tell the story, as was his typical practice. This was no exception. John took a deep breath.

"Well, that's quite the story, that one," he began. "Ya see, Askon and I weren't fully acquainted yet, just assigned to the same area and company. Our task was to keep an eye out for Norill movements. If we saw any, we had two options. The first was to handle it ourselves, which we did from time to time. The second was much more costly in terms of, well, costs."

Askon stopped. "The alternative was to report a Norill sighting with a request for reinforcements, though that was up to the commander. It was costly in that a mistake not only wasted resources, it held consequences for those who made the report." He waved John on and continued through the tunnel.

"That's right," John said. "Now as you can predict, nobody wanted anything to do with this half-sprite recruit of ours."

Thomas thought he saw Askon flinch at the term though John seemed to mean nothing by it.

"We drew lots to see who'd be assigned with him for watches. We did 'em two by two so as to be sure nobody was sleepin' on the job."

"People did anyway," Askon interrupted. "Certain people especially."

John sniffed. "Yeah well, we all have our vices, I figure. Anyway, we set the watch every night that winter up above our camp. Thing was, we'd built the camp up against the side of a cliff— four, five hundred feet high if it were an inch."

Askon laughed, throwing his head back. "Then it *were* an inch, John. Sometimes I wonder at the parts of a story you choose to embellish. What difference does it make if we were on a hundred foot cliff or a five hundred foot cliff?"

"It just does," John replied, a little childishly.

Thomas smiled at Elise but chose to keep quiet.

Unruffled, John went on. "At any rate, we were up this cliff every night, and the wind would howl somethin' terrible. Chill ya right down till you could feel the ice inside yer bones. Frostbit more'n one person that winter."

"So why 'the Face'?" asked Líana.

John looked up the mountainside where a spray of snow shot out over them beyond the tips of the rock. "Well, the lookout was on the edge of the cliff, as I said. Thing was you had to climb down to it from a bluff above."

"So it was a cliff on top of a cliff?" Elise folded her arms. Whether as a sign of her disbelief or because she was simply cold, Thomas couldn't tell.

"It was," said Askon heavily. "That part, at least, is true."

"See?" John said to Elise. "Now give me some space to tell this the way it was."

While John collected his thoughts, they emerged from the tunnel and into the open mountainside again. Wind whipped their cloaks, and it occurred to Thomas just how much the rock formation had sheltered them. Despite the wind, though, they now at least had a brilliant sun to warm them whenever the gusts relented.

"You know, Líana only asked about the Face, John," Askon said. "You've told her. It was a lookout ledge on a cliff below a bluff."

John laughed again. "That may be right, but ya don't think I'll leave out the best part on account of it bein' an informatational query, do ya?"

Thomas considered correcting him, but thought better of it.

"So I had drawn the short straw, as it were, and was set to watch with the half-sprite." He put out a hand. "No offense meant to present company, o'course, that was the way of it then." When no one replied, he went on. "We're up on the face. It's colder than it is now, wind just full steady. I'm noddin' off a bit, as you do."

"A bit?" Askon called from the front of the line. "You were dead asleep. I could've hit you with a rock and you wouldn't have more than stirred."

John grinned. "Maybe, but that just makes the next part even better." He adjusted the fur at his neck, scratching a bit for effect in his thick black beard. "It was about midnight when I woke—I mean, well—when my attention was called to a frightened squeak. For a quick breath, my heart beat a little faster. Thought it might be a young noble maiden callin' out for assistance."

Askon made an inarticulate sound, shifted his cloak, and trudged ahead.

"But I got my bearings, realized such only a pleasin' dream, and turned to find our half-elf recruit wide-eyed, breathin' like a cornered kitten, sword drawn and leveled as if an angry ice giant might come lumberin' around the corner." He thought for a moment. Just long enough, Thomas assumed, to sharpen their attention.

"There weren't much room up there on the Face, but Askon's backed right out to the edge. Now I'm about as strong and brave as they come, as you rightly know, but even I have to take a soldier seriously when he looks like to jump the cliff at what he's seein'. So I turn around, hand on sword hilt, heart beatin' a little faster'n it ought, and I see what his blade's pointed at."

A sigh erupted from the front of the line.

"A little shrub, rattlin' in the wind. My hand drops from my sword. The shrub shakes again, and I hear your brother's foot scrape as he inches toward the ledge. And out hops a jackrabbit."

John roared with laughter. The others laughed as well, though perhaps not quite so heartily.

"It fell off the bluff and landed on me," Askon said weakly. "I might have been dozing as well."

Thomas laughed a bit more, remembering when he had first encountered Askon, how foolish he'd felt at the offered hand, at his recovered horse, the whole business of their meeting.

"And the whole time," John chuckled, tears in his eyes, "he's lookin' to fight it like its some demon beast out o' the Great Darkness."

Thomas smiled. It felt good to laugh again. And by the looks on their faces, the others felt the same. He took a deep breath.

And lost his footing.

He hadn't seen the ice, hidden as it was beneath a thin bit of snow. He watched it happen, as if time had slowed—the way

Askon described the power of the fragment. His foot slid over the path, through a tuft of snow, where it stuck fast against a stone. His shin snapped with a sickening crack and nauseous pain took him.

✝ ✝ ✝

"Thomas!" Elise cried, diving on her husband's body where he lay broken upon the icy rocks. He had lost consciousness, but she felt the gentle rise and fall of his chest, listened to his heart beating. It had all happened so fast: the slip, the fall, the twisting and breaking. Ignoring the gory shaft of bone protruding from his leg, she cupped his face, gently tapping either side. "Thomas, wake up," she said in a shadowy whisper that all but vanished in the wind. "Wake up."

"Líana!" she shouted. "Help him!"

The half-elf woman knelt by her side before she had even finished calling. When they'd first met, Elise worried that the beautiful face, the glittering eyes of green and blue, the lithe dancer's body would be a threat, a challenge for Thomas's attention. But she knew better now. Líana was in some ways hardly more than a girl then, lost in the world's ways, especially those of women. And despite that, her skill with a sword had been what Elise took in trade, one teaching the other. As they knelt beside Thomas's pale form on the sparkling mountain path, they might have been sisters, one dark and one light. Both dangerous as sharpened knives.

"Can you help him?" Elise asked after a moment.

Líana cringed at the spike of blood-covered bone, torn through flesh and clothing, exposing itself to the cold. Like a too-green willow branch one tries to snap from the trunk rather than to cut, Thomas's shin bone had broken only partially. The rest clung together in frayed spiral strands.

"I…"

Elise knew this kind of break, had heard this kind of response from healers in Dalstone when careless boys climbed too high, jumped too far. They would shake their heads, wear solemn frowns, say nothing could be done. And then the boys would die.

"You carry the Life fragment," she said with more venom than she'd meant. On her wrist she could feel her own piece of Alora's Tear, like heat smoldering through the bracelet's metal band. She brushed the hair from her face. "You saved yourself with it. You saved John with it. Do something!"

By then the others had gathered. Askon with his condescending eyes. If she could hear his mind, she knew what it would say: *Poor girl, she doesn't know it is the sort of break that kills. Living with those Norill savages, she probably has no idea that even if he lives, he will never walk the same again.*

And John with his, *"That's how they are,"* and his *"Best thing a woman can do is…"* She didn't even allow him to finish it in her head.

Edward simply looked sad, as if all the weight of the world were upon him, as if he might with his own hands carry Thomas back home and place him where he belonged, where both of them belonged, with their son.

"Please!" Elise cried, taking a long ragged breath and letting her head fall against him. She lay there for a moment, trembling. When no one spoke, she sobbed, no pretty sound, but an explosive animal bark that echoed across the snow.

"If we use the fragments, especially for something like this, we don't know what will happen," one of them was saying.

"I do," John's voice. "That commander and his chanting pack o' Norill will be back here quick as a flash. That's what'll happen."

"Can we carry him?" Líana.

"We could," Askon.

A breath and then the half-elf man again. "We would risk the same fate as Thomas. For a few feet, or maybe a few hundred, John, Edward, and I could carry him. But we'd be spent in less than a mile. Or injured as well."

"Won't that be the same risk if Líana helps him?" Edward.

A familiar worry laced the new king's voice. He was feeling the same pangs for Líana as Elise felt for Thomas. If Líana used the Life fragment, not only could she bring on the Norill they'd worked so hard to evade, but Líana might become an equal burden, unconscious and unresponsive after helping him.

Elise listened to the empty pause and knew they felt it too. It was the moment when Thomas would have interjected, correcting John or offering some clever solution. Now there was only silence. She sat up and turned what she hoped was an imploring gaze on Líana. Neither of them spoke.

Líana removed her glove, the Life fragment glowing on her finger. She gripped Elise's hand and squeezed. John stepped forward to intervene, but Askon held him back. Light bloomed over the snow, purple as a sunset before a storm. So bright it grew that Elise had to look away. She felt Líana's grasp loosen, and the light faded. After another moment Thomas's leg was whole, and he stirred. Líana collapsed heavily.

And another purple light grew.

In a heartbeat, they were surrounded by Norill with dangling arms and empty eyes. "*Sors*," one said.

"*Sors*," another.

And now they were all chanting, at least a dozen of them, all carrying the same long knives as before. The others had never asked, of course, but she'd known from the first that these Norill were not of Grafmark, not of Brâghda's proud people. For one, the knives were too polished, too clean, unmarked by use. The Grafmark Norill kept no weapons for display. Art was art and work was work, battle was battle. *And the world is how it is*, she finished to herself.

Drawing her sword, Death fragment aglow on her wrist, she stepped away from Líana and Thomas. She could sense them both breathing behind her; they would survive, if she kept them safe. Directing her attention to the nearest Norill, she sneered and waited for its attack.

It stared back, chanting again and again with the others, "*Sors. Sors. Sors.*"

Then it leapt forward, knife gleaming. Elise exhaled and it fell, dead, in the snow. She turned to the next, and it too died, though she gave it no chance to charge. With a shudder, she breathed again, killing them without ever lifting her sword. When six had fallen, her balance wavered, and she dropped to one knee.

Askon, Edward, and John formed a line in front of her where another dozen Norill remained.

"Oh, you're just a forge fire disguised as a candle flame aren't you?" said an unfamiliar woman's voice.

Elise turned to face the way they'd come. She heard a soft click.

"We could use one of your fiber—your spirit—especially with poor Gaelin injured," the voice said with gentle pity. "You'll probably choose death instead. Unfortunate."

There with her arm raised, carrying the same weapon as the commander, Gaelin, stood a woman in her middle years, her blond hair cropped short at the jawline.

Gritting her teeth, Elise reached again for the power of Death. The woman fired her weapon, and the fragment's power slipped through Elise's fingers. She braced for the impact, the shuddering tremors she'd seen wrack Líana's body when the commander's shot had struck her. But it never came.

Of course it hadn't. In the space between the woman's appearance and her attack, Askon had put himself between them. Hoping, Elise assumed, to pluck the object from midair as he'd done with the arrow in Dalstone or her own body after Apopsé had pushed her from South City's wall. This time, he did not succeed.

Heaving and struggling to stay upright, Elise watched as Askon appeared, shuddered, and crumpled to his knees. For a moment, she thought he might rise, but another tremor came and he fell spasming to the ground, his arms and legs stirring the surrounding snow.

Above stood the short-haired woman, her pointed ears showing through the dingy gold. She smiled greedily, stepping toward Askon's flailing body. "Finish it," she said, and to Elise's surprise, turned away.

As if from nowhere, a pair of Norill appeared at either side of the path. They dove on Askon. Elise reached again for the Death fragment's power, but it eluded her. She charged, colliding with the Norill on the right, her sword impaling it. Drawing the blade back she rounded on the other, only it was too late. The creature hunkered over the green cloak, lifted its weapon and drove it down.

With a hoarse, roaring cry, she lunged at the Norill, her sword whipping through the air. Metal met flesh, cut bone, came free in a spray of red across the snow. The Norill's body gurgled as it choked and died beside Askon.

The woman turned to face Elise, her expression pure disbelief. On her forehead a circlet—like the one they'd seen on the commander and the girl in the vision—glittered a shifting color so deep it may as well have been black. "How valiant," the woman said kindly. "I suppose he's helped you before. Saved you? Loved you, even?"

"Not loved," Elise said.

"Oh, it's another of these then?" the woman said. "Well. They'll all be just as dead when we're finished."

No call came this time. Two more Norill appeared and rushed Elise and Askon. Behind her she heard John shout. A white light rose up all around her, first bleaching the snow, then the path, and finally the sky.

Everything around her was endlessly white. Like glass or polished stone. Then the others appeared. First, Askon beneath her, then Edward and John behind her. And when she turned to look, Líana and Thomas. She sighed and fell from knee to hip in the snow.

Snow. That's what it was. Endless snow all around, as far as she could see. Something wasn't right. She looked again. The tunnel was gone. The Norill were gone. The bodies of the fallen and the red streaks their blood had left were gone. And that woman, with her kindly mothering voice, she was gone too.

Then Elise understood. Wherever they were, it was far from the place where Thomas had broken his leg, far from the attack. Edward had moved them.

"Elise!" she heard John shouting. "Don't lie down! Stay on yer feet. It's colder here. Like to freeze to death if ya don't keep movin'."

He grabbed her shoulder and hoisted her up. "Ya did good work back there, but we've got to keep goin', get the others up too, or we won't get far."

Thomas was already upright and helping Líana. Elise wrapped her arms around him and clung tight. Then she pushed herself away. "Askon!" she called. "The Norill got to him before I did. He's hurt. Líana, we need to help him!"

Askon had propped himself up, his green cloak blackening at one side. His eyes were unfocused, and he stared into the distance, his face pale and bloodless.

"You have to leave me," he said when John had walked Edward down the slope. "If Líana heals this wound—" He winced and sucked a breath through clenched teeth.

"No," said Elise. "We'll be ready."

Askon smiled and took a shallow breath. "How? They appear from nowhere. Their weapons—" He coughed. "We're exhausted."

"We are," said Edward, "but we're not leaving you to die. Líana will heal you, they'll appear, and I'll make us disappear. Once more will be enough."

Askon coughed again. "But look at where we are! It's empty wilderness…"

"No it isn't," said Thomas. To Elise, hearing his voice again was like warm sun after weeks of rain. "Edward's taken us right where we needed to go." He pointed up the slope.

"And I'll freeze to death here before I leave you," Líana said. "We didn't come this far for you to sacrifice yourself. We have the Tear, and they know where we are. They probably know where we're going. I say we use it."

Líana didn't give her brother a chance to answer. Elise preferred it that way. She watched as the Life fragment healed the wound, though his cloak did not receive the same benefit. For now it would remain a bloodstained reminder of how close they'd come to failure.

Askon held his sister as she steadied herself. The purple light rose behind them. Elise saw the tall woman's silhouette in the blinding sun. She strode forward. The world again grew white, starting with the snow, and the woman stepped closer. She sneered, Norill appearing on either side. Their gray hands reached out, and the white crept up over them, over Elise herself. Their fingers closed tight, and all grew still.

"I was right. You are in love with one of them," the woman's voice echoed. "I wish I didn't have to take him."

Beside her, Thomas's eyes widened with surprise as the Norill fingers tightened around his wrist. Frantic, he fought against their grip. When the arm didn't come free, he looked into Elise's eyes, her grip tightening as well. The white light crept higher, touching the horizon.

Pulling with all her strength, she felt her hands slip, the bracelet with the Sight fragment sliding from his wrist. Elise screamed, fierce and feral, her sword slashing at the woman's placid smile.

Cloud and sky and sun and Thomas dissolved into unending white.

CHAPTER THIRTY-ONE

Destinations

Elise was screaming. Thomas was gone. Askon stared down the hill, his sense slowly returning, as she slashed and screamed, slashed and screamed, the Death fragment blood red at her wrist. Shouting Thomas's name, she cried, lifting the sword until her arm no longer had the strength. Then she collapsed in the snow.

"Where is he?" asked John.

Edward's shoulders fell. "They took him. We were too slow—I was too slow."

"Someone needs to get her on her feet," Askon said. "We can't stay here."

Líana's eyes narrowed and she frowned. "That's all you can say?" she snapped. "After Elise pulled you along, despite the danger, that's what you have for her? Get her to her feet? She's not a soldier, Askon."

His sister was right, of course, but they had no guarantee the Norill and their new leader would be content with a captive. He had known the order lacked compassion when he gave it. They needed to move and soon; however, rushing Elise would only make the situation worse.

"Alright," he said. "Give her a moment. And then you should be the one to convince her to keep moving."

Líana frowned. "Well it certainly shouldn't be you," she said, marching down the slope toward Elise's huddled form.

Askon turned to John and Edward. "Are we close?" he asked. "We don't have Thomas to tell us. Edward, can you tell?"

Edward gestured up the slope. With determined steps, Askon trudged through the knee deep snow. Fifty yards from where they'd landed, at the top, his heart stopped and his breath left him. Below, a wide crater spread, as if a huge boulder had fallen from the sky, left its imprint upon the mountain, and then dissolved into nothing. All around the edges, a thick forest of shifting evergreens grew. A lake, shimmering and clear, filled the center. And beyond, an ancient stone keep crouched in sullen biding.

In his mind's eye he imagined the girl, Alora, running toward the edge of the lake. He saw the low wooden buildings, with his own eyes, where the weapon they'd now used on him and his sister had brought her down. Tracing backward he found the patch of tufted grass where the girl in the vision had hidden the fragments, buried them in the chest by the waterside. And he knew, understood finally what it all was, and what he would have to do.

"John! Edward!" he called, turning back toward the slope, resisting the fear that Dalkaldur might very well vanish if he looked away. "I need the fragments—all of them."

Further down, Líana coaxed Elise to her feet. Askon looked instinctively for Thomas, felt the pain again in finding he was not there. Thomas, he realized, would have known by now, probably did know, wherever he was. With the answer clear in his mind, Askon sensed that they could find him, as long as he was still alive.

In a swirl of wind-whipped snow, under a brilliant sun, all five of them climbed to the summit and stood upon the rim looking down into the crater. Askon took the rings from Edward and Líana, removed his necklace, steadied his balance against John, and fought the nauseous churn of his stomach. Then he took the Death fragment from Elise, and finally, Sight. For a long moment Elise clung to the bracelet as though Thomas might appear again within it. When he did not, she let it go.

With the whole of Alora's Tear cupped in his hands, he stared out over the rim. "Stand close to me," he said.

Then, from the echoes of his memory, he recalled a spacious hall, a lavish table set with cups from which they sipped sun-gold wine, and the ancient voice of Morrowmen cawing like a hungry raven:

Wait for them.
The morning light be blinded by.
On mirror lake or crystal stream,
As long as things of green reside,
If you seek them,
They will find you
By the waterside.

Closing his eyes, he drew upon the Time fragment and the vision of the girl; he drew upon the remembered voice of his friend Thomas and the advice of those who had already passed on: Morrowmen, Caled, his mother and father. He felt the pieces pull at one another, straining to be together, thrumming with the nearness of each other. Then he opened his eyes.

All around them a wide field of white flowers bloomed. The sun shone yellow in the sky, and though the wind rustled the petals gently, the crisping air grew warm and the field filled with shadow. A hundred feet beyond, the snow appeared again, blinding bright, harsh and cold as ever.

"I understand," Askon said, his face bathed in the light of the five fragments. "The Tear is both door and key. They are the *source*. It's what the Norill have been after all along. We should have seen it, should have guessed it much sooner."

Slowly, carefully holding tight to his concentration, he pointed to Dalkaldur below. "She's not in *our* Dalkaldur. She's in *theirs*."

"Whose?" John's voice said, though it felt faint and distant.

Liana's face lit with awe. "The elves," she whispered.

"This is where they entered our world," Askon said, unable to suppress a smile. "Or near enough. It's how we get to her as well."

Edward shook his head. "I can't stay here, Askon. We don't know for sure what they want, and even if it is the Tear they're after, the kingdom will panic when word of the attacks spreads. I have to go."

"Then go," said Askon. The fragments vibrated together, as if breathing, as if speaking. And now Askon was listening. He'd said the words to free his friend, to give Edward what he needed, but the wound was clear in the king's expression. Askon thought back to the day when Codard and Iramov had interrogated him concerning Austgæta, the day John had let them escape.

"It's alright," Askon said. "Go." And in his hands, though the others would never hear it, Alora's Tear echoed him.

Like a shimmering window, the air split and the throne room at King's City with its heavy curtains and ornate fixtures shone through.

Then another window split the sky, just as clear, just as impossible. In it glimmered the small room at the back of the Tolarenz Town hall. The small table, the upholstered armchairs, all was in its place.

"And what is that one for?" Edward asked.

"It's for Elise," said Askon. "He's there. Go to him."

But Elise turned sharply away. "I can't," she said. "If Thomas is out there, and I have strength left to find him, I can't go back."

"But your son…" said Líana softly.

Elise's eyes welled again with tears. She pushed them away with a tight fist, and the veil of ink-black hair went with them. "My son needs his father!" she cried. "If I have to fight, kill, *die* to bring him back…"

In his hands, Askon watched as the Death fragment glowed red, and for a heartbeat the seams at the windows' edges wavered. The stone grew warm.

Elise looked to John, her eyes wild and pleading.

Askon expected a refusal, thought that John, stubborn as he was, would argue. He didn't. The big bearded man simply nodded and put a hand on Elise's shoulder. "You say he needs his father? Seems what you're doin' is a lot closer to that anyway," he said. "So you bring Thomas back. I'll keep the boy safe, and I'll warn Dalstone. It'll take more 'n a couple slack-mouthed Norill to get past the guards I'll set. And in the evenin's I'll watch over him my-self."

He released her shoulder and approached the window, then turned to face Askon. "I know I told ya—"

"You did," Askon interrupted. "You went with me. And now, someone else needs you."

John stared at the window as if it might reach out to swallow him. "So I just…walk through it?"

Askon nodded and John stepped gingerly over the threshold into Tolarenz, miles upon miles distant, and yet only an arm's length away. The window dissolved, leaving nothing but the white-flowered field and a wall of snow beyond.

Edward held Líana in a tight embrace, speaking quietly so only she heard the words. He kissed her, lingering, holding her face in his hands. Then he approached the window. As it had so many times before, the Time fragment told Askon the story of Edward's last look: he'd known she wouldn't come back to King's City, where she was at best a caged bird, waiting for a chance at flight. Askon saw too that Edward knew she loved him, and that some-how she would return. With a smile, the King of Vladvir vanished into his throne room. Líana stifled a cry and turned away.

With Elise on his right and his sister on his left, Askon too turned from the crater, from the empty air where John and Edward had once been. The fragments hummed together, whispering for him to face the long frozen slope. "Close your eyes," he said.

They did.

The wind stopped, and it grew suddenly warmer. In the emptiness behind his eyelids, Askon felt a shift, electric like the air before a thunderstorm. He opened his eyes, to darkness, and knew they had left Vladvir behind.

Above them a wide sky unfurled in a moonless night. Beyond the jagged ridges of the Southern Mountains he saw the Breaker and the Mender, starry figures forever reaching out to one another. But the other stars were dim and few. He looked down the slope.

An endless array of lights glowed in clusters, like embers hidden at the base of a campfire. Thousands upon thousands they numbered. Much brighter than candles and much steadier than bonfires, they shone unfailingly. He looked closer, each light inside, beside, or between a building. There were short, low structures, but most were tall, almost impossibly tall, rising from the valleys below nearly as high as the outer wall in South City or the battlements of King's City Castle.

Between the rows of towering buildings, more of the eerie lights floated steadily along. He tried to follow them but lost track. There were so many. He looked further, higher, and found the highest of them all, a spike of a pillar standing tall enough to reach above the very mountains themselves. And though it was many miles distant, at its point, like a beacon, a light as brilliant as a full moon glowed.

Líana and Elise drew closer to him, their faces awash in awe.

"The Glittering World," Askon whispered to the air above the endlessly flickering city of his people—each light a sign of the elves, each elf a possibility, an answer to a question unanswerable by even the greatest minds in Vladvir. Askon smiled. It was a thousand questions inside the one. It was a question for his elven half. Only here, there were no halves. Here, they were whole.

Acknowledgements

To everyone who made it to these last pages, thank you. I cannot express how important you are to me. Without readers, the story, these characters, these people exist only in my head. Now, Vladvir and the Glittering World live and breathe in your mind as well.

To my wife and family, your support is measureless. So many drafts, so many hours of me rambling through ideas that might not ever make it into a draft, and all the while dealing with my constant obfuscations meant to preserve the surprises and secrets. Kel, you never rush me out of the writing room. You always find a way for there to be enough time. That and a million other reasons are why there's no book, no *anything* without you.

James—who will stop at nothing to make the invisible people visible. Dansil is here because of you. There was always someone for John in Finnestre, but he wasn't clear to me until you sent the article about Riordan and Alex Fierro. I thank you, and I imagine readers who have stories similar to Dansil's will thank you too. The world needs more Dansils, and it needs to see the Dansils we already have. I'm proud to have placed a stone on that path.

And as promised, many thanks go out to the students of my Advanced Creative Writing class: Kylie, Chloe, Kelsey, Emily, Ashley, and Hannah, who in a giddy bout of vengeance dissected an early Chapter 10 with more than a little relish. Without them, Alora's father would never have rapped about accomplices and locations, readers would have been mired in a veritable fleet of muckducks, and I might never have realized how instantly charming a character could become simply by rattling off a list of book titles.

About the Author

Nathan spends most of his working days with the students of Genesee Junior-Senior High School in Genesee, Idaho. Whether it's essay structure, a classic literary work, an invisible ball of energy and deep breathing on stage, or the occasional impromptu dance routine, he strives to keep students interested in the fun and the fundamentals of the English language.

When he's not teaching, he wears a number of hats, though the one that says "Dad" is the most careworn and cherished (it says "Husband" on the back). It hangs on a hook in a house where music is a constant and all the computers say "Apple" somewhere on their *aluminium* facades. From time to time it is said that he ventures into the mysterious realm called *outside*, though the occasion is rare and almost exclusively upon request by son or daughter.

Sign up for Nathan's newsletter:
www.barhamink.com/subscribe

Connect with Nathan:
Website: barhamink.com
Twitter: twitter.com/natebarham
Facebook: facebook.com/BarhamInk

CPSIA information can be obtained
at www.ICGtesting.com
Printed in the USA
FSHW021637170120
66007FS